Flirt

Flirt

TRACY BROWN

K'WAN

ANGEL MITCHELL

 ST. MARTIN'S GRIFFIN ≈ NEW YORK

These are works of fiction. All of the characters, organizations, and events portrayed in these novellas are either products of the authors' imaginations or are used fictitiously.

 For information, address St. Martin's Press, 175 Fifth Avenue, New York, N.Y. 10010.

www.stmartins.com

Library of Congress Cataloging-in-Publication Data

Brown, Tracy, 1974–
Flirt / Tracy Brown, K'wan, and Angel Mitchell. — 1st ed.
p. cm.
ISBN 978-0-312-53701-2
1. African Americans—Fiction. I. K'wan. II. Mitchell, Angel. III. Title.
PS3602.R723F57 2009
813'.6—dc22

2009017039

First Edition: December 2009

10 9 8 7 6 5 4 3 2 1

CONTENTS

Flirting with Disaster

TRACY BROWN

For Ashley, Teona, Jade, Tamara, Savannah, Kenisha, and all the other young ladies I know who are starting to date. Beware of the false motives of others. Watch out for the wolves in sheep's clothing. And remember that your parents don't want to ruin your fun or run your lives all the time. It's just that sometimes we can see things more clearly than you can. You're all beautiful, intelligent, and talented ladies with the world at your fingertips. Stay focused. I love you, divas!

As she sped down the ramp like a track star, Chloe prayed she hadn't missed it. On the way to the ferry, she'd felt like the bus driver was going extra slow on purpose. The bus had finally pulled into the St. George terminal at 7:39 A.M., giving her exactly one minute to catch it. Not even—because if the guy whose job it was to close the doors wanted to be an asshole that day, he'd close them faster on purpose. Then all anyone could do in their frustration was curse and stare at him through the glass partition. Chloe hated that guy, and had always wished that one day someone would wait until he opened the doors for the next ferry and then punch him dead in his face.

She ran as fast as she could this morning. If she missed this one, the next boat wouldn't come for another twenty minutes, and she had no patience to wait around that long. Just as she entered the terminal, she could see the doors slowly closing. She ran faster and slipped between them just in the nick of time. She looked victoriously at the son of a bitch pressing the button. *Bastard!*

She boarded the Staten Island Ferry and swore for the thousandth time that she was going to start waking up earlier so that she wouldn't have to run like a wide receiver anymore. Winded—and annoyed that her morning was off to such a bad start—Chloe plopped down in an empty seat and tried to catch her breath. She put her bag on the floor in front of her and sucked her teeth. As usual, she hadn't had time to pick up a copy of the New York *Daily News*, and now there was nothing to read during her ride to Lower Manhattan.

It was Monday morning, and Chloe hated Mondays! She preferred to take her time, sleep late, and get her day started at her own pace. Mondays meant she had to get up on time, catch the bus on time, be at the ferry on time. She had never cared much about being on time for things. It wasn't that she didn't respect other people's schedules. She just wasn't a morning person. And the earlier she had to be someplace, the more likely it was that she'd be late.

Still struggling to regain her breath, she looked around. She noticed a guy sitting across from her, with a smirk on his face. Wondering what the hell he found so funny, for a brief moment she had an attitude. But then she noticed how handsome he was.

He was honey-hued with a neat mustache and goatee and a low-cut Caesar. He reminded her somewhat of the rapper T.I., with his laid-back style and neat, well-groomed appearance. He looked older than she was, and he was fine. But she still wondered what the hell was so funny.

"Tough morning?" he asked, still smirking.

She looked at him. Suddenly her week wasn't off to such a bad start after all. She glanced down at his feet—since footwear mattered to her when meeting a guy for the first time. This one wore a pair of crisp black Nikes, blue jeans, and a Coogi polo shirt. Chloe liked what she saw, so she smiled back.

"Yeah," she said. She shook her head and sighed. "I'm always late for this boat."

"So you should be used to running by now, then," he said. "You seem a little out of breath."

She thought his lips were perfect. He had nice eyes. She noticed that he was using them to size her up as well. He looked her up and down.

"I just hate it when I don't get the chance to pick up the newspaper before I get on," she said. "This ride is not the same without my *Daily News*." He had no cuts on his face, but he still looked as if he'd lived a lot. Like he'd seen a lot of things. Chloe was intrigued by the sexy stranger, and she absentmindedly toyed with her charm bracelet.

He nodded. "I got the *Post* if you want to read it." He offered his newspaper to her, but Chloe shook her head, frowning.

"I hate the *Post*," she said. "But thanks, anyway."

They looked at each other for a few quiet seconds before

Chloe glanced around to see if anyone had discarded a copy of the *Daily News* nearby.

Often passengers left their newspapers on empty seats after they'd finished reading them. Normally, Chloe turned her nose up even at the thought of touching a "used" paper. She'd seen many a passenger pick their nose as if digging for gold, then turn the pages of their newspapers, leaving booger residue behind. The idea of coming into contact with anyone else's boogers repulsed Chloe to no end.

But sitting across from this cutie, she suddenly needed something to do with her hands. He made her feel a little shy, for some reason. And without something to distract her, she knew that the twenty-five-minute ride to Manhattan would feel like an eternity. There were no discarded copies of her preferred paper, so she resigned herself to enduring an awkward boat ride.

The handsome stranger shrugged and set his newspaper down beside him. He extended his hand to her. "My name is Trey," he said.

Chloe thought his voice was so sexy. "Chloe," she said, shaking his hand. "I've never seen you on this boat before." Trey had a face Chloe would have remembered seeing.

He thought she was pretty as well. Chloe was a coffee-complexioned girl with shoulder-length hair and big brown eyes. When she smiled, her deep dimples were clearly visible, and her lips were full and sexy. Her nails were well manicured, and her makeup was light. She was a stunner, and her skintight jeans didn't hurt either. She had Trey's undivided attention. He looked at the knapsack at her feet.

"You go to school?" he asked, hoping that she was a college student and not a high schooler.

She nodded. "Yeah. Medgar Evers College."

He breathed a sigh of relief that she was indeed of age. "What are you taking?"

"Journalism." She looked at his casual clothes and wondered how old this guy was. "How about you?" she asked.

Trey hesitated for a moment and said, "I'm a student like you."

"Yeah, right. You look like you're about twenty-five. You're still in college?"

He smiled. "First of all, thanks for the compliment, 'cause I'm about to turn twenty-eight. And, yeah, I'm in school. After high school, I made a detour, so it took me a minute to get back on track. Now I go to BMCC."

Borough of Manhattan Community College, aka BMCC, was located in Downtown Manhattan. Chloe had considered going there when she graduated high school, but opted instead for Medgar Evers, in the heart of Brooklyn. "What's your major?" she asked, even more intrigued than before.

Trey cleared his throat. "I'm taking up psychology."

Now it was Chloe who smirked. "Wow. That sounds exciting," she said sarcastically. "You want to spend your life analyzing a bunch of psychos?"

He shrugged, picked up his newspaper again. "I find it interesting getting inside people's minds and trying to understand them." He looked away for a moment, watching a bum nearby rummaging through a garbage can. Then he turned back to

Chloe. "I work for transit, too," he said. "I'm a track worker, but I work nights. I take my classes in the daytime."

Chloe was impressed. Trey was pursuing a degree *and* had a good job. She couldn't believe her luck! The guys her age weren't this focused. They were either hustling—which Chloe found ridiculous in this day and age—or working some menial job, trying to make ends meet. This handsome stranger seemed like he was different from the lames she was accustomed to. Chloe herself still lived at home with her mother and younger sister. She didn't want to work, didn't want to pay bills. She figured it was easier to live at home while she took her time getting her life in order. She was twenty years old, and she loved having the freedom to come and go as she pleased. But she didn't want all the responsibilities that went along with adulthood, and for that reason, she still lived in her mother's house.

"You have any kids?" she asked. A guy this fine—with all that he had going on—must have a crazy baby mama, she assumed.

"Nah, no kids. No girlfriend. None of that."

"You live out *here*?" she asked, wondering how a guy this perfect had evaded her for so long on Staten Island.

He nodded. "Yeah, I just moved here, though. I'm from the Bronx originally. I've only lived out here for like a year. I live over on St. Marks."

She smiled. St. Marks was just a few blocks from her home. This was all too good to be true. "Really? So, we're practically neighbors. I live on Jersey Street. But in the houses, not in the projects!" She crossed her legs.

Trey frowned a little at Chloe's disdain when she'd clarified that she didn't live in the projects. "Well, I grew up in the projects in the Bronx all my life, sweetheart," he said. "So it wouldn't matter to me if you lived in the projects or not. I'm not like that."

Damn! Chloe wished she could eat her words. She hadn't meant for her statement to sound so demeaning.

"I wasn't saying it like that," Chloe backpedaled. "Not at all."

It wasn't that she was stuck up. Chloe and her sister, Willow, were the product of a single-parent household. Their mother had raised them on her own after their fathers—Chloe's a deadbeat from the get-go, and Willow's a guy who supported her financially but was never around—took off. Rachel Webster constantly reminded her daughters that even though they lived in the hood, they didn't have to act like hoodrats. She never wanted them to limit themselves. She taught her children that there was no goal outside their reach and that they should *never* settle for less than the best.

Rachel Webster worked hard at her clerical job at a Midtown Manhattan bank so that she could afford for her daughters the luxuries most girls their age could get only from their drug dealer boyfriends. It was no big thing when guys tried to lavish Chloe and Willow with designer clothes or expensive gifts. They had already been lavished with all of that. Monthly shopping sprees and biweekly hair and nail appointments were the norm for them. Rachel insisted that they look like classy young ladies whenever they went out, monitored their grades like a hawk, and never let them date thug niggas.

Not that she raised her daughters to be bourgeois. In fact, they lived in federally owned housing, so they couldn't be stuck up even if they wanted to. Granted, they didn't live in the projects. No pissy elevators or crackheads in the hallway.

Instead, they lived in the "McDonald's houses" right up the block from Staten Island's New Brighton projects. They were known as the McDonald's houses because they resembled the color and shape of a McDonald's restaurant on the outside. The patch of grass in the front and the two-family town house–style layout made them feel slightly more privileged than their counterparts in the apartment buildings. But it was still Jersey Street, and it was still the hood, no matter how superior they'd convinced themselves they were.

"You live alone?" Trey asked, changing the subject. "Or you got a man?"

"I live with my mother and my younger sister, Willow. She goes to Murry Bergtraum High School. And no, I don't have a man." Chloe knew she was telling only half the truth. She was a pretty girl with a nice body, so she had no shortage of male companionship. She was seeing a few different guys, but not any *one* exclusively. She was a free spirit. The kind of girl whose motto was Life is short, play hard! She was young, single, flirtatious, and was living her life like it was golden.

He nodded. "So you think I can call you, take you out or something?" He licked his lips as he asked her, and Chloe had to fight the urge to pounce on him. All her nervousness faded.

"Sure," she said, smiling.

Trey pulled out his BlackBerry and programmed her phone

number; then Chloe entered his number into her Sidekick. The announcement came on that the boat was about to dock, and they stood to join the throngs of other passengers preparing to get off the ferry. Chloe adjusted her over-the-shoulder North Face book bag and stood beside Trey. Now that they were standing up, she could see he was maybe six feet tall and very well proportioned. His shoulders were broad, and his walk was strong and sexy. As they exited the boat, they made small talk until they reached the R train station.

Chloe turned to Trey and smiled again. "Don't wait too long to call me," she said.

Trey smiled back. "Don't worry. I won't," he assured her.

Chloe skipped down the stairs and boarded her train—just in time. She caught her balance on the speeding train, holding on to the pole. Suddenly Mondays weren't so bad after all.

Her school day held no surprises. It was business as usual, with Chloe eagerly devouring the knowledge her professors dispensed. She took notes, asked questions, and offered insight in each class and was almost pissed that class had ended just when Professor Burke was getting deep in his Sociology lecture. Chloe loved being a college student and felt smarter with each credit she earned. She liked the luxuries she enjoyed, and she watched how hard her mother had to work in order to provide her children with those things.

Rachel Webster always reminded her daughters that a college degree was the difference between the meager wages she received as a bank teller and the six-figure salary her boss pulled down. She drilled it into her daughters' heads that ignorance, men, babies, marriage—those were things that weighed a woman down. She told them that children were a blessing, but only *after* you've lived a little yourself.

Chloe didn't care to be burdened with any kids or responsibilities at this point in her life. Instead she wanted to stay focused, get educated, and live a fulfilling life. She didn't want to fall in love. She'd had one serious boyfriend when she was in high school. He broke her heart during her senior year by cheating on her with one of her biggest haters.

Because of their doting mother, who stressed education and the dance classes Chloe and her sister took after school two days a week—while most of her peers came from homes where these things weren't priorities—Chloe was hated on by most of the girls she knew. When she was in high school, many times girls from around the way had hissed that she was a "prissy bitch" as she walked by or picked fights with her purely out of jealousy.

Chloe was pretty, built like a brick house, smart, and she caught the attention of males wherever she went. She was also picky about which boys she gave her attention to, and most often ignored the advances of boys most girls were swooning over. Chloe was not interested in guys with no future, no potential. She could look at a boy and size him up after only a few seconds of conversation. If there didn't appear to be potential, Chloe would move on. Her refusal to entertain the advances of most guys only made her more coveted by them. Every guy wanted to be the first to hit it. Most girls hated her for this popularity, and the slights only drove Chloe to be better than ever. It drove her to succeed in school, always look her very best, and try her hardest to be the envy of all those bitches.

She had only two females whom she considered true friends. Dawn and Kim were like sisters to her, and the three of them were always the center of male attention and usually the target of female envy.

During senior year, Chloe had been going out with the captain of the football team—Daniel Grand. She really gave her heart to Daniel and had been devastated when she learned that he had slept with Nikki Means—the girl who hated on her the most and who also tried the hardest to be like her. Chloe was crushed, more out of embarrassment and anger that he had cheated on her with *Nikki*—the same pimple-faced no-flavor-having chick who taunted her and dissed her under her breath whenever she walked by in the hallway.

After their breakup, Chloe had spent only three days crying and listening to sad songs in her room. It was enough to show her that she never wanted to feel brokenhearted again. Her mother had consoled her, told her that everything would be fine given some time, that soon she wouldn't hurt so much, and that she didn't ever need any guy to make her feel special.

"Your name is Chloe Webster. If you want that to mean something, *you* have to make it mean something. Go out there and make your mark in the world. Nobody's gonna make it for you." Her mother had smiled at her, stroked her hair. "Don't waste your tears on idiots. When a good guy sees that you're about your business, that you have it together and you're independent, he will fall at your feet."

That had been Chloe's mantra ever since. She thought about her mother's advice as she passed the Aldo shoe store on her way to the train station. If she was gonna have dudes falling at her feet, she just oughta have some hot shoes. She knew that the debit card her mother had given her was supposed to be for emergencies only. But the honey-colored shoes with the stacked heel in the window were calling her.

She didn't resist them, and after she went inside, she thought of Willow. She picked out a cute little purse for her sister and charged that as well. Chloe loved her younger sister and always looked out for her. Even though her family was far from rich, Chloe often fantasized about living the life of the rich and powerful. She wanted to have enough money to shop whenever she felt like it, wanted the chicks from high school to see her and hate even harder than they had before. It was the three Webster women against the world, in Chloe's mind. She had plans to run her own media conglomerate someday—TV, print, radio, the whole nine. She was determined to be the next Oprah, just more stylish. Chloe wanted nothing more than to be That Bitch—the woman all the guys wanted and all the women envied. She wanted to be the Beyoncé to the next Jay-Z.

Chloe walked to the train station with a gentle sway in her hips that had the fellas calling out to her at each step. She smiled, feeling like she had the world eating out of the palm of her hand.

The next morning, as she ran for the boat once again, Chloe thought about her encounter with Trey the day before. She was pleased that he hadn't called her yet. She hated meeting a guy only to have him call the same day. It made them seem eager or desperate. Chloe enjoyed the thrill of the chase. The fact that he hadn't rushed to call her was a plus.

As usual she barely caught the boat. She huffed and puffed, out of breath from her sprint down the ramp, and headed for the same seat she'd occupied the previous day. She was pleased to find Trey there once again.

Chloe smiled, tried to catch her breath faster than she had the day before. "So up until yesterday, I never saw you before. Now I see you two days in a row. Must be my lucky week."

Trey smiled back. "I see you've been running again," he observed.

She laughed and so did he. "I'm always late," she said. "I gotta work on that."

Trey shrugged his shoulders. "We all have our faults." He handed her a folded newspaper and watched her face light up.

"You got me the *Daily News*?" she asked, grinning from ear to ear. *Nice touch!*

He smiled. "Yeah. You said you never have time to get it in the morning so I figured I'd pick it up for you."

Chloe could not stop smiling. "That's so sweet! Thank you." She loved the fact that he had obviously been listening closely to her during their conversation yesterday. It was nice to see that a man as fine as this one could also be so attentive. Her cheeks burned from smiling so hard. She was thinking that if she could get him to buy her a newspaper from one conversation, there was no telling what else she could get him to buy for her while attempting to woo her.

Chloe believed that all men were ultimately after one thing only—sex. She knew that's what had crossed Trey's mind the second she'd first sauntered in his direction in her painted-on jeans. She was no fool and wasn't blinded by a few kind words and thoughtful gestures. She wondered how soon he thought that surprising her with newspapers would net him some ass. Little did he know, Chloe's sole intention at that point was to flirt with him enough to bleed his transit paycheck dry.

Just as they'd done the day before, the two of them talked during the half-hour boat ride to Lower Manhattan and got to know each other a little better. Trey hung on her every word as she told him about an assignment she had to do for her creative writing class. She asked him about his own course load, but Trey seemed more interested in her than in talking about himself. How refreshing. Chloe had become accustomed to guys who were so self-involved that it was tough to get them to listen to the things that were important to her. Trey was different, and she was definitely feeling that!

By the time the boat docked, they had established a tentative courtship. When they parted ways at the train station, Trey watched her walk down the stairs to her train, and then he smiled. Chloe was definitely the kind of girl he could see himself with. She turned and smiled at him before she disappeared into the crowd. She was fantasizing about a shopping spree on Trey's payday, and that put a spring in her step.

WORDS OF WISDOM

"Yo, what the fuck is his problem?" Kim asked, her face twisted in a disgusted grimace. She slammed her cell phone shut and tossed it into her fake Gucci bag.

"I don't know why you keep answering when he calls you!" Chloe chastised.

Kim's boyfriend, Chris, was blowing up her phone and cursing her out over and over. Each time she answered, he asked some rhetorical question like, "You think you're smarter than me, huh?" Then he'd launch into a verbal assault, and Kim would hang up on him.

This had been going on for close to an hour, and both Chloe and their mutual friend Dawn were fed up with the bullshit.

Kim rolled her eyes. "That nigga's just mad 'cause I found out about him and Lynn. That filthy, nasty bitch!"

While there was a break in Chris's phone calls, Dawn decided to try once again to get the whole story.

"So explain this to me from the beginning," she said. "You went through Chris's cell phone?"

Kim nodded, lit a Newport, and exhaled the smoke. "Yeah. And I saw all these messages from her about how she wants him to go down on her, and she can't wait to suck his dick—"

"What!" said Dawn in amazement. Things this exciting never happened to Dawn. She lived a very drama-free life, for the most part. Dawn was a pretty girl with a two-parent household complete with a picket fence—though it was brown instead of white. *Beyond fucking boring!* she thought. She craved the excitement and drama that peppered the lives of her friends. She loved days like this, when she could sit back and be regaled by Kim's and Chloe's adventures with the guys in their lives. This rainy Sunday afternoon in March gave them the opportunity to do just that. Dawn's parents had gone away for the weekend to celebrate their twenty-fifth wedding anniversary, and Chloe and Kim had come over to Dawn's house in Rosebank to hang out.

"Yeah!" Kim continued. "The bitch was talking real reckless in her text messages." She puffed the cigarette again, exhaled the smoke. "And he wasn't innocent either. He was texting back, asking if she takes it in the ass and all kinds of crazy shit."

"So what did you do when you found out all this?" Dawn asked. She was hanging on her friend's every word.

"I wrote a message to that bitch as if I was Chris and told her that she need to back off 'cause he's not trying to mess up his relationship with me. Then I wrote that she should lose his number, and I sent that shit. I deleted the text from Chris's phone memory so he wouldn't know I was going through his phone."

Dawn nodded. "That was smart."

"Exactly!" Kim said, cosigning on her own cleverness. "So I'm thinking the bitch is just a potential jump-off or whatever and that she would get the point and leave Chris the fuck alone. But no! This skank went and *replied* to the text and told Chris that she thought he was *different* and all this other bullshit!" Kim blew the smoke out and tapped her foot on the hardwood floor in frustration.

"And now he's mad at *you*?" Dawn asked.

"Yeah! That bastard got the nerve to be mad at *me* for going through his funky-ass cell phone. It ain't the first time I did that shit! It's just the first time I had a bitch *respond* to the text!"

Chloe shook her head. She hated how men always tried to turn the tables and get mad, when they were the ones who fucked up in the first place. "Let him be mad, then! He's just pissed that he got caught. Rather than be a man about it and admit that he fucked up, he's pissed off at you for finding out what he was up to. Fuck that nigga!"

Kim nodded in agreement, but inside she was scared to death. What if Chris really dumped her over this? She didn't let her friends know she was scared to lose him, but inwardly Kim was in turmoil. "I just wish he'd stop calling me over and over again. If it's over, so be it! I'm fine with that," she lied. "Just stop calling out my name!"

Chloe shook her head. Was she serious? "Stop taking that nigga's calls and kick *him* to the fucking curb, Kim!" Chloe felt like she needed a cigarette, and she didn't even smoke! She was tired of having to give this bitch motivational speeches and pep talks all the time. "You're sitting there, waiting for him to decide if it's over or not, when you should be the one to make that decision. He fucked up, not you. You don't need his broke, unmotivated ass! All them bitches hate on you 'cause you got your shit together. You're not sitting out here every day, going to the corner store with your EBT card and having kids like the rest of these females out here. They hate on you, Kim. So they gonna wanna try to fuck your man to get back at you. The point is, he shouldn't be out here playing you like that, embarrassing you in front of these hoes. Dump that sorry nigga. He ain't shit—you know it and he knows it, too. You can do better than him!"

Kim scowled at Chloe. "Please, bitch. This ain't the Tyra show."

Chloe laughed despite her aggravation. She didn't mean to preach to Kim. But Chris was such a fucking lame, and she hated to see her smart and cute friend keep putting up with his bullshit. Kim's self-esteem was low enough as it was.

Kim was one of those girls who yearned so badly for the love she never got from her father that she fell into the arms of unworthy guys as a result. She tended to latch onto the sorriest dudes and always wound up with her heart broken. Chloe was sick of helping Kim get over one breakup after another, sick of constantly reminding her friend that she deserved better. It was time that Kim broke the cycle and for once left a guy before he had the chance to leave her first.

Chloe was glad she didn't have that problem. She was having the time of her life with Trey. He was spoiling Chloe rotten, and she was loving every single minute of it. After their initial encounter a month ago, he met Chloe on the ferry each day, and each day he had a copy of the *Daily News* for her. It had all started as a subtle flirtation between two strangers, and it blossomed into the start of something with potential. They began calling each other and getting together every so often. And each time, Trey spent money on her. He took her to dinner at swanky, celebrity-filled restaurants in NYC. He bought her flowers, gave her money to get her hair done, and even paid for two textbooks she needed for her creative writing class after she'd maxed out her debit card.

"I'm just saying, you could save yourself a lot of headaches if you live by my rules of dating." Chloe rattled off a list, using her fingers demonstratively. "I don't tolerate cheating. I don't date broke niggas. We're not fucking on the first date, because my pussy is special. You can't disrespect me or lie to me and think everything is gonna be all right. And the first time a dude acts shady toward me when he's around his boys, it'll be the last time he sees me. Period." She looked at Kim. "As soon as you realized that he was texting raunchy messages to bitches, you should've cut him off." Chloe shook her head. "Talking 'bout 'this ain't the first time' . . . you must be crazy!"

Kim knew her girl was telling the truth. Still, she couldn't help hoping this would all blow over and that Chris would forgive her. "All I want is for him to be faithful to me. I can tolerate all the rest of his bullshit. I just feel like if he expects me to be faithful to him, he should give me the same respect."

Stupid bitch! Chloe nodded. "You're right. But he's not! That ugly nigga is fucking everything in a skirt, and you're tolerating that shit. Instead of playing phone games with chicks, you should cut his ungrateful ass off. You were doing him a favor by dealing with him in the first place. His no-job-having self! Instead of sending those text messages to Lynn, what you should have done was send a text to Chris's bum ass. A text that said, 'Hope that nasty bitch Lynn was worth the fact that you will *never* touch my pussy again!' That should have been the end of that!"

Dawn was dying laughing. "You really treat guys like that?" she asked, astounded. "You tell them all that?" Dawn didn't have much experience with dating. She'd been with her boyfriend, Darius, since high school, and their bond was stronger than ever. She was intrigued by Chloe's no-nonsense approach to guys.

Chloe shook her head. "Nope. I don't have to tell them that. Look at me," she said, gesturing at her hair, clothes, and shoes. "When you look impressive, men know not to come at you half-assed. When you keep your hair done and your nails and toes neat, and carry yourself with class and self-respect, no man in his right mind would think to treat you as anything less than a queen. You know that, Dawn." She pointed to her friend. "Look at how Darius treats you. I've seen you two together. He holds doors for you, pulls out your chair, tickles you, and all that. That's the way we *all* deserve to be treated!" She looked at Kim for emphasis. "A guy could tell from the moment he first sees me that I ain't a bum bitch. And when a guy sees that you're about something, he will always treat you like you're about something." Chloe was quoting her mother almost verbatim. Rachel would've been proud.

"That's true," Dawn said, nodding.

Kim wondered if Chloe was implying that she didn't carry herself as if she was about something. "Well, I know I'm a queen."

"So why do you care about Chris so much when he treats you so bad?" Dawn asked.

" 'Cause I like him, that's why." Kim was tired of explaining herself to her friends. "And if I want to forgive him, that's my business."

Chloe shook her head in disgust. "Trust that you won't catch *me* going through no man's phone or worrying about who he's with. Please!"

Kim frowned. "I know you ain't trying to play me, bitch." She couldn't stand Chloe sometimes. Especially when she was being condescending and acted as if she had everything all figured out. It made Kim reluctant about sharing the negative things in her life, for fear she'd be criticized or put down.

Chloe looked at Kim and calmly shook her head. "Not at

all," she said. "I'm just saying what *I* would be doing if I were you. And I would *not* be listening to him call me out my name and letting him hang up on me every ten minutes. I would *not* be answering my phone if he called me. That's all I'm saying. I think females—all of us, at some point in our lives—can be really silly when it comes to guys. We spend so much time worrying about them, when they spend so little time worrying about us. It's all a game. It's just a matter of who's the better player."

Dawn smiled. "I like that," she said, giving Chloe five. "So you think that so far you're a better player than Trey?"

Chloe nodded. "Absolutely. I got him spending his money trying to get in my pants. I'm getting everything I want from him. Meanwhile, I have no intention of giving up any pussy any time soon."

Kim shook her head. "Then he won't spend money on you much longer," she said. "Once he sees that he's not getting the panties, he will move on. Trust me!" She was hating just a little.

Chloe shrugged her shoulders. "No problem. Next!"

They all laughed, and Chloe's cell phone rang. She looked at the caller ID and smirked. "See?" she said. She showed the screen to her friends, and the name JASON was displayed. "He's the one I'm actually fucking. He has already graduated to that point. He spends money on me consistently, knows not to call me unless he's ready to spend *more* money, and the sex is out of this damn world!" She answered her phone as her friends looked on admiringly. They listened while she made plans to see Jason that night, and they both had to hand it to her. Chloe knew how to play the game!

When she was done talking to Jason, Chloe turned her attention back to her eager pupils. "Eventually, I'm sure I'll sleep with Trey. But on *my* terms. Not his!"

"I hear you," Kim said. She turned her cell phone off for the time being, changed the subject, and the three friends enjoyed each other's company for the rest of the rainy Sunday afternoon.

Chloe met Jason at his place late that night. He only had the basement apartment of his mother's house, but it was a start. Most of the guys her age were still living in the same home and sleeping in the same bed they grew up in.

In Jason's apartment, the ceiling was so low that he could barely stand up straight in there. But it didn't matter. They didn't spend much time standing upright at all.

"Did you miss me?" she asked as she stepped inside, unzipped her dress, and let it fall to the floor. She stood before him, wearing nothing but a sexy smile.

He nodded and walked over to her, kissed her and scooped her naked ass into his large hands. He tossed her on the bed unceremoniously and then climbed on top of her and licked and sucked her until she called out his name. They spent the entire night in bed, with Jason making her climax four different ways.

She thought about calling Kim and letting her listen so that she could take notes on how to live life to the muthafuckin' fullest! In the morning, she woke up, showered, dressed, and joined Trey in their usual spot on the boat. Chloe felt like the queen of the world.

DON'T TALK, JUST LISTEN

Rachel had just gotten home after a night out with her man. Robert was a mechanic who owned two cars and a house, and he had money to spend, which Rachel absolutely loved about him. They'd met in Lower Manhattan when Rachel was on her lunch break. Robert had been coming out of Chase Bank, not watching where he was going, and had bumped into Rachel. After apologizing profusely, he'd suggested that maybe it was destiny. Then he invited her to join him for lunch, and the rest was history.

In the year since their initial meeting, Rachel had learned a great deal about the man. In his youth, he'd been in the streets hustling, making money, and living the high life. A stint in federal prison tamed him, though, and Robert had reformed his life. Now he had a legitimate hustle as a mechanic, making good money. But Rachel still found herself wondering how he managed to have such deep pockets. Mechanics got paid, but not *that* much! Still, she didn't question him or rock the boat. She was more than happy to help him spend his dough, whether it was ill-gotten or not. His appearance was pressed and polished, and he behaved like a perfect gentleman. Robert had explained that while he was locked up, he realized it was time to change his lifestyle. He decided to become a mechanic because he had always enjoyed working with his hands. With Rachel he used those hands well, and she loved it! Robert wined and dined her, and she spent several weekends each month at his house, which gave her a much-needed break from her everyday grind.

Today, she came in whistling and practically skipped to the bathroom to take a shower.

"Ma," Chloe called out from her room. "Don't forget that Trey is coming over to meet you in a little while."

Rachel had almost forgotten. "Okay," she responded, then slipped into the bathroom with thoughts of Robert etching a smile on her face.

As she showered, Rachel thought about her journey as a single mother and was happy with the way things had turned out. She wasn't living in the lap of luxury as every woman wished she did. But she wasn't doing too badly either. Her job was comfortable, and so was her home. Her daughters were developing into well-rounded young ladies, and her love life was at an all-time high. She whistled some more as she lathered her body, feeling better than she ever had before.

In her bedroom, Chloe opened the shoe box as if there were a treasure inside and displayed the contents to her sister.

"He bought those for you?" Willow asked, wondering how much money transit workers made.

Chloe flaunted the Coach sneakers Trey had given her, then checked her reflection in the mirror. It was amazing what a new hairstyle could do. Trey had also paid for her trip to the hair salon, which had done wonders for Chloe's already lovely appearance. She felt better than ever.

She smiled at her younger sister. "It's for my birthday. Twenty-one and legal, baby! Don't hate!" she teased Willow. "I didn't think he'd really get them for me, but I'm not complaining. He's like that all the time. If we go out, I never have to reach for my wallet. He takes care of everything. I love that about him."

Willow was jealous. "Tell him I'm a size eight and a half."

Chloe laughed and plopped down on her bed in the room they shared. "I can't wait for you to meet him. He said he'd be here at four o'clock. And he's never late."

Willow looked at the clock and saw that it was close to one thirty. She was eager to meet the guy her sister spoke of so often. It had been close to two months, and Trey was all Chloe talked about. Willow knew that Chloe still talked to and flirted with other guys. But Trey was definitely high on her list of priorities. Chloe always took his calls and took extra time whenever she got ready for one of their dates. Willow hadn't met a guy who was worth her time yet. At fifteen, she was going through an awkward phase. She was slightly chubby and had occasional outbreaks of acne. But still, she was a cute girl with a brilliant mind. There were guys in her school who she thought were cute, but none of them seemed to notice her. Willow was enchanted by the whirlwind romance her sister seemed to be involved in with Trey.

"You said that when you met him, he just struck up a conversation with you. What did you have on? How were you wearing your hair? 'Cause guys like that never strike up random conversations with me."

Chloe smiled at her sister. "It's important to pay attention to how you wear your hair or how you dress. But guys don't get as caught up in all of that as women do. It's all about the vibe between you and him. It's all about being sexy. Not slutty and easy. Just flirt a little. Flutter your eyelashes, smile, soften your tone. It goes a long way. If you like a guy, you can let him know it without telling him in words."

Willow was taking mental notes. "So when I meet a guy and I like his style, I should smile at him and hope he gets the message?" Willow frowned. "I don't think I know how to flirt. I come across like Ugly Betty, and it's real awkward."

Chloe smiled. She was definitely the more social one. Willow, on the other hand, was somewhat shy and didn't really know how to approach the boys she liked. Chloe was the queen of flirtation, and she liked to impart some of her knowledge to her younger sister.

"So, let me guess. There's a guy you like at school, right?"

Willow smiled shyly and nodded. "This guy named Eric Hall. He is so cute, Chloe! All the girls like him, though, and I don't know how to get him to notice me when everyone else is trying to get his attention."

"Okay," Chloe said. "You have to act like you're not that into him. Sounds crazy, but it will work. I promise. He's probably used to having chicks lavish him with attention. They're probably throwing themselves at him every day."

Willow nodded quickly. "Yeah! They are! You should see these girls at school. They act like groupies! And he just smiles and loves every minute of it. He sits next to me in my art class, but I don't know what to say to get his attention."

"Well, here's what you do. You're already halfway there because you're pretty and you dress nice and you're a genius! He'd be a fool not to like you. Just step it up a notch. Make sure your lip gloss is popping every time you step into art class. Check your hair in the mirror every time you know you're going to see him. Make sure you smell good when you're around him. And flirt with him, Willow."

"How?"

"Just soften your tone when you speak to him. Ask him for help with things you don't really need help with. Guys love to feel like they're teaching us something. Let him think he's doing that. I'm not saying act dumb. Just let him take the lead sometimes. Become his friend, and as a 'friend' ask him if he saw a certain movie or if he read a certain book. Ask him to help you with your art project. Eventually, if he has any sense, he'll notice that you're different from the other girls because you're not putting yourself right on out there. He'll respect that, and soon you'll have him eating out of the palm of your hand."

A knock at the front door interrupted Chloe's speech. She sprang up from her bed and checked her hair in the mirror. She glanced at the digital clock as she made for the front door. Trey was almost ten minutes early. She got to the front door at the same time her mother did. Rachel smiled at her daughter, who was visibly excited that her new boo was finally about to meet her family.

When Chloe opened the door and ushered Trey inside, Rachel's smile broadened. He was such a handsome man. He wasn't a baggy-pants-and-a-do-rag kinda guy like she saw walking around the city each day. Instead, Trey seemed much older than Chloe, not just in years but in life experience as well. His appearance was neat and pressed. He smelled good; his hair was groomed. And when he smiled at Rachel, she felt herself blush.

Chloe introduced him, shyly. "Ma, this is Trey."

"Hi," Trey said. "It's nice to meet you." He shook her hand, and she noticed that his grip was firm and strong. His hands were hard, presumably from his job in the subway. He looked around the apartment and smiled again. "Your house is so nice. And neat!"

Rachel's cheeks hurt from smiling so hard. "Thanks, Trey. It's nice to meet you, too," she said. Willow cleared her throat, and Rachel snapped out of it. "This is Willow."

Willow smiled and waved her fingers at Trey. He smiled back and nodded in her direction. "Hello," he said. "I heard a lot about you."

Willow forced another smile. For some reason, Willow already didn't like him. She couldn't put her finger on why. But something about him made her feel hesitant to welcome him with open arms. Willow figured that maybe it was pure envy, since Chloe was having her socks knocked off while Willow had yet to even be kissed. She brushed off the jealousy as Rachel ushered them into her living room and offered Trey something to drink. He politely declined, and they all sat down.

Rachel wasted no time. "So, Trey," she began, crossing her legs. "You're new to Staten Island?"

He nodded. "Yeah. I like it, though. It's quiet."

"Where did you live before that?" Willow asked. She was curious as hell about this man Chloe had brought home.

"The Bronx." He brushed imaginary lint off his shirt and shifted nervously.

"Your family still live there?" Rachel asked.

Trey looked at the floor. "My father does." He looked up at Chloe and then smiled at Rachel. "I see where Chloe gets her good looks from. No disrespect, but you're very pretty."

Rachel felt herself starting to blush again. She thanked Trey for his compliment and cleared her throat.

He looked at Willow now. "You, too. Chloe talks about you all the time."

"So you work in the subway, huh?" Willow asked.

Again, he nodded. "Yeah. I help maintain the subway tracks

at night. It's cool. A lot of rats and homeless people. But I'm used to it."

Willow frowned. Rats made her skin crawl. She looked at Trey and wondered how a guy this cute could have such an ugly job. "You must make a lot of money doing that, since you keep buying Chloe so much nice stuff!"

"What kind of stuff?" Rachel asked, frowning slightly herself.

Chloe shot a glare at her sister. She didn't want Rachel to know the amount of money Trey spent on her, because she knew her mother wouldn't approve. Rachel had always lectured her daughters about not letting guys trick their dough on them. *It makes a man feel powerful over you, like he owns you*, she'd always say. Personally, Chloe felt her mother was being hypocritical, since she knew that Rachel accepted gifts from the man she was dating. But out of respect, Chloe had never said that to her mother.

Rachel looked at Chloe, then at Trey, then back again. She looked Chloe up and down and noticed the Coach sneakers she was wearing and the big diamond hoop earrings hanging from her ears. "Did Trey buy you those earrings?" she asked.

Chloe nodded uneasily. "Yes, he did," she said, sensing her mother's disapproval.

"And those sneakers, too?"

"They're birthday presents, Ma."

"Expensive ones," Rachel observed.

"She deserves it," Trey replied, smiling at Chloe and then looking back at Ms. Webster.

"Why does she deserve them?" Rachel asked. "Don't get me wrong—she *does* deserve nice things—but I wanna know why *you* think she deserves them." Rachel was really wondering if Chloe was already screwing this boy. And if she was, Rachel didn't even want to imagine what her daughter was doing to get such expensive tokens of affection.

Trey cleared his throat. "Because she's a true lady. She was raised well, carries herself like a princess, and so I treat her as such."

Rachel noticed that Trey was saying all the right things. Still, her intuition tugged at her. "How old are you, Trey?"

"Twenty-seven."

"I see," Rachel said simply. The six-year age difference between Trey and her daughter bothered her, but Rachel decided she'd speak with Chloe about that later.

"Trey goes to school part-time at BMCC. He's studying psychology." Chloe smiled proudly as she said it.

Trey simply nodded in agreement.

Rachel raised an eyebrow, impressed. "Psychology is a very interesting field of study."

He nodded again. "It is. I like it. It's interesting to find out what makes people tick. What sets them off and things like that."

"What sets *you* off?" Willow asked, curious.

"Willow!" Rachel chastised her youngest daughter. "That's not a polite question."

Willow couldn't believe her mother was offended by a simple

question. "What?" Willow asked, genuinely confused. "I just want to know what kind of guy he is."

Trey smirked. "It's okay," he said. He looked at the teenager. "I'm no different from anybody else, really. We all have things we dislike about people. But I'm pretty normal. Nothing out of the ordinary."

Chloe shot her sister another evil look, and Willow shrugged. She was just being protective of Chloe. She loved her sister and wanted to make sure this guy was worth her time. He answered all the questions right, he wore the right clothes, bought her sister the right gifts. But she wanted to make sure he wasn't too good to be true.

Willow decided on a softer approach. "So, what do you do for fun?" she asked.

Trey smiled and looked at Chloe. "Well, lately Chloe takes up most of my free time. Between my job and my classes, there's not much time to do too much else."

Rachel nodded. "Well, it seems like the two of you really enjoy each other's company. I think that's great. But just try not to move too fast. Things can get complicated if you do."

An awkward silence followed.

Chloe cleared her throat. "Okay, well, we have reservations for dinner. We need to leave so we're not late." She stood up, and Trey happily followed suit.

Rachel stood as well. She walked over to Trey and shook his hand. "It was very nice to meet you," she said. "You'll have to come over and have dinner with us soon."

Trey smiled, relieved that his meeting with Chloe's family was finally over. "Thank you," he said. "I'd like that."

Willow watched in silence as Chloe and Trey left. She couldn't wait till she could meet a guy who would lavish her with designer clothes and sneakers, days at the hair salon, and expensive dinners. Some girls had all the luck.

"So," Trey said as he sat beside Chloe in the taxi zipping through the streets of Manhattan. "What did you do today?"

Chloe shrugged. "Nothing, really. Just hung out with my friends for a little while—that's about it." She left out the fact that she'd spent part of her afternoon getting her back dug out at Jason's place.

Trey stared at her for a long time, but said nothing.

Chloe looked at him and tried to think of some way to change the subject. "Well, now that you've met my family, tell me about yours." She was eager to meet Trey's folks, curious to see his old neighborhood.

Trey shifted in his seat. "What do you wanna know?"

"I don't know. Do you have any sisters or brothers?"

He shook his head. "Nah. I'm an only child. I always wanted a brother or sister. I used to be jealous of kids who had siblings to chill with. Like you and Willow, for instance. You two seem real close. Y'all look out for each other."

Chloe nodded. "I love my sister. She's a pain in the ass sometimes, but we're very close. She listens to me and she looks up to me."

"That's wassup," Trey said. "It's good that she has somebody she can talk to when she has to deal with the shit teenage girls go through. Having you around should help her avoid some of the bullshit."

Chloe nodded. "I can't believe how many of the kids she went to junior high with are pregnant or have kids already. It's fuckin' sad. I'm just happy that shit hasn't happened to her."

Trey smiled at her. "That's 'cause she has you to keep her on track. You're in school, focused on your future. That's a good look. You're a good example for her."

The driver pulled up in front of the pricey restaurant, and Trey paid the man. She looked at him and smiled, proud to have a guy like Trey in her life. This was how it was supposed to be—the way women were supposed to be courted. He was so mature, and being with him made her feel more grown up. They ate dinner, made small talk, and laughed together. They had a beautiful night. When it was over, Trey once again footed the bill, and they headed back to Staten Island. On their way back to the ferry terminal, Chloe let Trey's hands roam up her skirt and underneath her blouse in the backseat of the taxi. She wondered for a moment if the driver knew what they were doing in his cab. But as Trey fingered her and stroked her breasts, she forgot all about the driver. She rubbed him through his pants and then unzipped his pants and pulled it out. He had a big, beautiful dick, and she was impressed.

Trey could barely contain himself, wanting her in the worst way. But it wasn't long before they arrived at the ferry terminal. Trey paid the driver, hating that the ride had to end.

As they walked inside the terminal, they held hands. Chloe felt like she was floating on a cloud.

While they waited for the ferry to prepare for passenger boarding, Trey turned to Chloe. "You should spend the night with me," he said. "We already catch the same boat in the morning. It would be nice to wake up next to you."

Chloe shook her head. "I'm not ready for that," she said. The last thing she wanted to do was sleep with Trey and have him stop lavishing her with the things she enjoyed. Chloe was a firm believer that having sex too soon could fuck up a good thing. Especially with an older man like Trey. She didn't want him to lose interest, so she was holding out. She kept Jason around for sex and was satisfied with the arrangement. At this point in their romance, she was happy just to spend time with Trey, talk to him, flirt with him, and help him spend his money. She would take things as slowly as possible.

"We don't have to have sex," Trey assured her. "We can just talk or lay in bed and watch TV. It doesn't have to be physical."

You just finished feeling me up in the cab! she thought. But she had to admit that it all felt so good.

Chloe thought about it as they boarded the ferry. She really liked Trey. In fact, she was hopeful that he would be "the one." But they had only been seeing each other for close to two months, and she just didn't want to mess up a good thing.

"I think that's sweet," she said. "But I just wanna go home tonight and get some sleep. I'm really exhausted. And I'm sure you have better things to do than to watch me sleep."

Trey finally dropped it and settled for making the most of

the ride home. As the ferry headed from Lower Manhattan back to Staten Island, Trey pulled her closer to him and wrapped his arms around her. She nestled into his embrace, and together they watched the beautiful New York City skyline melt into the distance. Chloe's smile broadened when she saw Nikki, the girl who had hated on her in high school, watching from a distance as Trey showered her with affection. Chloe was loving this—being the center of attention, the envy of hating-ass bitches like Nikki. This was something she could definitely get used to.

Meanwhile, Trey thought to himself that he would be as patient as he needed to be. Because he was definitely falling for Chloe Webster.

Chloe got home from her date and found her mother waiting up for her. She smiled, surprised to see Rachel awake at such a late hour. "Hey, Ma."

"Hey," Rachel said. "Sit down for a minute."

Chloe did as she was told, and her mother sighed. "So I think Trey seems like a nice guy. He's handsome, he's respectful, polite."

Chloe folded her arms across her chest. "But . . ."

"But from what Willow is telling me, he's spending money on you like crazy. Coach sneakers, Tiffany bracelets and necklaces, trips to the hair salon . . . that's a lot for him to be spending on you, Chloe. You just met the guy."

Chloe couldn't believe her ears. "You're kidding right?"

"No, I'm not kidding at all," Rachel asserted.

"Ma . . . how much would you say Robert spends on you in a week?"

"Watch it, now, Chloe," Rachel warned. "Robert and I are grown and—"

"Well, I'm twenty-one, so I'm grown, too." She met her mother's gaze. "I understand what you're saying, Ma. Thanks for your concern. But there's nothing to worry about."

"It's my job to worry about you." Rachel sighed. "You think you know everything. But don't be blinded by expensive gifts and wining and dining. That can be deceiving."

Chloe tried to resist the urge to roll her eyes. "Ma, Trey's not the boogeyman. He has no tricks up his sleeve. He's just a nice guy. That's it."

"He's older than you," Rachel observed.

"And?" Chloe frowned, confused. She didn't think the age difference between Trey and herself was a big deal at all.

"And," Rachel said, "I just think that maybe Trey is a little more experienced than you are, and maybe he's expecting you to be impressed by all the money he lavishes on you. You have to think, Chloe. You're thinking he's a nice guy, when all along he could have ulterior motives."

"Ma, stop." Chloe sighed in exasperation. "It's nothing like that. Trey is not that much older than me. And he's not trying to manipulate me or impress me. He's just a nice guy. Just like your friend Robert is a nice guy. Okay?"

Chloe got up and went to bed, leaving her mother sitting in silence in the living room. Rachel took a sip of her wine and shook her head. She hoped Chloe knew what she was doing.

Chloe and Dawn stood in front of Kim's building on Jersey Street and watched the spectacle before them. Chris was embarrassing Kim in front of all the passersby, and Chloe was appalled.

"Don't worry about where I was last night," Chris said, looking Kim up and down like she disgusted him. "I keep telling you I ain't your man. Don't ask me shit."

Kim didn't seem the slightest bit embarrassed. "So stop fucking me like you're my man, then!" She had her hands on her hips and steam coming out of her ears.

"I'm tired of telling you the same thing over and over. I like you, Kim. Word. I really do. But it ain't serious with us. I'm not your man, ma. Period."

"Kim, fuck that nigga!" Chloe had seen and heard enough. This was too much!

"Fuck you, you gold-digging bitch!" Chris shot back. He looked at Kim. "Stop hanging around with bitches like that constantly putting thoughts in your head all the time."

"Bitch?" Chloe asked, amazed that this bum-ass bastard had the nerve to address her that way.

"Yeah. You heard me, bitch." Chris walked off, storming up the block and away from Kim and her friends before he had to hurt one of them.

To Chloe's shock, Kim went after him. "Kim!" Chloe called. "You gonna leave us here to chase his broke ass?" She couldn't believe it.

"I'll call you later," Kim cried over her shoulder, not bothering to so much as glance back at her friends. She continued to chase Chris, calling after him until he finally stopped walking and turned to talk to her.

Chloe and Dawn stood stunned as they watched Kim talk to Chris, seemingly begging and pleading with him. In disgust, the two women walked off toward Chloe's house. "She's a stupid bitch!" Chloe lamented to Dawn. "Choosing that asshole over her friends."

Dawn shook her head. "You can't tell her shit. She's one of those chicks who has to learn shit the hard way."

It was a Sunday afternoon, and Trey was following Chloe around the mall like a puppy follows its owner. He had called her that morning and suggested they get together. Chloe proposed a trip to the mall for some retail therapy, and he had happily agreed. They always did whatever Chloe wanted to do, and she liked it that way. Trey enjoyed her company so much, he never complained.

Most guys hogged conversations, talking about bullshit. Trey was always willing to listen to Chloe, whether it was during their hours-long late-night phone conversations or face-to-face during the times they spent together. He was demonstrative, generous, and attentive. Plus he was new to town, and everywhere they went together, they attracted attention. Trey was uncharted territory for the girls she knew. He was fresh meat—handsome, well-dressed, affectionate, and attentive—and he only had eyes for Chloe. She couldn't ask for much more than that. Chloe thought Kim was crazy to believe she didn't deserve similar treatment herself.

While she looked through a stack of jeans in the Guess store, she glanced up and caught Trey staring at her. She smiled, slightly uneasy, and stopped browsing. "What?" she asked.

Trey was embarrassed that she'd caught him staring at her. He cleared his throat and shyly looked away. "I don't mean to stare at you," he said. "Sometimes I can't help it, 'cause you're so pretty." The truth was, she reminded him of someone in his past so much sometimes that he couldn't help but stare.

Chloe blushed. "Awww! That's so sweet!" She walked around the rack and kissed him deeply. Chloe's kisses were like liquid sex, and Trey felt his temperature rise as she kissed him. "You make me feel so good, Trey," she said, her voice dripping seductively.

Trey felt his dick get hard as Chloe's voice took on a sultry, sexy cadence. She noticed him trying to hide his erection and she laughed. Trey was flustered and appeared to be a bit pissed off as the vein in his temple throbbed. He walked out of the store without another word before any of the other patrons noticed his condition, leaving Chloe standing there alone. She lingered a few moments, hoping he'd come back in so that she could get him to buy the blue jeans she had her eye on. But Trey stood outside the store, waiting. Chloe left the jeans on the shelf and walked out to where Trey stood. He seemed annoyed.

"You mad at me?" she asked. "Did I do something wrong?"

Trey looked her in the eye. He wanted to tell her he was sick of her teasing him, that he was tired of her leading him on. Trey wanted to have sex with Chloe. But he didn't want to appear impatient and scare her off. He forced a smile. "You didn't do anything wrong, sweetheart. I just didn't want the other women in there laughing at the guy standing by the rack with a hard dick."

Chloe laughed and linked her arm through his. They passed a store, and Trey stopped short. He noticed a pale yellow pullover sweater in the window and pointed it out to Chloe. "That's pretty," he said. "Let me buy it for you."

Chloe looked at the sweater and then back at Trey. She shook her head and frowned. It was a modest garment, prim and proper. Definitely not her style. "No. Let's go to Macy's. I saw a DKNY jacket you can buy for me instead." She led him by the hand, and Trey followed just as he always did.

THE SILENT TREATMENT

Trey stood in the ferry terminal, scrolling through the images in his camera. Picture after picture of his beloved Chloe appeared, causing him to smile. He was really feeling her. She made him forget so much of the pain in his past—but at the same time, she reminded him of the mother he'd lost when he was just ten years old. The resemblance between them was uncanny. He looked at one picture of Chloe as she emerged from school, backpack slung across one shoulder and the wind in her hair. He couldn't get enough of her.

He knew that Chloe kept secrets from him, and he was a little bothered by it. He had long suspected that she wasn't always out with her friends the way she claimed to be. He wasn't as dumb as she thought he was. And he wondered how long she would continue to see someone else behind his back. Trey wasn't seeing anyone else, and he wanted to take his relationship with Chloe to the next level—wanted to make her his and his alone. But he also didn't want to spook her. They had met only a few months ago, and in the past he had come on too strong in his relationships with women. This time he didn't want to make the same mistake. Still, it killed him to think of her in another man's arms. The more he thought about it, the sicker it made him feel.

Meanwhile, Willow had a half day at school and was glad. High school was tough, and as the end of the school year drew closer, she found herself swamped with papers to hand in, tests to take, and one deadline after another. She was relieved to be going home early, with no homework. She couldn't wait to spend an afternoon on the couch with the remote control.

She entered the ferry terminal and saw that the boat was already loading. She joined the packs of other passengers as they boarded and noticed a guy who looked familiar. It was Trey. She maneuvered through the crowd until she was at his side. "Hey, Trey," she said. Shc wondered what he was doing on the ferry so early in the afternoon, since Chloe had said that she and Trey had nearly identical schedules. It was Wednesday, and Chloe didn't get out of school until around six o'clock. She met Trey at the train, and each Wednesday the two of them went out to dinner after class. So Willow found it somewhat odd that Trey was on the ferry so early in the day.

He didn't even look at her. She wondered for a moment if he hadn't heard her over the sound of the crowd. She looked for headphones in his ear. Maybe he had his music turned up so loud that he couldn't hear her. She smiled again, waved her hand in front of him until she got him to look at her finally. He stared at Willow in silence. "Trey, hi. It's me, Willow. Chloe's sister."

He stared at her blankly, sending a chill up her spine. She waited for him to say something, but he never did. She got no response other than a cold, blank stare that made her so unsettled, she walked ahead of him. She found a seat on the ferry that was not too close to him, but still close enough that she could watch him.

She kept staring at him, wondering if he was indeed her sister's boyfriend. Maybe she had spoken to the wrong guy. Maybe it wasn't Trey after all. But as she sat there several feet from where he sat alone staring out at the water, she was sure that it was Trey. He was the same guy Willow and her mother had met in her living room weeks ago, who had said all the right things. And now here he was, acting like he had never met Willow before in his life. He hadn't said a single word to her, and she was confused. When the ferry docked, she waited for him to get up so that she could follow him. But he never moved from his seat, even as the announcement came on that "all passengers must depart the ferry at this time." Finally, Willow rose to leave and glanced again in Trey's direction. He was looking at her, watching her make her exit and staring at her with the same icy glare that he had before.

Willow couldn't wait for Chloe to get home that night. When she did, Willow was pacing the floor in their bedroom. "What took you so long to get home?" she demanded as soon as Chloe walked in the door. "I've been waiting for you all day!"

Chloe frowned. "Why didn't you just call me? I had my phone with me. What's wrong with you?"

Willow shook her head. "I wasn't going to call you while you were with *him*!"

"Trey?"

"Yeah, Trey!" Willow could hardly get the words out, she was so anxious. "I saw him today. Did he tell you?"

Chloe set her backpack down and sat on her bed. "No. I just had dinner with him, and he didn't mention anything about you. Where did you see him?" Chloe backtracked in her mind and thought about her conversation with Trey over dinner. She tried to recall if he had mentioned Willow at all, but he hadn't. She was certain of that. In fact, most of their conversation had centered around Trey asking her for details of how her day had gone at school. That had been difficult for her to answer, since she didn't actually go to school today. Chloe had skipped class and spent the day holed up in a hotel room in Midtown with Jason. It was a great day of one earth-shattering orgasm after another, and Chloe still glowed from the sex. She had pried herself out of Jason's arms just to meet Trey at Mr. Chow's in time for their reservation. When he'd pressed her for details of her day, she had to think on her feet and make up a bunch of stuff on the spot. And when Trey stared at her in silence, her guilt caused her to wonder if he was onto her. But he wasn't, and the night had gone smoothly after that. She was certain he'd made no mention of running into Willow.

"I saw him on the boat. I walked over to him and said hi. But he didn't say a single word to me. He just stood there, staring at me like he'd never met me before. At first I didn't think it was him. But I kept looking at him, and I *know* it was. I know it was him. I waited for him to get off the ferry, but he didn't. He just sat there like he was riding it back and forth to Manhattan or something. And the whole time, he just kept staring at me." Willow was talking a mile a minute.

Chloe frowned. "Really?"

"I'm telling you it was him, Chloe. And I told him who I was, thinking that he must not recognize me. He ignored me and just stared at me. He had on a pair of black jeans, a Rocawear jacket, and some black sneakers. But he didn't have a book bag. Does he usually carry one?"

Chloe mulled it over. Willow had described Trey's outfit perfectly. And it was true: he wasn't carrying a backpack. In fact, now she tried to recall if she had ever seen him carry any books since the day she met him. She shook her head and dialed Trey's number. "Hey," she said when he answered on the first ring. "Did you see my sister today on the ferry?"

Willow listened as her sister questioned Trey. When Chloe hung up, she could hardly wait to ask her, "What did he say?"

Chloe shrugged. "He said that you must be mistaken. He said he didn't see you and he wasn't even on the boat this afternoon. His last class is at five o'clock on Wednesdays, so it couldn't have been him." Chloe stood up and pinched Willow's chubby cheeks. "You're just being too suspicious, Nancy Drew." Chloe went to use the bathroom, leaving Willow sitting speechless in her wake.

No matter what Trey said or what Chloe believed, Willow knew it was Trey she'd seen that day. And the thought of his icy stare sent chills down her spine.

QUESTIONS

Over the next several weeks, Trey ran into Chloe in a number of places. He saw her at the mall while she was shopping with her friends, and he bought them all lunch before leaving them to continue their shopping spree. Of course, he peeled off a couple of large bills for Chloe before he left. Her friends loved him!

Kim was still going out with sorry-ass Chris, and nothing had changed. He was up to his usual bullshit. Seeing the way Trey doted on Chloe made Kim realize just how sad her relationship with Chris was. Trey was the perfect gentleman, and

Kim and Dawn had finally seen why Chloe was always bragging about him.

"You really like him, huh?" Kim asked as they looked at fake designer sunglasses.

Chloe smiled. "Yeah. I do." She stared off in space, thinking about him.

"So what about Jason?" Dawn asked. "How come you're still messing with him if you're so crazy about Trey."

"Jason is familiar. He gives me good sex and good conversation. That's why I keep him around."

"You're still not having sex with Trey?" Kim asked incredulously.

Chloe shook her head. "Nope. Not till I'm ready."

Kim made a face and wondered how long Chloe's luck would hold up with a guy like that.

Trey later ran into Chloe at the supermarket when she was out with her mother. He'd shopped along with Chloe and Rachel and helped them load the groceries into their car before he went home himself. Chloe had been happy to see him and was even happier that Willow opted not to go shopping with them that afternoon. Willow was still convinced that Trey had given her the cold shoulder, despite Chloe's assurance that it wasn't him. Rachel still had her doubts about Trey as well. But Chloe believed their insistence that Trey was nothing but trouble was just a case of the green-eyed monster rearing its ugly head. Chloe knew she had chosen the perfect gentleman.

Trey even ran into Chloe at the bodega on Jersey Street one day, and she was surprised to see him.

"Hey," she said. "I didn't expect to see you here. Don't you have class this afternoon?" It was a Tuesday, and Chloe's one class had been canceled for the day.

"I was tired this morning, so I didn't get up when my alarm clock went off." Trey paid for his Sprite, and together they walked out of the store.

For a brief moment, Chloe wondered why Trey was at this particular store, since there was one much closer to his house. She wondered if he was coming from seeing another girl, and she was pissed. But then Trey said, "I'm glad I ran into you. I have a surprise for you."

She beamed and forgot all about her suspicions. "You do?"

"Yeah." Trey opened the passenger-side door of his white Camry for her, and she climbed inside. He got in the driver's seat and smiled at her. "Wanna go to the movies? I don't know if you had plans for this afternoon, but I want to see that new Tyler Perry joint."

"Sure," she said impatiently. "Now, where's my surprise?"

Trey laughed and kissed her. Chloe's enthusiasm was visible. "It's in the backseat."

Chloe saw a box in the backseat and reached for it before she even buckled her seat belt. She tore at the box and then quickly moved the tissue paper aside to reveal the same pale yellow sweater Trey had pointed out in the store window days ago. She tried to hide her disappointment. "Thank you!" she said, feigning excitement. "That was so nice of you!" But she was really thinking, *What a fuckin loser! I don't even like this ugly shit. Shows how much he listens.*

Trey smiled. He couldn't wait to see her wearing it. "Ready to see the movie?" he asked.

Chloe pretended she was thrilled. "Yup!" she plastered an Oscar-worthy smile on her face and tossed the wretched sweater in the backseat.

She noticed Trey's cell phone kept vibrating, but that he never answered it. She felt another unexpected twinge of jealousy as she wondered whether another woman was calling him. Chloe was still seeing Jason on the low, so she really had no right to be upset.

Still, as the phone vibrated for the third time in twenty minutes and Trey continued to ignore it, Chloe turned and looked at him. "Who's that you're ignoring? Your other girlfriend?"

Trey took his eyes off the road briefly and glanced at her before returning his attention to the traffic. He was honored to see Chloe so obviously jealous. And had she just implied that he was her boyfriend? Trey liked the sound of that.

"Nah," he said, setting his phone down. "It's my job calling me, trying to get me to come in and do a double shift. I don't feel like going into work early, so I'm ignoring them." He saw a gas station and decided to stop and fill up his tank.

Chloe nodded, feeling slightly silly. As they pulled into the gas station, she admitted to herself that Trey's explanation sounded perfectly logical. He climbed out of the car to go and pay for his gas, leaving his cell phone lying invitingly on the driver's seat. Chloe figured she should trust what Trey had told her, since he had never given her reason to doubt him. Just to be sure—and as usual, being slow to trust a man—Chloe slyly reached for Trey's phone and looked at the list of missed calls. Seven missed calls from MOM.

Chloe was confused. Why would he lie about his job calling him, when it was really his mother? His mother . . . Chloe had never heard him mention his mother before. She tried to recall if Trey had ever talked at length about his family. She couldn't think of one instance when he had divulged much about his family, his friends, or anything personal. Chloe realized for the first time that she had been so caught up in what a great listener Trey was that she never noticed how little he spoke about himself. She decided to ask him about the phone calls from "Mom" when he got back in the car.

Meanwhile, Trey finished paying the Arab guy behind the counter for his gas and a bottle of water. But he was preoccupied as he did so, thinking about the phone calls he'd been ignoring for days now. Why couldn't everyone just leave him the fuck alone?

As he stepped out and headed toward the pump where his car was parked, Trey yawned. He was exhausted after spending yet another late night sitting up, watching videotapes. As he stepped off the curb, a Nissan came to a screeching halt just inches from hitting him. His heart racing, he realized how close the woman had come to running him down. Scowling at the driver, he took a deep breath and told himself not to overreact. She hadn't hit him, so no harm, no foul.

The woman behind the wheel couldn't believe this idiot had the nerve to give her a dirty look. She stuck her middle finger up at him and yelled out her open window, "Move out of the fucking way before you get yourself killed!"

Trey erupted in rage. "You stupid bitch! You should watch where the fuck you're going!" He charged over and kicked her car, then reached through the open window as if to grab the horrified woman. The entire time, he cursed her out viciously. The gas station attendant came running over and pulled Trey away from the driver, who had shrunk to the passenger side of her own car to get away from the raving black man.

The attendant tried to calm Trey. "Calm down! It's okay."

Trey was pumped and ready for battle. His chest was heaving and his muscles bulged. "That crazy bitch almost ran me down!"

"I saw it, my friend. I saw the whole thing! She was wrong. Just go. It is not worth it!"

The woman sped off, checking her rearview to make sure that crazy nigga wasn't following her. Trey stood in her wake, furious, his chest heaving. He walked over to his car and pumped his gas as Chloe sat petrified in the passenger seat. Once he'd pumped his gas, Trey climbed back into the car and started it.

Chloe looked over at him. He was sweating, and the vein was throbbing in his temple again. She could tell he was pissed off. "What happened?" she asked, now too distracted to even question him about the mysterious calls.

Trey didn't answer her. Instead, he shook his head, turned up the music, and peeled out of there.

Chloe sat in her anthropology class and text-messaged Jason for the hundredth time. She hadn't seen him in weeks, and he wasn't returning any of her phone calls. She didn't want to just pop up over his house, because their relationship wasn't like that. It wasn't like he was her man or anything. Still, Jason had never ignored her phone calls, text messages, and voice mails until now. She wondered what had made him switch up so suddenly. Then she shrugged it off. *Fuck him*, she thought. At least she still had Trey to keep her occupied.

Weeks had passed since the incident at the gas station, and Trey had done everything he could to show Chloe he wasn't a ticking time bomb waiting to explode. He hated the fact that she had seen him lose his cool, and he assured her that the behavior she'd witnessed wasn't typical of him. Chloe told him that she understood, that everyone gets angry sometimes. But just to be on the safe side, Trey lavished her with more gifts and more attention than ever before. And Chloe was loving every minute of it.

One day, as Trey drove her to the library, he looked over at her and sized up her outfit. She wore a pair of denim capris that were so tight, he wondered how she had gotten into them. And her T-shirt looked like it was sized for a preschooler. "Why don't you ever wear the sweater I bought for you?" he asked.

"Oh," she said, caught off guard. "It doesn't fit. Too big. I gave it to Willow."

She noticed that Trey gripped the wheel a little tighter. Still, he said nothing. Figuring she was coming across as an ungrateful bitch, Chloe changed the subject and talked about all the compliments she was getting from the girls at school on the Coach bag he'd bought for her. She knew she would never wear that ugly-ass sweater, no matter how it hurt Trey's feelings. With all the other countless articles of clothing he'd bought for her, why did that damn sweater matter so much, anyway?

The following month, Rachel Webster warned her daughter again that she was letting Trey spend too much money on her. She liked Trey, but was wondering whether her daughter was in fact leading the generous young man on.

"Chloe, be careful, I'm telling you. You let a guy spend this much time with you and money on you, and they start to feel like they own you. Trey's a nice guy and I don't think he's like that. But I want you to be sure that you're not leading him on and taking advantage of his generosity. Playing with people's emotions can be dangerous. Especially because you two have been seeing each other for only a few months."

"Ma, I'm a grown woman. I can take care of myself." Chloe hated when her mother acted like she was still a kid. Rachel should be saving all her lectures for Willow, who was still young, naive, and impressionable. Chloe was anything but.

"I know you can take care of yourself, Missy. I'm just making sure that you're not getting caught up."

"I'm not," Chloe said simply. "But thanks for your concern." She grabbed her new Bebe handbag and headed out for a day in the park with her two dearest friends.

Dawn and Kim were sitting in Mahoney Park on their usual bench. It was a beautiful and sunny May day, and the girls were eager to show off their new gear. School was officially out, and that meant lazy hot summer days ahead. Dawn waved at her friend as she approached. Chloe walked over to where they sat and smiled brightly as she greeted them.

"Wassup, divas?"

"Nice bag!" Kim snatched up the pricey clutch as soon as Chloe set it on the bench beside her. "Trey still ain't tired of spending dough on you, huh? After three months of no ass, I'm surprised he hasn't given up on you."

Chloe laughed. "First of all, my mom bought me that bag."

"But I bet Trey bought the matching shoes," Dawn said, smirking.

Chloe cut her eyes at her friend, but then chose to ignore her. She sighed. "Second of all, I think I'm finally going to give him some pussy."

Dawn gasped and clapped her hands. "Finally!"

"Oh my God!" Kim's mouth hung open in shock. "What brought about the change of heart?"

Chloe shrugged. "I don't know," she said. "I really like him. He pays attention to me, he spoils me, and he's very thoughtful and romantic. Plus he's fine."

Kim nodded. "He *is* fine!"

Chloe laughed. "I think he might have potential. I like spending time with him, talking on the phone with him, and he was a big hit with my mother. She loves him."

Chloe knew that was a lie. Both her mother and her sister had reservations about the man in her life. But Chloe liked him. In fact, Rachel and Willow's hesitation to embrace Trey only made Chloe like him more.

Dawn nodded. "That's major. When the parents like a guy, it's a good sign. Usually no guy is good enough for their daughter. So if Miss Rachel likes him, he must be a keeper."

Chloe smiled. She wished what she'd said was true. It used to matter to her a lot more what her friends and family thought. So far, Trey was scoring high marks with everyone. Well, yes, except for her mother, who Chloe felt was just hating. And Willow, too, was still very suspicious of her sister's boyfriend. But Chloe told herself she didn't care what they thought. *She* liked Trey, and that was all that mattered. Plus, it had been weeks since she last heard from Jason, so she figured Trey had won by default.

Kim took a sip of her wine cooler, which was wrapped in a brown paper bag in case the police passed through. "I'm glad you're gonna give the man some ass. He earned it. Trey seems like a good dude. Even though I'm all for taking advantage of niggas, I would hate to see a good dude get his heart broken."

Chloe frowned slightly. "I wasn't taking advantage of Trey."

Her friends gave her looks that said, *Give me a break!*

Chloe laughed. "Well, not intentionally, anyway. I'm just not gonna be pressured into giving up my goodies too soon. No amount of clothes, dinners, or material things can make me see my sex as any less precious than it is. That's all. It's just as important for me to get what I want as it is for him to get what he wants. So I got most of the things I want—now he can finally get what he wants."

Kim nodded. "He'll be as happy as a faggot in Boystown when he hears that he's finally gonna get his dick wet." They laughed. “Damn,” Kim said. “I really wish I could find a good guy like that.”

Chloe sympathized with her friend because she knew Kim attracted the biggest losers. “I know,” she said. “I wish he had a brother we could hook you up with.”

Kim thought about that. “Does he have any cute friends?”

“I haven't met any of his friends,” Chloe admitted, realizing once again just how little of Trey's world she'd explored.

Dawn looked at her. “What? All this time you two have been spending together, and you haven't met a single friend?”

Chloe shook her head.

“Well, who does he hang out with when he's not with you?” Dawn asked.

Chloe smiled. “He's always with me,” she said. “When he's not at work or doing schoolwork, he's with me. He seems to like it that way.”

Dawn shook her head. “Maybe he just doesn't trust you.”

“That's not true. He trusts me. He just likes spending time with me.”

“Well, he met your mom and Willow. Have you met his family?” Kim asked.

“No. Not yet.” Chloe thought back to the incident at the gas station and the way he'd ignored the phone calls coming from his mother. After Trey's battle with the woman in the Nissan, Chloe had forgotten to ask him about those calls. But now she wondered what the story was with Trey's family. He never spoke about them, aside from telling Chloe's mom that his father still lived in the Bronx. And he'd mentioned that he didn't have any siblings. But as she sat in the park with her friends, she realized there was still so much she didn't know about her man.

"So then how do you know if he's even serious about you?" Kim asked. "You haven't met his family or his friends, and it sounds like you don't know much about him at all. This could just be a fling to him. Who knows?"

"It's not," Chloe said, waving her hand as if to dismiss the absurdity of her friend's remark.

Kim shrugged. "All I'm saying is that Trey is older than you, and he's probably been in more than a few relationships and maybe this just isn't as serious to him as you think it is."

Chloe was pissed now. "What, are you jealous, Kim?"

"What? Jealous of who? You?" Kim looked offended.

"Yeah. I mean, what's with all the twenty questions?" Chloe sat back and folded her arms across her chest.

"You're crazy," Kim said, though she *was* slightly envious. She laughed weakly. "I'm happy you found a good guy. You deserve it. Shit, we all do. I'm just asking things that I would want to know if it was me getting ready to have sex with someone."

Chloe waved her hand at her friend. "Well, it's not you. It's me. And everything is fine. I have forever to find out the things I don't know yet. I'm not gonna interrogate the guy."

Kim could see her friend getting emotional about this, and that's not what she wanted. She figured that if the lack of information was all right with Chloe, it would be all right with her, too. "Here comes your sister," Kim said, nodding in Willow's direction as she made her way over to their bench.

Willow sat with the girls. They all greeted her and then listened as she filled them in on some "he say, she say" drama she was dealing with at school.

Chloe and her pals offered advice, and Chloe was grateful for the change in topic. But the rest of the afternoon, in the back of her mind she was thinking about Trey and all the mystery surrounding him. Soon, she shrugged it off, figuring that her envious friend was simply planting seeds of doubt in her mind. She wasn't going to let Kim, Willow, or her mother cast a shadow on her good thing, no matter how hard they tried.

BREAKING NEWS

Chloe couldn't stop crying. Willow wrapped her arms around her sister and tried to comfort her as best she could.

"It's okay," she said, rocking her in her arms. "It's okay, Chloe."

"I don't understand!" Chloe wailed, tears and snot running down her face. Rachel rushed into the room with a glass of water and some tissues and sat down at her daughter's side.

"Chloe, calm down. You're gonna have a heart attack if you don't relax. You can't keep getting all worked up like this. I know it's messed up what happened to Jason, but falling apart isn't gonna bring him back."

Chloe couldn't calm down, no matter how hard she tried. Jason's body had been found in a wooded area of his Grymes Hill neighborhood. He'd been gunned down with three bullets in his back. The *Staten Island Advance* had reported that Jason was shot in broad daylight by an unknown assailant, and yet there were no suspects in the crime. "Who would want to kill him?" she asked her mother. "He never bothered nobody. He didn't do shit to deserve that, Ma." Chloe cried, hating herself for being mad that Jason hadn't returned her phone calls, when all the while he'd been rotting away in a swamp!

As Willow cradled her sister in her arms, Rachel read the newspaper article again.

> Todt Hills resident Jason Meadows, 20, was found dead last night as a result of multiple gunshot wounds he received the week of May 11. His decomposing body was found in a wooded area off Wescott Avenue in the Todt Hill section of Staten Island. No witnesses have been identified, and there are no suspects at this time. Law enforcement officials have appealed to the public for any information relevant to the case. The investigation is ongoing.
>
> The Meadows family had become increasingly worried about the youth after not hearing from him for close to three weeks. "It just wasn't like him to up and disappear like that," explained Linda Meadows, 52, the young man's mother.
>
> Meadows was a former local basketball star who graduated from Curtis High School in 2006. At the time of his death, he was pursuing a degree in education at the College of Staten Island.

Rachel shook her head. "I don't understand it either, Chloe." Chloe and Jason had gone to school together since elementary school, so he had practically grown up alongside the Webster girls. Rachel had never known him to be the kind of kid who got in any trouble or made any enemies. His murder seemed like a senseless tragedy. "You have to be strong," she told her daughter gently. "You can't fall apart, baby."

Chloe's cell phone rang, and Rachel reached for it. She glanced at the caller ID and then looked at her daughter. "It's Trey," she said. "You want me to answer it?"

Willow rolled her eyes, wishing Trey would fucking disappear. The guy gave her the damn creeps!

Chloe shook her head. "I can't talk to him right now."

Rachel stroked her daughter's hair. "You need to relax, Chloe. Turn your phone off. Get some sleep."

Chloe shot an evil look at her mother. "How, Ma? Huh? You think I can just relax and fall asleep when I just found out my friend was killed?" Jason was more than a friend to Chloe, but that was her business. She was devastated for reasons her family couldn't understand.

Rachel didn't get upset at the way her daughter was speaking to her. She understood that Chloe had to grieve for her friend. "No, Chloe," she said. "But you're not doing anything but laying around and crying." She took a deep breath. "Jason was a good young man. He was robbed of his life, and I can fully understand you being upset about that. But you can't keep going like this. It's been two days, and you're not answering your phone, you're not eating anything. All you do is sit in here and cry. It's dark in here, and it feels gloomy and sad, Chloe. We're worried about you."

Chloe ignored her mother and continued to cry, distraught that Jason had been slain so viciously. An hour later, Trey was at her front door.

Willow answered it and looked Trey up and down. Neither of them spoke at first. Willow refused to acknowledge him after he had so coldly ignored her the last time they saw each other.

Trey cleared his throat. "I just came to see if Chloe is all right. I been calling her, and she's not answering—so I got worried."

Willow smirked. For someone who was going to college he sure didn't speak proper English. *I been calling her.* . . . She looked Trey square in the eye. "Why didn't you speak to me that day on the ferry?" she asked him.

Trey didn't blink. He looked at her dead-on and said, "I don't remember seeing you on the ferry. Chloe mentioned something about that to me, but I didn't know what she was talking about. Pardon me, though, ma, if I didn't see you."

Willow stood her ground. "You saw me."

Rachel appeared in the doorway behind Willow, and her face bore a forced smile. "Hi, Trey."

Trey looked at Chloe's mother. "I'm sorry to come by unannounced, Ms. Webster. I just wanted to check on Chloe since I haven't heard from her in a while."

Rachel nodded slowly. "Everyone is just really upset right now, Trey. One of Chloe's friends was murdered, and she's taking it really hard."

"What happened?" Trey asked, concern etched on his face.

Rachel showed him the newspaper article, and Trey read it, shaking his head in disbelief. He could see why Chloe was so upset. "Can I see her?" he asked.

"Well, she's just trying to get some rest right now, Trey. I'm sure she'll call you when she's feeling up to it."

"I just hate knowing that she's upset. . . ." He had hoped to see her and offer his condolences. But Willow clearly had an attitude, and Rachel wasn't budging. So Trey shrugged and turned to leave.

Chloe came out and called after him. "Trey, come in." She stood there with eyes puffy from crying, her hair swept off her face in a messy ponytail. Her nose was red, and her Juicy Couture sweatsuit looked like loose loungewear on her.

Rachel touched her daughter gently on the shoulder. "Are you sure you don't want to try and lay down for a little while?"

Chloe looked at her mother sharply out of the corner of her eye. "I'm sure."

Rachel nodded, and Chloe led Trey down the hall to her room. He stepped inside, and Chloe shut the door behind them. He didn't know what to say, since Chloe's sadness was written all over her face. "I'm real sorry to hear about your friend."

Chloe didn't respond. Instead she stared silently at the floor.

"I was worried about you when you didn't answer my calls. I'm sorry if I shouldn't have come over. . . ."

Silence.

Trey sat down on the foot of her bed. "Your mother told me what happened. I guess you and him were close or whatever. So

I just want you to know that I'm sorry about what happened to him. I'm here for you if you need me."

Chloe nodded. "Thanks."

Trey took a deep breath. It really pained him to see her this way. "I don't mean to push you or nothing. I just want you to know that you can talk to me if you feel like talking. I know how it feels to lose somebody you love."

Chloe turned and looked directly at Trey for the first time. She could see the genuine love and concern in his eyes, and she began to cry. "He was such a nice guy," she said, feeling sadness for the loss of her friend, mixed with guilt over having cheated on Trey, another good man. He went closer to her and pulled her into his arms. Chloe cried on his shoulder and vowed to herself that from that moment forward Trey would be the only man in her life. She knew she didn't deserve him. Here he was being so supportive of her, and all along she'd been fucking Jason behind Trey's back. Now with Jason gone, all she wanted was to feel the strength and warmth of Trey's arms as she grieved for her deceased lover.

The funeral took place the next day, and Trey was by her side as Chloe said good-bye to Jason. He never asked her whether she and Jason had been more than friends, but Chloe figured that Trey must suspect that was the case. She had openly wept for Jason on more than one occasion, and Trey never pried, never questioned her. Chloe was so grateful for that. She wouldn't have lied to him if he had asked her, and she didn't want to risk losing Trey at a time like this. She leaned on him for strength, and Trey supported her in every way possible.

One night, as they sat together late on a bench in Mahoney Park, Trey looked at Chloe in the moonlight and swept her hair away from her face. She was more beautiful to him in that moment than ever before.

"I love you," he said. "I just want you to know that."

Chloe's heart melted, and she smiled. They had been through so much in so short a time. He had been there for her in every possible way, and she really appreciated him for it. She wondered if it was love and then realized that it might just be. Still, she wasn't sure if she was ready to say the words. She took his hand in hers, kissed it, and held it against her cheek. "I know you do," she said.

TOUCH ME, TEASE ME

Trey sat in his living room, watching one videotape after another as he jerked off. This was his favorite way to spend an afternoon—unless he could spend it with Chloe instead. The thought of her lips, the way she kissed him, and how soft her hands felt whenever she touched him made him weak. He fantasized about these things as he stroked his long, thick dick until he came in volcanic spasms all over his thighs and T-shirt. Laying his head back against the sofa, he sighed, relieved. The phone rang, and he was so physically drained that it took him a moment to gather the strength to answer it.

He paused the videotape and reached over to pick up his cell phone, which lay beside him on the sofa. MOM appeared on the screen once again, and he felt his heart race. He was so sick of these calls, sick and tired of deleting unwanted voice messages and e-mails. He sent the call to voice mail and had to resist the urge to throw the whole phone against the wall in frustration. He was about to turn his phone off for good, when he got a call from Chloe. Hurriedly he answered it.

"Hey, beautiful!" he greeted her.

"Hey, Trey. I just got off the ferry, and I stopped to talk to Dawn before she went to catch her train. Now all the buses are gone and I don't feel like waiting here. Can you come and get me?"

Before she could even get the question out, Trey had grabbed his car keys, locked his apartment door, and was heading down the stairs. "Of course," he said. "I'm on my way."

"Thanks, baby," Chloe said, smiling. She knew he wouldn't let her down.

As he drove to pick her up, Trey was deep in thought. He had noticed that since Jason's funeral, he and Chloe had become a lot closer. She had really leaned on him as she mourned her friend, and Trey had been her rock, comforting her when she was down, making her laugh when she felt like crying, and doing everything he could to take her mind off the situation.

Trey had professed his love for Chloe and couldn't help noticing that she hadn't done so in return. He wasn't used to that. Normally, women were the ones who craved the L-word and longed for commitment. But Chloe was different. She was independent and didn't seem to be in a rush to declare her love for Trey. He wondered what it was that made her hesitate to say it, since he'd done everything he could to win her affection. As he pulled up at the ferry terminal's passenger pickup ramp, he saw her walking toward him and frowned slightly. He wondered what the fuck she had been thinking when she got dressed that morning.

Chloe walked over to his car in a pair of tiny white shorts, a multicolored top, and stiletto sandals. She wore a pair of Gucci shades on her face, and she turned the heads of men and women alike as she strutted over to his car.

"Hey, sexy!" she greeted him when she climbed inside. Trey noticed a man nearby watching Chloe's ass as she got into the car, and he had to resist the urge to say something to the guy. Instead, he turned his attention to Chloe as she kissed him softly on his cheek and smiled at him.

"Why do you dress like that?" he asked.

Her smile immediately turned to a frown. "Dress like what, Trey?" It wasn't the first time he'd voiced his disapproval of her outfit choices, and frankly, Chloe was getting tired of it.

He put the car in drive and headed toward Richmond Terrace as he answered her. "So revealing," he said. "You don't leave much to the imagination when you wear shit like that. You got every guy out here checking you out. And I know it must've been worse in Manhattan. I know them dudes out there was trying to holla at you all day." He shook his head, bothered by the mere thought of men ogling her that way. "Where are you coming from, anyway?" he asked. "I thought you said you were gonna stay home all day and help Willow find something to wear for her date with that guy she likes."

Chloe looked at Trey like he was crazy. Was he interrogating her? Had he questioned her morals simply because of the way she dressed? And since when did she have to give him a planned itinerary whenever she decided to leave the house? "Pull over," she said.

Trey looked at her, then back at the road ahead of him. "Why?"

She reached in her bag for her cell phone and looked at him as if he had completely lost his mind. "Because I asked you to, that's why."

He reluctantly did as she requested and pulled over across the street from the 120th Precinct. "What's the problem?" he asked.

"You tell me!" Chloe took off her seat belt and turned sideways in her seat to face him. "What's with all the questions and the criticism?"

"What—?"

"You criticize how I dress, but it didn't bother you that I dressed like this when you met me. Now all of a sudden I'm supposed to change my style because we're together?"

He shook his head. "Nah, I'm not saying—"

"Well, what *are* you saying, Trey? I gotta tell you where I'm going all the time now? For your information, I took Willow to the city to look for an outfit to wear tonight. Then she got a call from the guy she's going out with, and they decided to meet earlier. So I helped her get dressed, took her to MAC to get her makeup done, and then left her at the movies on Forty-second Street with the guy. After that, I came back to Staten Island and called you." She sighed, frustrated that he was actually sitting there and letting her explain her whereabouts. "I'm not the type of chick who does this. I don't like having to explain where I've been, and I don't like being questioned about my style of dress. This is me, Trey." She pointed at herself for emphasis. "I like nice clothes, I like being spontaneous, and I *don't* like having to explain all that to you."

Trey sat silently and looked at her for a long time. He thought about what she was saying to him, and frankly, it pissed him off that she was asserting herself this way. But he had to respect her feelings. "Let me ask you a question."

"Go ahead," she said, sitting back to listen.

"Do you love me?"

She was caught off guard. She hadn't expected him to ask her that. "What does that have to do with anything?" she asked, sidestepping the question.

"Because I already told you that I love you. I guess I overreacted about what you got on. And I only asked where you've been because I knew that you were turning heads all day in that outfit. That's my way of saying that you look good."

Chloe had to resist the urge to be flattered by the compliment. At least he'd managed to acknowledge that.

Trey looked at her. "But I feel kinda insecure about where we stand. I'm not messing with no other girls, you know what I'm saying? I'm happy being with you. I try to show you that you make me happy all the time. And all I get in return is you asking me to pick you up or buy you stuff."

"So now you're gonna throw that in my face?" Chloe knew that he was right, but she still didn't like hearing him remind her of all the things he'd done for her.

He shook his head. "I'm not throwing nothing in your face, Chloe. I'm just saying that it feels like you're a tease sometimes. 'Cause whenever I want to have sex, you shut me down. You play with me, get my dick hard, and then you back off. I tell you that I love you, and you don't say it back. And now I'm starting to feel like a fool for feeling like this is serious if you don't feel the same way."

Chloe looked away, knowing that Trey was right. She had been teasing him, but not intentionally. She'd just gotten caught up in all the fun she was having, and she hadn't wanted to jinx a good thing. She looked at him again. Trey was the total package—handsome, smart, generous, and affectionate. Maybe sometimes he could be too sensitive. But in the grand scheme of things, that wasn't so bad. Chloe thought about it and realized she didn't want Trey to go out and find some other girl to spend his time and his money on. "I do love you, Trey," she said softly.

A slow smile spread across Trey's face. "Yeah?"

She nodded. "Yeah. I do." Even as she said it, she knew she didn't mean it. "And I want to make love to you—I don't want to just have sex. You're special, and I want our first time to be special. That's why I've been holding out all this time. I don't want it to be just ordinary." She knew as she said it that it was a lie.

She had held out for the most part because she hadn't needed to fuck Trey as long as she had Jason around. And then when Jason was killed, sex had been the furthest thing from her mind. But she wanted to make love to Trey now that she thought about it. In the four months since they'd met, he had earned it. She decided then that it was time for her to let down her guard.

Trey leaned over and kissed her. Then he stared at her with love in his eyes for several long moments before he spoke. "I want it to be special, too," he said. "Tomorrow night I'll come pick you up, and you can spend the night with me. I promise I'll make it special for you."

She smiled and kissed him back. "Okay."

She buckled her seat belt again, and Trey put the car in drive. He would plan the perfect night for her and make sure that their lovemaking was more special than anything she'd ever experienced. "Wanna go get something to eat?"

She nodded, glad that he was happy now. If giving him some pussy would keep him from worrying about what she wore or where she was going, then she planned to fuck him till he was speechless!

THE PERFECT NIGHT

Chloe couldn't figure out why she was so nervous. Tonight was the night she would finally make love to Trey, and she was feeling an odd sense of excitement and apprehension that she had never felt with other guys. This was different. She knew in her heart that if the sex with Trey was good, it would be the icing on the cake. Trey treated her perfectly, intrigued her, and spoiled her. If tonight went well, she might be willing to be his completely. For the first time, Chloe was ready to fall in love.

After he had helped her mourn the loss of Jason in her life, Chloe felt more connected to Trey than ever. He had been so gentle, so understanding, and so patient. And she felt that he had finally earned her complete devotion.

He came to pick her up outside her house and sat there for twenty minutes, waiting for her to come out. As she walked toward the car, he couldn't take his eyes off her. Chloe wore a short and backless black dress and black Mary Janes. She climbed inside, leaned over, and kissed him.

"Look at you," he said.

"Thanks!" Chloe hoped her unexpected nervousness would subside soon. She couldn't seem to shake it. They made the short trip to his place and held hands as they walked inside the building. Chloe couldn't help feeling disappointed that they weren't going to dinner at some new hot spot. She wouldn't have bothered to get all dolled up if she'd known they were only going to get right to the point.

They rode the elevator in silence from the parking garage to the fifth floor. Once they reached his apartment door, he unlocked it and they stepped into his home. Chloe saw roses by the dozens all over the place. They were every color imaginable, scattered throughout his place. Some were in vases around the apartment, while the petals of others were scattered across the floor. There were candles lit, and several feet away, she could see a table set for two.

"Wow!" she exclaimed, holding her hands over her mouth in amazement. "You did all of this for me?" Her disappointment faded.

Trey smiled shyly and ushered her into the living room. She

noticed how empty his apartment was. The crisp white walls and clean floors were the centerpiece, it seemed, peppered with only a small number of items. Stacks of videotapes were piled next to the wall unit by the floor, and she paused, frowning. "VHS tapes? Those went out with the Jheri curl."

"Oh, those? I've had those for years." Trey seemed a little embarrassed that she'd noticed them, and Chloe dropped the subject. She hadn't meant to make him feel uncomfortable.

She saw a large television in the corner, but noticed no cable box, no DVD player. She wondered what he did for fun in the absence of all these things she couldn't live without. But not wanting to embarrass him further, she kept silent about it. He showed her to the kitchen, where several dishes sat atop the stove. He was cooking salmon, wild rice, asparagus, and dinner rolls.

"Damn," she said. "You can cook all of this? I can hardly scramble eggs."

Trey laughed, and showed her the Patti LaBelle cookbook he'd studied all evening as he prepared the meal.

Chloe laughed, too. "Oh, okay. I feel better now." Silence fell between them, and Chloe figured that Trey was just as nervous as she was. She thought it was cute. "Can I use your bathroom?" she asked.

"Sure," he said. "Let me show you where it is." He walked her down a short narrow hallway and directed her to the bathroom. She stepped in, peed, and washed her hands. She left the water running and, just out of sheer curiosity, looked in the medicine cabinet. She found the usual contents. A tube of toothpaste, some Band-Aids, Robitussin. Then she noticed a half-empty bottle of pills with no label. She wondered what they were, so she opened the bottle and looked at them. They were tiny blue-and-white pills, and she wondered what they were for. She put them back in the cabinet, noticing that everything was lined up perfectly, facing forward. Chloe marveled—for a young man, Trey was extremely neat. She smiled. "That's nice," she mumbled softly to herself. Finally, she turned the water off, opened the door, and gasped. Trey was still standing there.

Her heart beat rapidly in her chest. "Did you wait for me? I can find my way back down the hall." Chloe was taken aback, and the hairs on the nape of her neck stood on end.

"I was just coming to see if you were all right. You were taking a long time."

Chloe's heart was racing. He smiled at her, and it put her slightly at ease. Still, she couldn't shake the feeling that something was strange. They headed back to the kitchen, where Trey had dinner laid out on the table. An old Roberta Flack tune played softly from his old radio.

"I'm an old soul," he explained.

"I see that! No cable, VHS tapes, a radio from the sixties."

They both laughed about it.

"Seems like you're stuck in your father's era," she joked. As soon as she said it, she thought she saw a flash of anger in his eyes, and he immediately stopped chewing.

"I'm nothing like my father," he said flatly, never taking his piercing eyes off her.

Chloe got chills and felt goosebumps while Trey stared at

her so coldly. She thought back to what Willow had said about seeing Trey on the boat a few months ago. Willow had described a cold stare—just like the one Trey was giving her now. She cleared her throat. "My bad. I didn't mean to hit a nerve."

Trey said nothing and instead kept right on eating.

Chloe ate in silence for a few minutes, then took a sip of her wine. "How come you never want to talk about your family, Trey?" she asked.

He still kept eating, and for a minute, Chloe wondered if he'd heard her. But Trey had heard her loud and clear. He was recalling his father, the tyrant. Thought about the way his pop's fists felt all the times they had come in contact with his face and his ribs. Trey thought about his father's drunken and violent outbursts, how he'd beaten Trey until he cried out in terror. Beaten his mother, too, until she couldn't take it anymore.

Silence cloaked them again, and Chloe was on edge. Trey seemed kinda moody this evening. She tried to break the ice again. "Did you hear what I said?"

He shrugged. "Yeah, I heard what you said. I thought tonight was supposed to be special," he snapped. "Who wants to spend it talking about my family?" He shot her a look that told her to drop the subject, and she did.

"Okay," she said, confused by his sudden mood swing. "So, anyway, let's start over. First of all, I'm sorry I was a little late tonight," she offered. "I couldn't figure out what to wear."

Trey cleared his throat, tried to shake off the memories flooding his thoughts. "You should have worn the sweater I bought you."

Chloe noticed that instead of complimenting the bosom-baring dress she had on, he was almost complaining that she didn't wear that plain, unflattering thing she had already given to her sister. "Don't I look nice in this?" she asked.

Ignoring the question, he pointed at her plate and asked, "Are you done?"

She wiped her mouth with her napkin, pushed her plate away, and nodded. He took her plate and his and headed toward the sink. Chloe sat there, confused. *Who gives a shit about that ugly sweater?* She wondered what the fuck Trey's problem was tonight. He wasn't being himself. In fact, she'd noticed that over the past several weeks, he had seemed moodier than usual. She had attributed it to fatigue, figuring Trey had been putting in long hours or something. But today was his day off. What the fuck was wrong with him?

Trey returned with a pint of ice cream and two spoons.

"Chunky Monkey!" she yelled. "It's my favorite!" All was forgiven.

He smiled. Finally, the ice was broken.

"Oh my God! I love Chunky Monkey. I used to buy a pint every Friday after my anthropology class as a reward for staying awake. The bodega near my school keeps it stocked for me."

Trey smiled knowingly, scooped some out, and fed it to her. Finally, a romantic moment. They kissed, softly at first, and then with an intensity that made her tiny panties wet with anticipation. Playfully, they enjoyed the ice cream until they got so caught up in their foreplay that the Chunky Monkey began to melt. Trey stood up, took her by the hand, and led her down the now dark hallway to a door that had been shut since she arrived. Stepping inside his bedroom, she looked around. She noticed that he had nothing in there but a dresser, a bed, and a camera lying on its side.

Before she could ask about the camera, he pulled her close to him and peeled her out of the dress she wore. He sat on the bed, and she straddled him as Trey kissed her neck and stroked her full breasts. Chloe purred and clung to him. His hands explored her body, caressing her nipples, her back, her ass, and her juicy thighs. Chloe moaned softly, eager to feel him. He touched her perfectly shaved pussy, fingered her, and felt her wetness. He could barely contain himself. Just as she reached to undo his belt buckle, he ejaculated and was visibly embarrassed by it.

Shocked, she laughed and said, "Damn! You got too excited and came all over yourself." She laughed at the endearing situation, but Trey was sure she was humiliating him.

Trey snapped. It was her fault he couldn't help but bust so soon. If she hadn't been fucking teasing him for months, he wouldn't have done that. He pushed her off him. She tumbled to the floor hard and was instantly pissed.

"What the fuck is wrong with you?" she demanded as she scrambled to her feet.

"Don't laugh at me."

"You're bugging." Chloe put her panties back on and looked around for her dress.

Trey looked at Chloe and tried to calm down. He was enraged, embarrassed, and wanted to slap the shit out of her. True, he had stopped taking his medication for the past several weeks. But he felt fine. Chloe was the one overreacting.

"Why you acting different all of a sudden?" he asked.

Chloe couldn't believe her ears. "*I'm* acting different? You've been acting funny all night."

He shook his head. "You act like your sister, that stuck-up bitch."

Chloe turned and glared at him. "Don't ever call my fucking sister a bitch!"

"I didn't know you were one of those chicks that thinks a guy's supposed to cater to them all the time. I thought you were different."

Chloe was astounded. "Tell me how tonight going wrong is my fault."

"You laughed at me. And you made fun of the way I live, the things I have." Trey was especially pissed because the reason he had so few material things was because he kept lavishing Chloe with gifts. In truth, Trey had been spending most of his disposable income on Chloe.

"I'm just saying, Trey. I thought you was balling. And I only laughed so I wouldn't make you feel bad about coming before we even got it popping." Now she was beginning to see that Trey was just a lame in a baller's costume. And with the blinders finally removed, she immediately thought about Willow. Her sister had warned Chloe all along that Trey wasn't who she thought he was. Chloe made a mental note to tell her little sister she'd been right.

Trey clenched his jaw. "So, what, you feel sorry for me now?" He bit his lower lip.

Chloe finally located her dress and picked it up before turning back to face him. "Shouldn't I?" she asked sarcastically.

She looked at him, and the fury in her eyes quickly turned to fear as she caught the crazed expression on Trey's face. She was in trouble. He looked like a madman—so much so that she almost didn't recognize him. She turned around, grabbed her shoes off the floor, and made a beeline for the bedroom door.

Trey's mind flashed in and out of the present moment. Chloe was leaving. Just like his mother leaving him all over again. He saw his mother walking out the door when he was just ten years old, saw her leaving him behind with that monster of a father. He snapped. Trey snatched Chloe by the hair, pulling her roughly back inside the bedroom. Chloe screamed, and he slapped her to shut her up.

"You fuckin' nut!" she yelled, laughing nervously and fighting to get out of his grasp.

That only added fuel to the fire. He punched her in the mouth, silencing her immediately. She scratched him and punched him back, which only made him even angrier. Again and again, he punched her in the face, slammed her head against the cold hard floor, and pummeled her mercilessly.

He saw his mother abandoning him and heard her laughing at him, laughing at what he'd had to endure because of her. When she left him, a mere child, his father had taken his rage out on Trey. Day after day, he'd beaten him, and Trey beat Chloe the way he'd been beaten—no, worse. He pounded her so savagely that her face—the face that had reminded him of his mother's face so many times—was disfigured. Now he was blinded by pure fury as he beat her the way a man would beat the crap out of another guy. He punched her until she lay motionless on the floor.

AFTERMATH

Out of breath and covered in Chloe's blood, Trey paced the room. He felt like a ten-year-old boy all over again. He recalled the way his father used to beat him and his mother until they begged for mercy. He could hear his own cries in his head; he relived the terror.

Pacing back and forth, Trey began to cry, just as he had as a child. He thought about how he and his mother had clung to each other for support during those violent times. It hadn't taken much to set his alcoholic father off. And during those tirades, there was no telling how far it would go. Trey and his mother had suffered countless bruises, broken bones, and black eyes over the years. And when his mother couldn't take any more, she left. She walked out one day, telling Trey and his dad that she was going to the store. She never came back. Trey's dad had been furious, searching for her for days and taking his frustration out on his son each night.

From that moment on, he'd hated his mother—although part of him still loved her for the bond they'd formed during their shared terror. Chloe reminded him of that. She had reminded him of the love he felt for his mother—he loved Chloe the same way. Chloe, who had tried to leave him. In and out of the present reality, Trey sobbed, his mind playing horrible tricks on him.

He remembered the time when he was thirteen and his father had beaten him until he was unconscious. After that beating, Trey had finally gotten the courage to speak up and had told his story to a teacher at school. They'd removed him from his father's custody and placed Trey into foster care. But the damage had already been done. Trey inherited a violent streak that surfaced whenever the women in his life tried to leave him. When they left him, he saw his mother walking out the door. When women hurt him, he became the monster that was his father, beating them until they begged him to stop. But Chloe hadn't begged him. She had just cried and tried to fend off his blows. She even had the nerve to try to fight back.

He looked down at Chloe's motionless body and realized that this time it had gone too far. He sat down on the bed, weeping over what he'd done and knowing that he was in serious trouble now. He hadn't meant to hurt Chloe. But it was too late. He thought about her face and how she had reminded him so much of his mother. They resembled each other a lot, and he had often caught himself staring at her for that reason. Her face was unrecognizable now. And he cried even harder.

He had lied to her about being a college student. On the day they met, Trey had actually been going to see his psychologist as part of his therapy for his issues with women. But from the moment he'd laid eyes on Chloe, he had fallen for her. She was everything he wanted in a woman, and he stopped seeing his psychologist and stopped taking his antidepressants. Instead, he spent his days following Chloe, even videotaping her at times. That was the reason for the countless VHS tapes in his living room, and by following her, he'd learned about her relationship with Jason, her love of shopping, and her affinity for things like Chunky Monkey ice cream. Chloe had become his obsession.

He'd followed Jason after the last time Chloe had left the man's basement apartment. Trey knew Chloe had spent hours at a time fucking Jason behind his back. He had to get rid of the competition. So he had stalked Jason, waited until he caught his rival alone, leaving the corner store late one morning. Then he shot him in the back of his head and dumped his body in the woods. Chloe had grieved for the son of a bitch, not knowing that Trey, the man whose arms she cried in, was the man who'd murdered her friend. Trey had watched her cry for him, had wiped her tears, and even gone to the fucking funeral with her. And this bitch had just tried to *leave him*. She had laughed at him. Trey wiped tears from his face, the sorrow over what he'd done now replaced with pure rage once again.

He scrolled through his cell phone until he found Mom—that's how he had saved his psychologist's number in his phone, since his mother was the reason Trey gave for his violent tendencies toward women. Trey got the counselor's voice mail. It was one o'clock in the morning and, as expected, she didn't answer, so he left a message.

"Dr. Hollister, this is Trey Gilmore. I know I haven't been coming to see you like I was supposed to. But I'll be there tomorrow morning. I had another setback. Bye."

He cleaned the bloody scene and wrapped up Chloe's body in an area rug. The whole time, he repeated the same twisted phrase again and again: "She deserved it. The bitch deserved it."

Trey carried her down to his car in the underground parking garage and loaded her heavy body into the trunk, carefully ensuring that no one saw him. It was late, and he hoped everyone in his building was asleep. Once he got her in the car, he drove down to an empty pier near the ferry terminal. Careful not to be seen by any of the dockworkers, Trey opened the trunk so that he could tie the ropes tighter around the rug Chloe's body was wrapped in. But just as he opened the trunk, a car passed and he panicked. Shutting the trunk quickly, he waited until the car was out of sight.

Once it was gone, he dragged her to the water's edge and dropped her in. He ran back to his car and peeled off before anyone else saw him.

As Trey headed home, the rug around Chloe's body unraveled in the water. She floated to the surface just as he got home to finish the clean-up. For the rest of the night, he sat in his living room, watching the surveillance videotapes he'd made of her. She never knew that he had been there, watching her in the shadows from the moment they met.

FADE AWAY

Trey arrived at the St. George ferry terminal the next morning to find that it had been shut down. Ferry employees were directing commuters to an alternative slip, where smaller boats were ferrying groups of passengers to Lower Manhattan. Trey panicked again, wondering if he'd been spotted dumping Chloe's body the night before. Nearby, he overheard a woman asking a ferry official what had happened. Trey stood there and listened as the ferry worker explained, "They found a woman's body this morning."

"Oh my God!" the woman yelled out as Trey was walking off, blending into the crowd and promising himself that he would never neglect his therapy again. This time, he had gone too far. Next time, things would be different, he told himself. He hurriedly boarded the next boat bound for Lower Manhattan. He didn't want to be late to his appointment with Dr. Hollister.

Meanwhile, at Richmond University Medical Center, paramedics rushed a nearly lifeless body into the ER. "She still has a pulse, but it's weak. Hurry!"

It was eleven o'clock in the morning, and Chloe had never come home. She hadn't called either, and her phone kept going straight to voice mail. Rachel and Willow were worried, so they started calling all of Chloe's friends. One by one, each friend told Chloe's family that they hadn't seen or heard from her the previous day. It wasn't long before Rachel realized she had no phone number for Trey, no address, nothing. He had always contacted Chloe on her cell phone, and her friends knew nothing about him either. None of them even knew his last name.

By seven o'clock that night, panic set in, and Rachel called the police. They came by her house and told her Chloe needed to be missing for more than twenty-four hours before they would consider her a missing person.

"But you don't understand," Rachel explained. "Chloe would never go a whole day without calling. She left here last night, and she hasn't called any of us—not us, not her friends—all day. She's not answering her cell phone. That's not like her. I'm worried about her."

The Latino officer felt sorry for Rachel, but his hands were tied. He couldn't file a missing persons report for anyone over the age of eighteen until the twenty-four-hour period had passed. But as a father, he could understand Rachel's anguish. "She probably spent the night with her boyfriend and turned her phone off for privacy."

Rachel shook her head. "Chloe never turns her phone off. She texts more than she talks."

The officer sighed. He had a soft spot for mothers whose children had gone astray. "Tell me about her boyfriend. Where does he live?"

"On St. Marks Place," Willow said.

"Which building?"

Willow shrugged and looked at Rachel. She shrugged, too, and shook her head. "I don't know?"

"Do you know where he works?"

Rachel nodded. "He's a track worker for the MTA."

The officer wrote that down. "And you said his name is Trey. Do you know his last name?"

Both ladies shook their heads.

"What kind of car does he drive?"

Rachel wasn't sure. She hadn't noticed that. "It's a white car," she said. "That's all I know."

The officer looked at Rachel and shook his head. "There's not much here to go on. There's probably a million white cars in New York City, ma'am."

Willow was getting pissed. "I wasn't investigating him, so I don't know those things. But I can tell you that I had a strange feeling about my sister's boyfriend from the beginning. And I know that if she was alright right now she would be answering her cell phone. She would answer my text messages. She's not answering any of us, not her friends, not me or my mom and that's not like her. The last time we saw her, she was leaving with him." Willow fought back tears. "If he hurt my sister, we should be out there trying to find him."

The officer rose to leave. "Then we'll need more information than this, unfortunately. See if you can look around her room for more clues about this guy. You said he's a black guy, six feet tall, short haircut, slim build. That's too broad of a description."

"He has a mustache," Rachel offered.

The officer shook his head. "Still—" He put his memo pad back in his pocket. "—we're going to need more than that."

Frustrated, Rachel walked the officer out, promising to call him if she learned any new information about Chloe's mystery boyfriend.

When he was gone, Willow began to cry. "I told you he was crazy!" she yelled. "I told you I saw him on the boat and he ignored me. I knew he was too good to be true."

Rachel hugged her daughter and took a deep breath. "We don't know that she's hurt, Willow. Maybe she's okay. We can't assume the worst." She comforted her daughter until Willow stopped crying. Then Rachel began calling the local hospitals and explaining the situation. She asked if anyone fitting Chloe's description had been admitted and was told that Chloe hadn't been brought into Staten Island University Hospital. Finally, she called the Richmond University Medical Center and was told that an unidentified black female had been brought in that morning with no identification and no clothes.

Rachel's heart galloped in her chest. "What?" she asked in disbelief.

"Ma'am," the woman on the phone said gently. "This young lady is in grave condition. Her face has been terribly disfigured, and she has nothing on her to identify her. You should get here as soon as you possibly can. I'm sorry."

Rachel hung up with tears streaming down her face. She and Willow rushed out the door, praying to God for a miracle.

Trey got off the 1 train at South Ferry after his session with Dr. Hollister, feeling worse than ever. He had told the therapist about the past few months he'd spent courting Chloe. He had explained the way she'd flirted with him, enticed him, and teased him until he was eating out of the palm of her hand.

"I didn't push," he said. "I didn't try to rush her into settling down like I've done in the past. I just let her take her time. I went at her pace. But she played me. She was cheating on me."

Dr. Hollister wrote something down then. Trey wondered what it was.

"Did you confront her about the cheating?" Dr. Hollister asked.

Trey shook his head. "Nope. I didn't. I just ignored it, and I never even mentioned it to her."

"How did it make you feel, knowing that she was giving herself to another man while she held out on you physically?"

Trey stared at the therapist for a while, unsure of how he should answer her. "It made me feel small."

"Small."

"Yeah."

Dr. Hollister wrote something down again. "Like a child?"

Trey didn't answer.

"Tell me what happened yesterday," the counselor asked.

Trey took a deep breath. In his mind, he could hear Chloe laughing at him. He could see her trying to leave him. He rubbed his hands across his face. "She tried to leave me, tried to break up with me."

"And?"

"I hit her. But not too hard."

"How did she react?" asked the therapist.

A slow, sinister smile spread across Trey's face. "She hit me back. And she laughed at me again. And then she walked out. She left me."

The counselor was writing like crazy now. Trey knew he wasn't telling the whole story, but he wondered if Dr. Hollister could tell.

Finally, she stopped writing and looked up at Trey. "In the past, whenever women have tried to leave you, you've lashed out. You've hit, kicked, punched, and even bound and gagged women who tried to abandon you. We've established that when you are abandoned in relationships, it conjures up memories of your mother abandoning you."

Trey nodded. That was true.

"What made you allow this one to leave?"

Trey didn't answer that question either.

He hadn't known what to say. Instead, he pictured Chloe's lifeless beaten body lying still on his bedroom floor, and he began to cry. Right there in front of Dr. Hollister, he had cried his eyes out until the psychologist announced that his session was over. Dr. Hollister made Trey to swear that he would come back for another session the next day and asked him to pick up a refill prescription of his Prozac. Trey had agreed, left the doctor's office, stopped at a pharmacy nearby, and was now headed back to the scene of the crime. He picked up the *Staten Island Advance* as he entered the ferry terminal and was shocked by the headline on the front page.

Unidentified Woman Clings to Life after Brutal Beating

Trey's heart skipped a beat, and he froze. Standing there in the terminal, he read the story. Chloe hadn't died. She was barely alive and in the hospital. They hadn't identified her. But when they did, she would surely tell what he'd done. Panicked, he looked around the terminal. He wondered if the police were searching for him *right now*. He had been careful to clean up all the bloody evidence in his apartment, but he had watched enough *Forensic Files* to know that one could never get rid of all the blood. There were tons of videotapes of Chloe in his apartment, too—proof he'd followed her relentlessly. And Dr. Hollister knew all about the violent episodes with women in his past. Trey faced the fact that he could never go home again.

He walked to the ATM in the terminal and withdrew enough cash from his account to last him a few days. Then he strolled back out onto the streets of Manhattan and joined the throngs of New Yorkers, fading anonymously into the crowd without looking back.

At the hospital, Chloe lay hooked up to a ventilator, her face wrapped in so many bandages that she looked like a mummy. They'd had to identify Chloe by her jewelry and birthmarks because her face and body were so swollen and disfigured. Willow cried softly at her sister's bedside as Rachel talked to the doctors.

"She's going to make it, Ms. Webster. But she will need plastic surgery to fix the damage done to her face. She hadn't been sexually assaulted," the physician explained, at which point Rachel breathed a sigh of relief. At least that bastard hadn't raped Chloe.

"But she did suffer some broken ribs and numerous facial fractures. Her road to recovery will be long, but she seems like a tough young lady. Many people couldn't have survived a beating that severe, let alone being dumped in the water and left for dead. She's a fighter. I think she's going to be fine."

Rachel was so relieved to hear that, she hugged the doctor. "Thank you," she said, finally pulling away and letting the tears fall for the first time since she'd arrived at the hospital.

The doctor gently touched Rachel's shoulder. "The police have some questions to ask you, and I'm sure they'll also want to question Chloe when she's able to talk again. That could take a while, since her facial injuries are extensive. But soon she'll be able to assist with the investigation, I'm sure." The doctor walked away, leaving Rachel to talk with the police.

Willow sat at her sister's bedside, stroking Chloe's hand. She whispered to Chloe, "It's gonna be all right. You'll be all right."

Chloe wished she could answer. She wished she could move her body enough to communicate with her sister in any way possible. But she was helpless to do anything but lie there and blink. She wanted to tell Willow that she had been right all along. Her knight in shining armor had turned out to be a devil in disguise. Instead, she squeezed her sister's hand limply and thanked God she was still alive. She had cheated death and would live to tell about it. She couldn't wait to do just that.

ACKNOWLEDGMENTS

Monique Patterson, I am your biggest fan. You're the greatest editor around and I will sing your praises until I go hoarse.

To libraries across the country, thank you for all that you do in urban communities to promote literacy. You're wonderful!

To the readers who faithfully read the books, comment online, and come out to events, a million thank-yous are not enough. You give a girl with a vivid imagination room to grow. Love ya!

Wild Cherry

K'WAN

Dedicated to every sista who woke up one day and realized that they didn't need someone to tell them that they were beautiful for it to be true.

ONE

Gina

"Gina, where the hell is my beer?"

The sound of his voice startled me so bad that I dropped the bottle I was holding, shattering it all over my freshly mopped tiles. Beer splashed on my cabinet doors and all over my new Max Studio Frida sandals. The damn things cost too much for me to be lounging around the house in them, but I wanted to represent for Jackie. I always tried to look good when Jackie's friends came over. Not because I wanted them ogling me—which they did anyhow, whenever they thought Jackie wasn't looking—but because I was a reflection of my man and liked to carry myself accordingly. To me, there was nothing worse than a clean-cut man with a busted female at his side. The snakeskin exterior of the shoes would survive the drenching, but the interior would end up smelling like mildew from the beer soaking in.

"Two hundred dollars down the damn drain."

"Gina, what the hell was that!" he barked from the other side of the door.

"Nothing, baby," I lied.

"Then bring yo ass on, a nigga thirsty!"

"Okay, I'm coming. One mess in the living room and one in here," I muttered to myself. "Relax, Gina," I said under my breath. The words sounded convincing enough, but I still didn't believe them.

I pulled open the right side of my stainless steel refrigerator to get Jackie another beer, and to my dismay we were out—at least out of Heinekens. Apparently the one now pooling on my kitchen floor was the last of the Mohicans. Thankfully, I had a Corona stashed in the vegetable bin. I was saving it for myself, but it looked like I'd be paying the house with it. Trying to ignore the beer drying on my feet and soaking into my instep, I sliced a lime for the lip of Jackie's beer and put my game face on.

When I stepped through the swinging door and into my living room, my heart sank as I beheld the mess Jackie and his stooges had made of it. The weed and cigarette smoke was so thick that my eyes stung. It would take weeks for me to get the stench out of my furniture. I hadn't taken two steps when I heard the crackle of a chip that had escaped from the bowl, pulverized beneath my soggy heels. I didn't even have to see the

Cheez Doodles stains in the soft cream carpet to know that I'd have to have it professionally cleaned . . . again. Beer bottles and cups were sitting on everything with a flat surface, including my autographed *Best of Patti LaBelle* CD box set. For all the hell I went through to get it signed, there wasn't a court in the land that would convict me if I went postal on those Negroes.

A card table was erected in the middle of my living room, with Jackie and his shiftless-ass friends huddled around it, engaged in a game of poker. If you added all of them together, Jackie's friends weren't worth a bucket of piss. They were loud, disrespectful, and just overall pains in the ass. But as the saying went, *birds of a feather.* In the center of the chaos sat Jackie, my husband and keeper of the last five years.

Jackie, for as much of an ass as he can be, is a prize catch. He had baggage, as most men do these days, but he kept his baby's mother at a distance, and spent time with his daughter. That turned me on about him. My dad was in and out of my life, so I really can't respect a man who isn't doing what he has to for his children. Back in those days, Jackie was working as an associate publicist for a major house during the day and working in the mailroom at another house at night. Considering that he had degrees in law and business management, I thought he was selling himself short. About nine months into our relationship, he made me eat my words. Jackie had taken the contacts he made—and stole—while working at the two houses and opened up his own literary agency. One by one, he started picking off authors and buttering up editors. By the time the industry even realized what was going on, Jackie had signed three of the top authors in urban fiction and was negotiating book and film deals for a former member of the 1925 New York Rens, whom everyone thought was dead. If you wanted talent, you had to see Jackie, and when you sat with him, you had better have your checkbook.

From the money he made off his clients, Jackie started flipping real estate. He bought a block of burnt-down row houses in Newark and opened up a book-distribution center and an hourly motel. If it had value, Jackie would buy and sell it. My man was making serious moves in the world, and he made sure I was at his side.

When he got his businesses up and popping, he made an honest woman out of me and threw a ring on my finger. Jackie went hard for the wedding. The cute little R & B singer with the funny face even came through to sing my wedding song. A bunch of hating-ass broads from the projects where I'd grown up were there, drinking my liquor and shooting me *prisons.* One of them even ended up throwing up all over one of the Porta-Potties we'd rented for the event. They tried to say it was from her drinking on an empty stomach, but I know the bitch was just sick with envy.

Once I jumped the broom, it was a whole different ball game. Jackie was good to me when I was his girl, and better when I became his fiancée, but when we got married, he made me feel like a queen. I was shopping two to three times a week and getting my hair done twice a week. Me even thinking about getting a job was out of the question: Jackie wasn't having it. He wanted me to rest, dress, and do away with stress, and I was content to do so. He insisted that if I wanted to work, it would have to be at one of his businesses. I did bookkeeping for the distribution and the agency from home, and time to time I'd act as the manager down at the club. Other than that, I didn't do much other than daydream and stay fly.

Don't get me wrong—I've been working since I was twelve years old, without missing a day. Like I mentioned, my dad was in and out of our lives between prison terms, so I had to help my mother hold it down for me and my little brother, Randy. My mother always drilled into me the importance of being independent, and until Jackie, I had lived by it. But I can't front. Being that I had worked for the last fifteen years of my life, nonstop, it kinda felt good to have somebody take care of me for a change.

Jackie was both a blessing and a curse in my life, which is probably true of 99 percent of husbands. He made sure life was good for us, and as his lady, I always stood in his corner, even when I might not have agreed with him. There was something about Jackie's character that made it hard for you to say no to him. He had that effect on most people. My Jackie is quite the character . . . and did I mention that he is fine as all hell!

Six feet tall, with chocolate skin and a low-cut Caesar, real throwback Harlem. Jackie was sexy, but in a clean-cut sort of way. He carried himself like a businessman but had plenty of thug in him, especially in the bedroom. Jackie knew how to split me just the right way. Damn, I'm getting moist just thinking about it. When his brown eyes land on me, I feel the hunger stirring low in my kitty, wanting to gobble that thick pole he calls a dick. As soon as he opens his mouth, the moment is ruined.

"You gonna just stand there, or you gonna give me my beer?" he asked, with a joint dangling from his mouth.

Jackie was never much of a smoker, but when his friends came around, he felt the need to step into character. From the way the air smelled, I knew they were blowing piff, not that crunchy shit, but that sticky-ass Broadway. I wasn't much of a smoker either, but I'd take a toke or two off the haze when Jackie brought it home on those rare occasions. There's something about that Barney that made me wanna get busy. Jackie usually bent me over and fucked me like a project bitch on those nights, but when he smoked heavy with his friends, I'd be lucky if he stayed awake long enough for me to suck him off, let alone bust mine.

"Here you go, baby," I sat the Corona on the table in front of him. I make sure I lean in a little extra when I do this so he can get an eyeful of the 36C's under my silk button-up blouse.

"What the hell is this?" He completely ignores my attempt at seduction, eyeing the beer as if it's something foul.

"Your beer, sweetie," I say in my sexy way, but it didn't seem to move him.

"Maybe you should've brought him one of them cherry smoothies his ass loves so much instead," Moe teased.

"Watch that—you know how I feel about them smoothies!" Jackie snapped. Lots of people had fetishes for weird things; Jackie's was cherry smoothies. What probably only me and José knew was the reasoning for Jackie's loving the fruity drink.

Jackie's father was a notorious womanizer, which led to him and Jackie's mother splitting up every six months. The separations never lasted more than a week, but whenever Jackie's father would come back, he would take the family out for smoothies on Coney Island. Cherry smoothies represented a piece of his childhood that Jackie wasn't quite ready to let go of.

"Sorry about that, boo, but it was the last beer in the fridge," I explained.

"Damn, baby, you know whenever I drink this Mexican shit, I get gassy," he complained, but still wrapped his lips around the beer.

"That's the last thing we need in here, wit ya rotten ass," Bilal joked. He was the youngest of their little clique. A reformed knucklehead from the block, Bilal proved to be the only one of Jackie's comrades at the time who had a little sense. Instead of blowing his money frivolously, waiting for Johnny Law's other shoe to drop, he made a little paper and dumped it into a business. Bilal was doing quite well with a dot-com he'd established with a college professor of his.

He was the portrait of a young dude who felt like because he had a little money in the bank, it made his dick bigger. Bilal was brash and had a mouth like gutter trash, but he was definitely eye candy. That afternoon, he wore his shoulder-length dreads twisted into three large braids that snaked over his head and tickled his neck. The blue Calvin Klein shirt he was rocking could've used a once-over with the iron, but he still looked neat. Without me really thinking about it, my eyes wandered the length of his body and stopped at the print of his baggy jeans.

Had it been a few years ago, I might've given his ass a little taste, not because he was cute, even though he was, but because there was no greater joy to me than making a so-called player recognize the power of the pussy. But those days were behind me. I was a married woman, and the only dick that my pussy would curve to was Jackie's.

"Fuck you, you fake-ass Rasta. Why don't you take your lil ass back up on the corner with the rest of them niggaz and grab a forty!" Jackie shot back.

"Nigga, don't play ya self, you know I ain't seen a corner in years." Bilal poked his chest out. "And while you're talking all reckless, you need to be glad she even brought it to ya lazy ass. I don't see a damn thing wrong with your legs."

It felt like all the sound was sucked out of the room. Seeing the fire burning in Jackie's eyes made me take a step back. I'd seen that stare enough times to know what came with it. Bilal had touched on a very sore subject, and he knew it. If you wanted to pluck Jackie's nerve, comment about how he ran his house or his woman. Jackie was one of the smartest men I had ever met, but he had a very Neanderthal way of thinking when it came to his possessions, including me.

Jackie leaned forward on his elbows and stared up at Bilal. "What, nigga?"

"Be easy, Jack, you know the nigga ain't mean it how he sounded, did you, Lal?" José tried to downplay it. He was a burly Puerto Rican whom Jackie had been friends with since high school. He now worked as head of security at Jackie's club, Paradise. José outweighed him by easily a hundred pounds, but even he didn't want to have to deal with Jackie if he was in one of his moods.

"Nah, I was just playing with you, Jackie, I didn't mean no disrespect," Bilal said in a less-than-sincere tone.

I knew it was a lie, and so did everyone else. It seemed like every time Jackie and Bilal got together and added alcohol to the mix, it became a dick-measuring contest. Bilal always went the extra mile trying to see how far he could push Jackie before he snapped. The young man didn't realize that he was threatening to open Pandora's box with his antics.

"Yo, pass the blunt." Moe spoke up, turning everyone's attention to him and away from the argument. He was a medium-built yellow cat who wore his head shaved. He definitely had his moments of ignorance right along with the rest of them, but overall, he had to be the most level-headed of the four.

"Do y'all want me to make some sandwiches or something?" I asked, trying to do my part in keeping the peace. When I saw Jackie's angry gaze turn on me, I knew I'd fucked up.

"Hell nah, these niggaz don't want no sandwiches!" Jackie half snarled at me. "This ain't Subway, if a nigga hungry, then he should've ate before he brought his ass over here." Jackie let his eyes sweep his crew, but in a flash they were back on me. Jackie frowned, before leaning in to sniff me. "Gina, you been drinking? And what the hell do you have on? Button that damn shirt!" he snapped.

When I had put the top on, I thought it was sexy, but the look of disgust on his face said I was wrong. As if the wet feet weren't bad enough, I really felt like a hot mess now. I could feel every eye in the room on me, and I suddenly knew what the whore of Babylon felt like. I tried to slink off to hide my shame, but Jackie grabbed me by the arm.

"Where the hell do you think you're going?" he asked.

"Upstairs to lie down." I tried to free my arm, but he held firm. Though nobody could see what he was doing, Jackie was digging his thumbnail into my forearm. He had that look in his eyes that I hated. The look that told me he'd had too much.

"Well, before you run upstairs to hop on the phone and talk our business to one of your hoodrat-ass friends or your faggot brother, go make a beer run."

"And some more blunts, ma," José added.

Jackie was trying to show his friends that he was the boss in the relationship—and the way I felt, I was in no mood to dispute it. The sooner I went and got the beer, the sooner I'd be away from them and Jackie. "A'ight, Jackie. Just let me go throw some sweats on, and I'll take care of that for you."

Jackie cast his bloodshot eyes back to me.

"Nah, ain't nobody got time to wait for you to primp and all that, Gina. You felt comfortable enough in ya little getup to flaunt it in front of my niggaz, so you'll be a'ight. If a nigga try to snatch ya ass, hit me on the speed dial." He looked me up and down as if I had just crawled in off the street.

I just looked back at him from under hooded eyes. I go and spend four hours in the salon and a thousand dollars on Fifth Avenue, and he all but calls me a whore for it? Excuse the hell out of me for going the extra mile to make my man seem like he has good taste. A bum bitch would've greeted Jackie's company in hoochie shorts, no bra, with a scarf on her head, but I catch the short end because I want to keep my marriage spicy. . . . Are you fucking kidding me?

A man can be good for holding you down or knocking the lining out of your pussy sideways, but they tend to be on the dull side when it came to dealing with things that they should've already figured out by a certain age. The comparison someone once made about men being so akin to animals because of their base natures was right on the money. They moved off instinct rather than rational thoughts. You show me a man who has 100 percent control over that little bell that goes off when a chick with a nice ass walks by, and I'll show you a closet homosexual.

"Don't trip, Jack. I'll go with her," José volunteered.

Now, of all Jackie's people, he trusted José the most. For as long as I had known him, he and I had always had a brother-and-sister relationship. Jackie knew all of this and was generally cool about it, but tonight it was about stripes.

"What, you trying to fuck, too?" Jackie asked venomously, cutting his eyes at Bilal before going back to José.

"Jackie, I don't give a fuck how much you had to drink or smoke, but don't come at me like that on some stunting shit, dawg. You know how me and Gina get down, homey," José told him. His tone wasn't hostile, but the words carried far more weight than when he normally spoke.

The two friends glared stone-faced at each other, neither moving, only glaring. A situation was fast on the horizon, and as usual I was in the center of it.

My rational brain told me to just go get my car keys and

skate, but the devil got the best of me. "Look, nobody has to go to the store with me, I'm a big girl. Jackie, you'll get your beers, but I'm taking these damn shoes off first." I made sure I flung my hair extra hard when I turned to sashay toward the stairs. About eight and a half seconds later, the world exploded into brilliant white stars.

TWO

Princess

Yo, I've never been a dick rider—well, at least not in the metaphoric sense, but I loved Harlem. Don't get me wrong, I was born and raised in Brooklyn, so my heart is always gonna be on Nostrand Ave., but I very much enjoyed my trips Uptown. Be it hopping off the A train, or out of some lame nigga's whip, I always felt a tinge of excitement when I touched these Harlem streets. In my mind, it was like the spirits that had passed through here were reaching out to the rejected and abused child within me, telling me that it got greater later. I've always held on to that belief, though I have yet to see it.

If the world were a perfect place, I'd be walking back and

forth across 125th, spending money on things I wanted but didn't need, but this world was far from perfect. In fact, I had started to see it as cruel. I was sweating like a runaway slave, though there was a comfortable chill to the air. My deodorant had melted away twenty minutes prior, and the damn duct tape pulled across my thigh felt like it was coming loose. My life had to get better than this.

As I crossed the different avenues, I could feel their eyes on me, the hungry eyes of men. Some were bold enough to say something—lame, of course—but most of them just watched in silence, wondering at what temperature did my pussy overheat. "You'll never find out, cocksuckers," I mumbled more to myself than to anyone else.

I couldn't be mad at them, though, because I was looking especially delicious that day. Mercedes had given my hair a thorough washing before sitting me under the dryer and eventually wrapping my hair. She didn't speak a lot of English, but that little Dominican chick knew hair like a gynecologist knows pussy. When I get my weaves, the Indonesian shit, I let her cut and style it. By the time I was ready to step out, my hair was falling just right, not even a pin mark.

I had on a gray wool skirt that I'd picked up at Marshalls. It wasn't tight, but it hugged my hips in a way that made me feel pretty. I loved that skirt because it showcased my figure without making me look like a slut. But when you have a thirty-one-inch waist and a thirty-nine-inch ass, lust will stir in the purest hearts. When I walked, I had a bad bitch's stride and the curves to match, which over the years I had learned to wear like a badge of honor. Niggaz went crazy over this, and for as silly as it may sound, it made me feel more like a woman.

I walked across the few avenues to Lenox, got a five-dollar pack of Newports, and slipped inside Starbucks. As usual, it was popping with people. I can't think of one time since they've been here that I'd seen the place empty. They had successfully made coffee a good business. It wasn't necessarily that they had the best product, but their presentation sold them. It was a relaxed little spot I could see myself sitting up in, poring over a good book, sipping something with way more sugar than I needed to have, but I wasn't there to daydream: I had to handle business.

Most of the people were young, hipsters, with laptops and paperback books, sipping drinks and making small talk amongst themselves. At the counter, I peeped a nice-looking chick drinking a latte and thumbing through a magazine. The red dress she wore hugged her so snug that I wondered if she'd bust the seams if she made a sudden movement.

The man I had come to meet with was sitting at one of the far booths, eyeing me over the newspaper he was pretending to read. I ordered an espresso from the pimple-faced young kid and made my way over to the table.

In true gentleman style, he stood as I approached. His hands slid down my sides and rested on my hips as he pulled me into a lover's embrace. I didn't pull away when he kissed me. The coarseness of his lips in contrast to the softness of mine brought back memories of eating dry toast in the mornings before school. It turned my stomach to kiss this man, but it was a delicate situation, and appearances were important. It wasn't until he tried to put his tongue in my mouth that I roughly slammed my hip into his groin, giving him the signal to back off. Smirking, he slid back into the booth and I slid in next to him.

"Damn, I missed you, ma," he said, draping his arm around me. He could've used another swab of deodorant, but I wasn't there to enlighten him on hygiene. "So what you been up to?"

"Nothing special, just trying to make it happen, ya know?" When I felt his hand under the table making its way up my leg, I reflexively shuddered. He lingered around my knee before continuing up to my thigh. For appearances, I traced the line of his jaw with my finger while gazing into his eyes like I was really interested in what he was saying. The duct tape stung when he pulled it off, but I'd take a few yanked-out hairs to pass that problem to someone else. I promised myself this would be the last time I let Slim talk me into toting his drugs.

I looked up when I heard the door open. A wiry young man slithered into the coffee shop wearing an Atlanta Braves cap pulled tightly on his head. His bloodshot eyes swept the joint, lingering a half second too long on me and my date. A frog jumped in my throat when he reached into his pocket, but to my surprise and embarrassment he pulled out his wallet and walked to the counter.

My date didn't seem to notice him, too preoccupied with his cell phone. I could tell he was ready to skate, and I can't say that I blame him, since he now had the ten years I'd been carrying. Truth be told, I wanted him and that package the fuck away from me as soon as humanly possible, but the business wasn't done.

The chick in the red dress had just noticed the kid in the Braves cap and had a chickenhead moment, squealing like a schoolgirl and draping her arms around him and putting her nasty painted lips on his. I watched them without watching them as they chatted it up for a few minutes before exchanging numbers and saying their good-byes. The slut in the tight dress was the first to boogie, big ass swinging as she went. A few ticks after that, the man in the Braves cap took the muffin and coffee he had ordered and left, too.

The minutes felt like hours as I waited the agreed-upon ten minutes before I was to leave. My date walked me out to the curb and waited around until I got into a taxi. He was a better person than me, because I sure as hell wouldn't have stood around with that weight on me. It wasn't until I was off 125th Street that I released the breath I hadn't realized I was holding. My days in the game were *so* over.

I had the taxi let me out at 135th and Fifth, in front of the bank. I walked into a store to get another pack of cigarettes, because I had lost the five-dollar pack in my rush to get out of Starbucks. My hand shook like Pookie in *New Jack City*, but I'd finally managed to get my cigarette lit when my green Honda Accord pulled up to the fire hydrant. Flicking my ash, I climbed in to the passenger seat and faced the sharp brown eyes staring out at me from under the Braves cap.

"You did good, baby," Slim leaned over and kissed me. There was no passion in the gesture, only approval. On his breath,

I could taste the lingering sweetness of red Alizé, the only kind of liquor Slim drank. "That lil move paid off nicely." He tossed the envelope the slut had passed him onto my lap and merged with the light Fifth Avenue traffic.

Just thumbing through the cheese, I figured it to be somewhere around five thousand, maybe a little more, but not much. I flipped through the bread once more before shoving it into my knockoff Bourke bag. It was a good little move, and we could damn sure use the paper, but I couldn't help but keep thinking that I could've gotten a year for every dollar in this damn envelope had something gone wrong. This was far from the life my mother wanted for me. I kept my game face and turned to my man.

"Yeah, it was a nice lick, but I ain't fucking around no more," I told him, trying to keep my voice from giving away my uncertainty. Slim was my lover, my friend, and my father, so going against something that he believed in felt funny. For damn near as long as I've known him, I've never been able to tell him no. Even when I put the pieces together, I still found myself loving him. Of course, the first thing he does is trace his finger from the back of my ear, down my neck, and across my collarbone. Bastard is using my spot against me, but I gotta stay strong.

Slim eased closer to me and placed his hand on my thigh. "Don't go rabbit on me now, baby. I thought we was trying to get this money up?"

"You know I am, but drugs ain't my thing," I told him.

"Princess, we in the street, ma. We gotta get it how we live."

"I feel you, Slim, but they're giving out too much time for

that shit, and I'm too pretty to go to jail." I pulled down the visor to check myself out in the mirror. Before meeting with the guy in Starbucks, I had applied a layer foundation that was two shades lighter than my actual mocha skin color. I was paranoid to the tenth degree, but it wasn't without reason. My face was correct, as usual, but I was starting to get bags under my eyes. I needed to slow down.

"So, you'd rather keep shaking your ass in them dives for shorts, instead of getting this long money?"

I rolled my eyes. "Shaking my ass won't get me time."

"But those backroom dances will," he muttered, loud enough for me to hear. It was a low blow, and he and I both knew it.

I sat stiff-backed in my seat and turned around to face him. "Nigga, you got some nerve. It's them backroom dances that hold you down when you blow your re-up money on dice games and strip clubs, trying to stunt for these lame-ass niggaz out here on some real birdshit!"

I never even saw him move. The only reason I knew he'd swung was because my head bounced off the car window. Tears welled in my eyes as the pain caught up with the deed and my lip started to throb. My hands suddenly began to shake, not because I was afraid, but because I knew I was about to kill this nigga. Slim must've felt it, too, because he quickly pulled over in front of the liquor store.

"Bitch, you better not start tripping—," he started, but that was as far as he got before I stole on him. The bum-ass engagement ring he'd gotten me a few months prior opened up a cut on his cheek. Slim was trying to undo his seat belt when I let him have two more. On open ground, he would've tore my ass up, but in cramped quarters, I had the advantage. I managed to visit his chin one more time before he was able to release the belt and lunge at me.

"You funky little cunt," Slim snarled, trying to grab a fistful of my hair. I managed to get the passenger-side door open and one leg out of the car, but not before he got a firm hold on the back of my shirt. Slim swung an overhand left that would've surely put me in la-la land had the top of the doorframe not absorbed most of the blow. Slim's fist landed on my jaw, sending me sprawling backwards and out of the car.

Half my shirt ended up being torn off in the process, but I had made it out of the car. I could only imagine how I must've looked, teetering on the curb with one of my tits hanging out of the shredded fabric, but I really didn't care as long as I had some distance between me and Slim. If looks could kill, I would've dropped dead from the way he was glaring at me.

"I'm gonna kill your ass, Princess!" he screamed across the car. This wasn't the first time he'd threatened to kill me, but it was the first time I actually believed him.

In the blink of an eye, I watched Slim go from my lover to a salivating maniac as he stalked around the car toward me. I tried to think of a getaway. I could've run—but I was wearing heels, and by the time I undid the laces on the back, he'd be on me.

The thought of survival took over my brain, and the word that fell out of my mouth surprised Slim just as much as it did me: "Rape!"

All right, all right, it was a low move. . . . I know this, but no more so than him trying to beat my ass after I had just risked going to prison for him. One thing that every man should know is not to play dirty pool with a woman; you'll come up short every time. Slim took another step toward me, and I said it again—this time a bit louder as I staggered backward toward the entrance of the pizza shop. The heel on my right shoe broke off, causing me to stumble and bang my shoulder against the door frame. All the hell we were raising out front and my screaming started to draw an audience. People were slowing up in their cars, being nosy, and even some of the corner boys inched closer to get a better look. Good—the more, the merrier. Slim was crazy, but he wouldn't be stupid enough to kill me in front of a crowd . . . or at least that's what I'd hoped.

"This fool is trying to kill me," I shrieked.

"You there, stop hitting that girl!" the owner of the pizza shop screamed, leaning out of the pickup window. "You keep it up, and I'm going to call the police."

"Mind your fucking business!" Slim snapped at the man before turning his attention back to me. "Princess, what the fuck are you doing?" he almost pleaded. It gave me a fucked-up rush to see fear creep into his eyes.

"Nigga, if you put your hands on me again, as God is my witness, I'm gonna put a case on you!" I yelled. Slim looked around cautiously before moving toward me again. His face had softened, but his eyes still said murder.

"Baby, I know I was wrong for hitting you, but don't go about it like this," he tried to coo, but that sweet shit wasn't working this time. Dick and sweet words had rocked me to sleep for the last time.

"I'm telling you, Slim, if you start this shit, Johnny Law is gonna finish it," I warned him. From the defeated look on his face, I thought the rational side of his brain was starting to take over and the threat kicking in, but I should've known better. Crazy people don't tend to think logically, and Slim's ass was nuts.

When whatever reasoning that had been keeping him off my ass finally gave, Slim rushed me. With my broken heel, I was like a wounded animal when the wolf came barreling down on me. He deflected my awkward swing and grabbed me by the biceps. The pizza shop owner was still spewing threats, but it was action that I needed to save my ass, not words.

Slim's lips were white, and he was breathing heavily when he hissed at me, "Princess, you better get your ass in the car before I cave the side of yo pretty-ass face in." I looked into the eyes of that deranged-ass young man and knew if he got me in the car I sure as hell wouldn't be getting out again, at least not on two legs. I had never been very religious, but whenever I found myself up shit creek, I called on God for a miracle, and as always he was right on time.

"Yo, fall back with that shit, son, you making the block hot right now," One of the corner boys was approaching. His was a face that required a special kind of love, but he was the most beautiful thing in the world to me at that point.

Slim glanced over at the young boy, giving me the chance to make my move. I shot my head at him like a bullet, aiming for his nose, but colliding with his bottom lip, cutting my forehead on his teeth. It probably hurt me more than it did him, but it made his crazy ass let go of me, which was all I needed. One heel or not, I tore around the corner and up toward Lenox Avenue as fast as I could. I heard Slim calling after me, but shortly after that, I heard the sound of glass breaking. He would have his hands full for a minute, so I didn't have to worry about him getting on my trail too soon.

Now here I was, bobbing and weaving up the block like I'm at a football combine, tits swinging and not really knowing where I was headed. One thing I did know was that if the corner boys didn't beat Slim too bad, he'd be on my ass sooner than later. It was a big city, and I knew all Slim's habits, so I could avoid him if I put my mind to it—but for how long? I needed to get my ones up so I could blow town. Luckily, I still had Slim's five thousand to get the ball rolling.

THREE

Gina

I could hear raised voices all around me, but I couldn't make out what they were saying over the ringing of my own ears. I'm not exactly sure what happened, but I ended up sprawled out on the floor, damn near under the card table. From the searing pain in the back of my head, I knew just what Michael Jackson must've felt like when that Pepsi commercial went to the left. Loose strands of hair were all over the front of my blouse, while a thick clump of it lay on the floor next to me. I touched my hand to the back of my head, and thankfully there was no bald spot, but it felt thin as hell.

Still dazed, I tried as best I could to gather myself. When I moved to get up, it felt like my kidneys shifted. I didn't have to see the bruise to know it was there; I'd had enough of them to know the dull ache just before the swelling. I managed to pull myself to my knees and peered over the table at my once-beautiful living room. The card table was now on its back, with beer and God only knew what else soaking into anything that could absorb it. Bilal was picking himself up from the floor, right next to the patio door. There was a slight gash over his eye that looked as if it would start leaking at any minute. He moved in my direction, and for a minute I thought he was coming for me, but his murderous rage went over my shoulder at Jackie. . . . My Jackie, who was smack-dab in the center of the chaos, with José restraining him.

"Nigga, don't you ever try to puff up on me in my spot!" Jackie foamed at the mouth, struggling against José's grip, with little success at getting free.

"Jackie, you're bugging the fuck out, word up." José was ushering Jackie toward the kitchen.

"Yeah, Jackie, this shit is bogus. First you slug your old lady and then you steal on Lal, what the fuck is your problem?" Moe stood between Jackie and Bilal, keeping the young boy in check, at least for the moment. Jackie was out of pocket, and he was surely going to let Bilal get a fair shake, but he didn't want it to go down in front of me.

Bilal stalked back and forth, trying to figure a way around Moe to tap Jackie's chin. "You got that one off, Jackie, but this shit is far from over." He touched the cut above his eye. "That shit was cute, but I ain't no bitch, homey. I'm gonna make you wear this shit."

"Word, you wanna get it popping, Lal? Yours ain't the only gun that works," Jackie threatened.

"Hey, the both of you niggaz watch that funny talk," Moe said seriously. "If you wanna shoot the fair one"—he raised his hands—"that's what it is, but it ain't gonna be no extra shit, so you might as well forget it." Both combatants stared at Moe, but they knew not to test the old head.

José stepped in front of Jackie and turned him so that they were eye to eye. "Jackie, you outta pocket right now. Look at what you did to your house—shit, look at what you did to your wife." He shoved Jackie in my direction. I looked for regret in his eyes, but saw only pity.

"Yo, this shit is real whack, fam," Bilal said. He was still pacing, but some of the tension seemed to have drained away from his body. "Every time you get drunk, you get on ya bullshit, Jackie, and one of these days a muthafucka ain't gonna wanna reason with you."

"Yo, Lal, you know who I be and where I be—" Jackie spread his arms. "—so quit kicking that gangsta shit like I'm supposed to be impressed. You always trying to call somebody out and then try to backpedal with the shit. You don't be knowing what to say out of your mouth."

"Both of y'all muthafuckas is faded, so ain't neither one a you gonna wanna see your own wrongs. Jackie, you need to slow up on that bottle, and Lal"—Moe turned to the youngster—

"that slick shit ain't gonna get you nowhere, know when to be easy."

If hadn't been for José reaching down to help me to my feet, I might've forgotten I was on the floor. Watching the scene unfolding between Jackie and his boys was surreal. Had it not been for the intense throbbing in my side and the pinpricks of pain shooting through my scalp, I could've easily been front row at the premiere of an action movie, but the embarrassed looks I was getting from everyone except Jackie were real.

"You okay, Gina?" José asked once I was standing on my own again.

My living room was a wreck, my blouse was torn, and I had managed to break one of the heels on the damn sandals. Was I okay? Hell no, but my pride wouldn't let me say so. "Yeah, I'm cool," I said, lying through my teeth. I watched Jackie scornfully as the reality of what he'd done seemed to soak in and his face finally softened.

"Baby girl." He reached out to me, but I moved away.

"Don't," was all I could say. I was angry and embarrassed. Had I been my mother, I would've picked up one of the tipped-over bottles and gone upside Jackie's head, but I didn't have that kind of willpower. Instead, I tucked my tail between my legs and headed upstairs to my bedroom.

With measured steps, I walked into my bedroom and closed the door. Against my better judgment, I went over to the vanity mirror to assess the damage. My hair was sticking up at an odd angle, and in some sections barely holding on by the roots. It wasn't as bad as it could've been, but I'd have to get it cut so you couldn't tell where Jackie had pulled it out. On the lower portion of my jaw, there were three red welts that were about the length of a man's fingers. In an attempt to make myself feel better, I told myself that it could've been a closed fist, but that didn't make me feel any better. I managed to keep my game face on in front of Jackie's company, but when I got a good look at the horror staring back at me through the looking glass, I broke down.

"This is not how your mother raised you," I said to the ugly duckling in the mirror. All my life, the importance of being an independent woman had been drilled into me like mental conditioning, but that all flew out the window when it came to Jackie. First there were the wayward friends whom he just couldn't seem to keep his dick out of, and then there was the occasional ass-whipping that I took for the team. I knew he didn't mean to hurt me, but Jackie had a bad temper. Whenever we would get into it, he'd feel bad and try to buy back my affection. I always said that the next time he hit me, I was going to leave, but I never did, at least not for more than a day or two, before I caved in and went back to him.

I'd heard older people say most marriages went sour in the first few years because young people didn't have the patience to work through their problems, but I'll bet the ones who started that bullshit weren't getting their assess kicked by the men who claimed to love them. Still, it gave me something to wrap my mind around in the hopes that Jackie would change, though I was starting to get the feeling he wouldn't. Every rational fiber of my body told me to leave his ass and go for the jugular in the divorce, but I couldn't do it. Jackie was my husband, and I'd vowed to stand by him for good or for bad, in sickness and in health. This is the mantra I repeated over and over so I wouldn't feel like such a fool. The truth of the matter was that I was a silly girl in love, and Jackie was the cross I'd chosen to bear.

Tap-tap-tap.

"Gina?"

Tap-tap-tap.

"Gina, open the door, baby."

I stood under the steaming water with my head pressed against one of the colorful swans carved into my porcelain shower tiles, listening to my husband requesting an audience with me. He had been out there for the last ten minutes, but I wasn't ready to receive him.

José had called me on my cell to find out if I was all right and to tell me that he'd cleared everyone out of the house. Thank God, because I couldn't bear the embarrassment of looking in their faces again today.

"Gina, I know I fucked up, baby, and I'm sorry. Can we please talk about it?" he continued to plead.

First he wanted to be Joe Frazier, and now he wanted to talk all nice? Nigga, please! I took my sweet time getting out of the shower and wrapping my hair in a towel. I had thought about trying to do something with it, but decided I didn't even want to see the damage. I'd just rock a scarf until I could get Mercedes to bless me at the shop. I knew that my sudden hair loss would be the topic of conversation the moment I left the salon, but I didn't really have a choice. I didn't let just anybody play in my hair.

Trying my best to ignore Jackie's insufferable pleading, I placed a hand towel over the commode so I could sit on it and dry off. The moment I bent over to dry my feet, I felt the pain shoot up through my side. My breath caught in my chest as I slowly sat back up to assess the damage. My ribs had turned a nasty shade of purple, and I wouldn't be surprised if one of them had been cracked. It wouldn't have been the first time. If it was broken, I'd have to just deal with it, because the triage nurse had already made it clear that the next time I dotted that door, she was going to call the police on Jackie. She was a no-nonsense woman, and I wasn't ready to call her bluff.

"Baby girl."

See, he had to go there. *Baby girl* is what he used to call me when we first started trying to build together. He called me that because he said he was going to raise me in the business like a father would his daughter, so that I knew the ins and outs of the game and could carve my own notch in the world. Well, if this is how he treats his other daughter, then his ass was an ACDC case waiting to happen. Still, when he called me baby girl in that silky voice, it did something to me.

"Baby girl, you don't know how sorry I am for what happened." He scratched at the door like a wounded cat. "Between

Bilal's mouth and that fucking purple haze, I just snapped. Gina, you know that haze is the damn devil in a dime bag, especially that shit from Uptown." He was trying to get me to laugh, and my dumb ass had the nerve to even crack a smile. "Baby girl, I know what I did was fucked up, but when you sided with that nigga, I just saw red and snapped."

No the fuck he didn't. With the towel wrapped around my waist and my breasts swinging freely, I stormed across the bathroom and snatched the door open. "Sided . . . I sided with Bilal?" I snapped at him. "Jackie, it was a freaking sandwich, and I extended the offer to everyone in the living room, including you!" I jabbed my finger into his chest.

"Gina, look—"

"No, you look!" I dropped my towel. "Look at my side—" I pointed at the bruise. "—look at my face—" I pointed to the throbbing point on my cheek. "Look at my hair!" I snatched the towel off my head so he could see the mess he'd made of my new hairdo.

For a while, Jackie just stared at me as if my bruised body were someone else's handiwork. He reached at me, but I backed away. I tried to storm around Jackie, but he grabbed me by the arm. When he tried to spin me around, I slapped him across the face, surprising both of us. Jackie's eyes flashed rage as he pulled me to him, and I tensed up for the blow that I was sure was going to follow, but Jackie didn't hit me. Instead, he hugged me to him and kissed me. He started with my head and moved to the bruise on my face before kissing a trail down my body.

"Get off me, Jackie, I hate you!" I said harshly, trying unsuccessfully to pull away from him. "I hate you for what you did to me," I sobbed.

"I hate me for what I did to you, too, baby girl." When Jackie looked up at me and I saw the lone tear twinkling in his eye, I was in love all over again.

I'm still not sure how it happened, but I ended up lying on the floor while Jackie planted soft kisses on my face. With one hand, he held both of mine pinned above my head while he explored me with the other. Every spot on my body that Jackie touched came alive with the intensity of a hundred suns, and I soaked it all in. When his fingers slipped inside me, I almost bit my tongue off. His prodding was aggressive, but not clumsy like a man looking for change in the couch. Jackie could be a brute with most things, but he knew my body and what it took to please me.

In no set pattern, Jackie ran his tongue over my collarbone and made his way down, giving each nipple equal attention. Blowing softly on the light trail of hair that lined my stomach, Jackie moved to my love cave and inspected it first with his fingers and then with his tongue. When his mouth met my coochie, I couldn't help but shudder. "You want me to stop?" he whispered, but didn't stop what he was doing. I think at that point I would've tried to kill him had he stopped that sweet trek across my body and my soul. For an answer, I forced his head back down between my legs.

Every time Jackie's tongue made contact with my clit, it sent waves of sinful pleasure through my body. Back and forth he went, lapping at my sex like a dehydrated dog in a puddle. I was so wet that I could feel the juices dripping down through the crack of my ass. Jackie must've noticed too, because his hungry mouth caught every drop. I tried to replay the incident from earlier and hold on to the anger I'd been carrying, but I couldn't seem to focus anymore. My head whipped back and forth as the fire building in my gut threatened to consume me, and Jackie drove his thick cock home. I swear that no matter how many times Jackie and I had sex, I still tensed up upon first entry. Jackie stroked me long, short, fast, slow, on my back, on my stomach, and finally came with me bouncing on top of him. Jackie seemed to explode inside me, filling every inch of my pussy and finally spilling down my legs and onto his stomach. When it was done, all I could do was lay on his chest with him still inside me. My last thoughts before I drifted off to sleep were how I hated this man just as much as I loved him.

When I woke up, I was still laying on Jackie, while he slept soundly beneath me. His dick was still lodged inside my womb, but it had gone soft. I gyrated my hips a bit, hoping that I might be able to get him up and go for another round, but Jackie was dead to the world. I looked down at his sleeping face and thought on how easy it would be for me to split his damn head open, but the thought fled my mind as swiftly as it came. No matter how many times Jackie hurt me, I couldn't bring myself to do the same to him . . . at least not at the moment.

I slid off Jackie's cock, leaving a trail of semen on his stomach.

Not only was my pussy sore, but it was also sticky with both Jackie's and my juices. I needed to take another shower, but the sun had almost set and I had some work to do outside, which was sure to require another shower afterwards, so I decided to wait. Slipping on my sweats, an old T-shirt, and some tennis shoes I went downstairs and out to the backyard.

The sun had started making its trip west, bathing the afternoon in a soft yellow glow. My half-an-acre private sanctuary had been a gift from Jackie. He knew how much I loved the outdoors, and he wanted to make sure I had a slice of it to call my own. I had a beautiful backyard, and everything in it had been planted by me when Jackie had the house built. From the trees to the rosebushes that bordered it, these were all my babies. I loved my backyard, but I got my greatest joy from my Tower of Joy.

My greenhouse stood off in an isolated section of the yard, which was off-limits to everyone, including Jackie. I'd started with the basics—sunflowers, morning glories, and lilacs—but as my love for gardening grew, I got into more exotic plants. I had successfully grown elephant ears, Mexican zinnias, and several other species of plants that weren't natives of big cities, but I spent the most time doting over my cherries—wild cherries, to be more precise. They were natives of Europe and northwest Africa, but my mother had managed to sneak me some back on her last trip.

When you hear wild cherries, you automatically think of the fruit, but my cherries were plants. They were still young, so the trunks were a purplish brown, but when they matured, they'd darken, leaning more toward brown. On the edges of the leaves there were small red glands that looked like underdeveloped cherries, which is how they got their name. I ran my finger along the smooth trunk and marveled at how erect the plant stood, just like I used to.

"Baby girl, what are you doing?"

Jackie's voice scared me so bad that when I jumped, I accidentally ripped one of the leaves off my plant. I cradled the beautiful green fold in the palm of my hand and wondered if it was true what they said about plants being able to feel pain. I turned my cold glare to Jackie. "You know, you're not supposed to be in here. This is my space, Jackie. That was the agreement."

Jackie raised his hands in surrender. "Sorry, but when I woke up, I couldn't find you anywhere in the house. I got nervous."

"What, you thought I'd finally grown a brain and left you?" I got up and brushed the dirt off my knees. "Don't worry, Jackie. I'm still an ass . . . at least for the moment."

"So you've thought about leaving?" he asked, a little more aggressive than I was comfortable with.

I added fuel to the fire: "Shouldn't I have?"

"Gina, you know I couldn't live without you," he was damn near pleading. Good, I wanted him to know what it felt like.

"Live without me? It seems like you can't stand to live with me. You shovel out all this shit, shit that any self-respecting woman wouldn't deal with, but not Gina. Like the obedient little jackass, I stand by my man, even if he ain't shit."

"Gina, you're not an ass. Please stop saying that," Jackie said.

"Why? I'm only speaking the truth." I stood directly in

front of him. There was a height difference, so I had to look up to see his eyes. "What kind of smart woman stays with a man that can't keep his hands to himself? When we took our vows, I don't recall agreeing to be your punching bag being slipped in there."

"Gina, I said I'm sorry. What more do you want?" he had the nerve to act like he was tired of hearing me talk.

"I want this shit to stop." I pointed at my face. "What's wrong with me, Jackie?"

"Nothing, baby girl." His voice sounded deflated. The usual Jackie bravado had drained away.

"Then why do I have to deal with this bullshit? I cook, clean, wash your nasty-ass drawers, and other than my gynecologist, a nigga ain't had the slightest whiff of this pussy since the first time you broke it in. To top it off, I *know* I'm a bad bitch, even if you seem to have forgotten. So if I've got all this going for me and you still treat me like a whore in the street, there has to be a problem somewhere." I felt the tears trying to come as I spoke, but I wouldn't give him the satisfaction. Composing myself, I continued. "Jackie, I used to think it was you, but the longer I stick around for this bullshit, I realize that it's me. A man will go only as far as you let him."

Jackie's jaw tightened, and so did my chest. He could've tried to act up if he wanted to, but before it was all said and done, those hedge clippers on my workbench would've surely found their way into his miserable heart. He must've been reading my mind because his eyes flashed to the bench.

"Gina—" He wisely took a step away from the hedge clippers. "—I agree with you one thousand percent. Putting my hands on you is whack, and I don't feel good about it." He sat on the stool by the front door and motioned me over. I went, but I made sure that I could still get hold of the clippers if I needed to. "I know it's no excuse, but I've been under a lot of pressure lately. Between the multiple businesses and hating-ass niggaz on the sidelines, my brain is all scrambled. Sometimes I confuse the people that hate me with the people that love me."

Damn, he was making it hard as hell to stay mad at him. "Jackie"—I took his hands in mine—"I can't speak for anybody else, but I know I love you and would place no one above you. When we got together, it was us against the world, baby. We might not get along all the time, but I still hold that in my heart." I drew him up so that we were nose to nose. "I just want it to be like it used to, Jackie—" I kissed him. "—you and me against the world."

Jackie embraced me, running his tongue along the roof of my mouth. "It will be, baby girl, I promise." Jackie sucked my bottom lip. "Now, start getting ready." He patted me on the ass.

"Ready for what?" I asked, still swooning from the kiss.

"You know we're doing that grand opening at Paradise tonight—you said you'd do the hostess thing, remember?"

Fucking Paradise, Jackie's boyhood dream and my nightmare. Yeah, I had agreed to help him with the grand opening two weeks prior, but at the time he had me benched over the couch and calling for my mama. "Jackie, I can't do the grand opening tonight with my hair being a mess, and let's not forget the little memento you left on my cheek."

Jackie cupped my face in his hands, turning my head this way and that. "It ain't too bad. Nothing a little makeup won't cover." He paused. From the look in his eyes, I knew his wheels were spinning. "You know what, I ain't gonna force you to do it if you don't want to. I understand you've had a rough night. I can get Kim to do it."

Oh, he must've really fell and bumped his head. Kim was a six-foot mix of Korean and black, with a size 5 waist and plastic titties. She had been working at Paradise for only a few weeks, but had already stirred up more trouble than her bubblegum ass could handle. It got so bad that Jackie had to stop her from dancing and put her on the door so she wouldn't keep getting into it with the other girls over the tricks—excuse me, clients. Whichever way you sliced it, I didn't trust that ho, and there was no way I was gonna sit by while she and Jackie played the don and diva of the night.

"No, I can do it. I doubt if Mercedes can squeeze me in on such short notice, but I've got a B-plan." I assured him.

Jackie smiled, but I saw the disappointment in his eyes. "That's my baby girl." He kissed me on the forehead. "I'm about to go hop in the shower and get out of here. The doors open at ten, but I need you there no later than nine thirty to make sure everything is set."

"Wait a minute, we're not gonna arrive together?" I asked.

Jackie's eyes blinked before he answered, and I knew before he opened his mouth that there was funny business afoot. "Nah, I gotta go down there now to make some last-minute arrangements and then I'm going Uptown to get a cut, so you'll have to drive in. As a matter of fact, take the keys to my CLK—I can't have my lady rolling up looking less than the queen she is. See you tonight, love." Jackie turned and started back toward the house, leaving me there to work it all out in my head.

I'd met a lot of men in my time. Some of them have been lucky enough to get inside my heart and body, while most of them haven't gotten past a kiss. But of all the men combined, Jackie had the biggest balls.

FOUR

Princess

I could feel them watching me, but I didn't care. I was dressed in one of those I ♥ NEW YORK T-shirts that I'd gotten from a vendor and a pair of dollar-store sandals. I'd scrubbed the ruined makeup off my face and pulled my hair back into a ponytail. I stuck out like a sore thumb in the lobby of Midtown's Marriott Hotel, but my strut said that I had just as much right as any of the well-dressed white chicks who were staying there. With an extra bounce in my step, I approached the check-in desk.

"Can I help you?" a man dressed in a charcoal suit asked from behind the desk. His name tag said TOM.

"Yes, Tom, I'd like a room for the night, please," I told him.

He must've stared at me in disgust for a full three minutes before responding. "I'm sorry, ma'am, but being that it's the weekend, we're very crowded. If you like, I can direct you to a Howard Johnson not far from here," Tom told me.

No this nigga didn't.

"Listen, Tom, if I wanted to stay at a Ho-Jo, then I'd have gone to a Ho-Jo. I've had a hellish day, and all I really wanna do is take a hot shower and lay down. Now, could you please give me a room?" I was trying to be polite, but if he kept playing, the project bitch was going to come out of me.

Tom scrunched his nose. "If you insist, but you'll have to pay the weekend rate on a standard room, which is five fifty per night." He smirked as if he'd said something slick.

My face faked indifference before I pulled out Slim's money and counted off fifteen hundred dollars. "Then you'd better make it a suite, Tom." I slammed the money on the counter. "And feel free to keep the change for yourself." As they said, Money talks and bullshit runs a marathon.

"Right away, ma'am," he said, fumbling with the keyboard. For as snobbish as people try to be, everyone respects the almighty dollar. He was so grateful that the grinning son of a bitch forgot to ask for my ID before giving me the room key. Oh well, it was his mistake, so it would be his ass when his supervisor caught wind of it. Within minutes, I had my room key and was riding the elevator to the twelfth floor.

"He's so sweet make her wanna lick the wrapper, so I let her lick the rapper."

I loved that ringtone when I had downloaded it, but as Lil Wayne's whining voice woke me up from my nap, I absolutely hated it. I felt like I had just gone to sleep, which I actually had. After checking into my room, I hit up a few stores to get some new clothes and retreated back to my hideaway. Then I took a hot shower, turned the air conditioner on full blast, and stretched out on top of the covers as naked as the day I was born.

Grumbling every curse word I knew, I stumbled around in the dark until I found the phone, wrapped in the skirt I had stepped out of. I started to let it ring, figuring it was Slim calling for the twentieth time, but when I saw Tashee's name flashing on my caller ID screen, I was glad I did. Tashee was a chick that didn't generally get out of bed before 9 P.M., so if she was hitting me up at seven forty-five, I knew it was about a lick.

"What up, bitch?" I yawned into the phone.

"*You*, skank," she shot back. Tashee and I called each other derogatory names all the time, and neither one of us ever took offense—but let somebody else try it, and it was on. "The word is that you're a fugitive from justice," she continued.

"I don't know about justice, but I finally dumped Slim's washed-up ass," I told her.

"So I hear. He's telling everybody you got him jumped and dipped out on him with ten stacks." News in the hood traveled as fast as the speed of sound, but nine times out of ten, the story always got twisted somewhere along the line.

"More like four and a half," I corrected her, "and he brought that ass-whipping on himself. If he hadn't have been trying to break fly, them dope boys might not have put the beats on him. They should've killed his ass for lumping a bitch up."

"Nah, they didn't kill him, but I hear his hand is gonna be in a cast for a while." Tashee snickered. Her ghetto ass loved drama, and I guess that's why it found her more often than it didn't. "So, y'all was on ya Ike and Tina again?"

"Yep, and I went Nutbush on that ass. I risk going to prison for that clown, and he had the nerve to try to break fly."

"Princess, you know this ain't the first time Slim done played himself, and it won't be the last."

"Now that's where you're wrong, T. I'm done, finished, end of the road. From now on, if I'm gonna risk my ass for someone, it's gonna be me!" In the back of my mind, I wished I was really as assertive as I sounded. I'd known for a long time that Slim was no good for me, yet I stayed. Some people would think that for as strong and intelligent as I am, I was a fool for sticking around, and they were right, but the heart was funny like that. I'd convinced myself to leave him on several occasions, but as soon as I looked into the puppy dog brown eyes, I was caught up again. I don't know what the fuck it was about Slim, but I just couldn't seem to get him out of my system.

"Church!" Tashee cosigned. "So what's up, you still on ya paper chase, or that lil five stacks you sitting on got you thinking you're hood rich?"

"You know I'm about my change twenty-four-seven, what's

the deal?" I knew between the hotel suite and my expensive-ass habits, it would be only a matter of days before I ran through Slim's bread, so I needed to get on one.

"Do you remember Harlem Heat?" she asked.

I had to think on it for a minute. I had danced at or been to over a dozen strip clubs in the five boroughs, so it was hard to keep them all straight. "Yeah, the spot Uptown that closed down a few years back?"

"Well it's back open and under new management. They're calling it Paradise now. This kid my peoples know renovated the place and is having the official grand opening tonight," Tashee informed me.

"I don't know, Tash. That spot has been shut down for a minute—it's probably not even gonna be popping."

"Princess, you know me better than that. I don't shake my ass nowhere if I ain't sure it's gonna be some bread floating around. The nigga who owns it is an ex-small-time hustler turned industry bigwig."

"What, he's a rapper or something?"

"No wit ya fame-thirsty ass. He's a writer or something like that. Anyhow, it's supposed to be all kind of big-Willy niggaz in there for the grand opening and all kinds of extracurricular activities to sweeten the pot," she told me.

"What kind of extracurricular activities?" I asked suspiciously. Don't get me wrong—I've been known to go above and beyond to make a few extra dollars—but Tashee's ass was off the hook. I once watched her do two guys and a girl at the same time. I enjoyed a little fish here and there, but I wasn't into the double-penetration thing.

"The usual: wet T-shirt contest, booty clap-off, and a dick-sucking contest for fifteen hundred," she said as if she were simply reading off a grocery list.

"Now the clap-off and the wet T-shirt contest, I'm down with, but I'm good with the suck-off."

Tashee sucked her teeth. "Princess, stop acting like you ain't never sucked a dick before."

"I ain't never said all that, but I'm just not with sucking some dude off in front of a bunch of thirsty niggaz for fifteen hundred dollars. Now, in private is something else," I half joked.

"You're so nasty." Tashee laughed. "But you ain't gotta worry about the suck-off, because we already know I got that on lock." She made a slurping sound into the phone. "So, you fucking with it or what?"

"Yeah, I'm fucking with it, but I got a little dilemma. When I bounced on Slim, I didn't take none of my costumes."

"Baby girl, that's a small thing to a giant. I'll bring you one of my joints," Tashee offered.

"T, you know damn well my titties can't fill them army helmets you call cups."

"Princess, stop making excuses and just have your ass ready when I come scoop you. Where are you staying?"

"At the Marriott Hotel in Midtown."

"I see you baller," Tashee sang into the phone. I could just picture her doing her silly little dance on the other end.

"Balling, my ass—this ride is on Slim."

"Well, in that case, you're buying the drinks tonight. I'll see you at ten or ten thirty." Tashee ended the call without waiting for confirmation.

Still naked, I slid off the bed and pulled the heavy drapes on the windows back. Below, the sun had set and the city was alive with lights and sounds. I was glad to know Slim had gotten his ass whipped, but the fact that they let him live meant I'd have to deal with him sooner or later.

"Fuck Slim," I said, stepping away from the window. I would cross that bridge when I came to it, but the order of business that night was paper, and I knew once those Harlem niggaz got a whiff of my cat, I'd be swimming in it by the end of the night.

By the end of my second shower, it was a shade before eight thirty, so I decided to get something to eat before Tashee got there. I knew once she arrived, she'd be too preoccupied with handling business to want anything other than a quick bite, and I was in no mood for McDonald's. My body craved a nice steak and a baked potato, so I slipped into the sweatpants I'd picked up from Modell's and a pair of white K-Swiss before slipping out of the room in search of a porterhouse.

I stepped off the elevator in the lobby and took stock of my surroundings. The hotel was more alive at that hour than it had been when I checked in that afternoon. There must have been some kind of party going on in the lobby's conference room, because I kept seeing well-dressed people sliding in and out. They were mostly white folks, and from the way they were stumbling about, I could tell they were partying down!

As I crossed the lobby on my way to the exit, I could feel the hairs on the back of my neck beginning to stand up. I turned around and spotted a middle-aged white gentleman staring at me. He was at least fifteen to twenty years my senior, but still kind of cute in a Harrison Ford kind of way. I expected him to turn away when I caught him looking, but he didn't. In fact, his stare only became more intense. That man had lust in his eyes and larceny in his heart, but as I'd come to learn, that was the story of my life. Men never loved me, only lusted after me. Our staring contest was broken up when he was joined by a silver-haired woman who I assumed was his wife. Playing the devil's advocate, I winked at him and exited the lobby.

Outside, the streets were teeming with people of all races and creeds, strolling along Times Square, snapping pictures or buying overpriced souvenirs. It's hard to believe that ten years prior, the place had been a breeding ground for sex and corruption; that was before the Giuliani administration. Overhead, one of the jumbo televisions was broadcasting the NBA finals, and the Celtics were beating the Lakers by twenty-five in the third quarter. I had been a Knicks fan since I was a little girl, but I wasn't mad at KG and his crew. They deserved a ring, and from the looks of the score, they were about to get one.

I felt a presence behind me and turned to see the man from the lobby and his wife. From their glassy eyes, I could tell they were both twisted, but the disturbing part was the way they were looking at me. It was as if they were two stalking lions and I was a gimp deer. Tired of being gawked at, I stepped to them.

"Is there something I can help you with?" I asked, placing my hands on my hips.

"I'm sorry, we didn't mean to offend you," he said in an accent I couldn't quite place, "but my wife and I were just talking about how beautiful you are. Melanie"—he nudged his wife—"isn't she gorgeous!"

"Yes, George, she's absolutely delicious," Melanie slurred. When she opened her mouth, I could smell the scotch rolling off her tongue. They tried to sound innocent enough, but the lustful looks in their eyes told me that something funny was going down.

"Well, thanks, but I gotta go," I said, turning to leave.

"Wait," George called after me. "I don't want to creep you out or anything, but . . ."

"Oh, George, stop beating around the bush and just spit it out," Melanie urged. I couldn't tell who wanted me more, him or her. "What my husband wanted to know was if you might like to join us for a drink?"

The gauntlet had been laid.

"Listen," I addressed the both of them, "I've been out here hustling for too long to go for the 'nice old couple holding candy' routine, so let's cut the bullshit, shall we? What your husband really wants to know is can he fuck me, am I correct?" The embarrassed look on his face said that I was. I started to scream on the both of their freakish assess and keep it moving, but seeing the ice around her neck and on his wrist, I decided to play the game. "Check it out, daddy. If you wanna sample this pussy—" I patted my crotch. "—it's one thousand dollars per hour, plus expenses, and I get all my bread up front."

They moved off to the side to discuss it, and I thought that I'd finally managed to scare them off, but to my surprise, they both came back wearing broad grins.

"I'll tell you what, we'll give you three thousand if you and my wife go at it and let me watch," George offered.

I looked at each of them seriously to see if they were bullshitting, and from the looks on their faces, I could tell they weren't. I'd heard stories about people like George and Melanie, but up until that point I'd never had the pleasure of meeting real swingers. I gave one more look around to make sure I wasn't being set up.

"Are you serious?" I asked.

"Quite," Melanie said. She didn't sound so drunk now.

"Are you cops?" I asked.

George laughed. "Heavens no, we're just an old couple trying to keep the marriage fresh—you know how it is, right?"

"No, I can't say that I do. Okay, where do you wanna do this? I know a motel not far from here and—"

"God, that'll never do." Melanie moved closer to me. A little closer than I was comfortable with. "We have a Presidential Suite upstairs. We can do it there." She reached out to touch my face, but I pulled away.

"First you pay and then you play," I told them in a tone that said it wasn't up for discussion.

"Oh, this one has spunk. I like her, George," Melanie purred.

"I knew you would, darling." He kissed her on the lips and began to fondle her right there in front of the hotel. I thought they might get arrested before I got a chance to get my money, so I hurried things along.

"If we're gonna do it, then let's do it. I don't have all night." I went back inside the hotel, not bothering to see if they were following, because I knew they would be.

By the time I got to the elevator, they were right on my heels. Before the doors had even closed, they were at it. George was kissing Melanie passionately, while she had her hands jammed down the front of his pants, jerking him off. I can't even front: my pussy got wetter than a nor'easter watching their raw display of passion. My watch said nine o'clock, so I still had an hour or so before Tashee would get there, but from the looks of George and Melanie, I had a feeling I'd be late for our meeting.

FIVE

Princess

George and Melanie's suite made my room look like a tenement. The common area was laid out with a beautiful cream sofa and love seat, with a large flat-screen mounted on the wall. George went to the safe in the closet and counted out thirty crisp one-hundred-dollar bills, which he laid on the table in front of me. I nodded in approval and stuffed the money into the pocket of my sweats. Once the transaction had been made, he went to fumble around in the minibar, while Melanie shed her shawl and flopped on the couch.

"Come in and make yourself at home." She patted the cushion next to where she was sitting. I was still a little suspicious, but I sat down. From her purse, she produced a small vial of white powder that I would've known anywhere. She sprinkled a little of the coke on the coffee table and turned to me. "Can I offer you a snort?"

"Nah, I'm good," I said, rubbing my sweaty hands on my sweats. I'd been with girls before, so that wasn't the cause of my nervousness; it was the couple. On the outside, they looked like the typical businessman husband and homemaker wife, but on the inside, they were stone freaks. It just goes to show that you never know until you know. Melanie had snorted two healthy lines by the time George had come back with the drinks.

"I hope you don't mind bourbon, because we've run through everything else." George handed me a glass of the mahogany liquor.

"This is fine," I said before throwing it back in one shot. The minute it made contact with my throat, I regretted it. It had smooth bite like Hennessy, but the gagging effect of Jack Daniel's. With watering eyes, I watched George and Melanie watching me.

"Being that we're on the clock, what say we get this party started." George slipped out of his jacket and began undoing his trousers.

"Hold on, you said you were only here to watch—we never discussed a threesome." I placed my glass on the table and stood up.

"Relax," he said, kicking off his shoes and stepping out of his trousers. He hadn't been wearing any underpants beneath, so his balls hung freely. Even though he was still limp, I could tell that George was relatively well hung. "I'm just getting comfortable for the show."

"Everything will be fine, darling, trust us." Melanie ran her hand up my leg and cupped my ass. "My, but you're a well-built one." *One what?* I wanted to ask her, but instead I just let her continue to grope me.

George had settled into an armchair with his drink and began to diddle himself. "Take your clothes off," he tried to order, but it came out like a gruff plea.

I turned my back to George and faced Melanie, while I pulled my shirt over my head. Seeing me standing there in just my yellow bra seemed to excite her. Next, I slid my sweats down around my ankles. Instead of stepping out of them, I bent over to pull them over my sneakers, giving George a clear view of my ass in the purple thong. The set didn't match, but I don't think either one of them noticed.

Melanie took another heavy snort before standing and giving me her back. "Unzip me," she breathed, and I complied. She turned slowly and let me admire her surgically enhanced breasts. Though they looked real enough, I knew they had to be purchased because they stood higher than mine. I reached out and touched them to find them firm yet soft. Melanie moaned as I let my thumbs flick her erect nipples. While I teased her nipples with one hand, I undid my bra strap with the other, letting it fall to the floor. Melanie gasped at the site of my tender breasts. With trembling hands, she reached out and touched one, and from the look on her face, I knew she was coming.

"Can I taste you?" she whispered. I didn't bother to answer; I just pressed her face to my breasts and let her devour them. Melanie suckled my breasts like a starved child while George moaned behind us. I looked over to see him stroking his cock, with his eyes narrowed to slits as he watched the show.

Melanie maneuvered me to sit on the couch while she knelt in front of me. She pulled my thong to the side and tasted my pussy. I'd had my pussy eaten by both women and men, but none of them measured up to Melanie. She worked me to a lather before dipping her tongue in and out of my asshole. All I could do was bite my bottom lip and curse as Melanie did her thing.

She flipped me on my stomach and started licking my ass from behind while I gripped the back of the couch. I felt an extra set of hands rubbing my ass cheeks and looked back to see that George had joined the party. He had mounted Melanie from behind and was hitting her with short, deep strokes. The force of his pumping forced Melanie's tongue deeper into me, escalating my pleasure. It wasn't until George reached around and tried to fondle my clit that I put the brakes on.

"George, we've already been over this. You paid for me to play with your wife, if you wanna join in, then that's gonna be extra." I hadn't intended on a threesome, but my pussy was jumping for some action. Melanie was handling her business, but I needed a stiff cock.

"Tell me how much and it's done. I just need to taste that sweet black meat," he whimpered. "Please, just a little."

I pushed Melanie off me and flipped over on my back. I raised my legs high in the air and looped my arms around them to keep them there. George looked like he was going to break out in a crying fit at the sight of my soaking pussy. "It'll be another two grand if you wanna play with this pretty kitty."

"Done!" he declared before almost shoving Melanie out of the way to get to me. In his lustful rush, George tried to slip it in me raw, but I wasn't having that.

"No glove, no love, daddy."

"Sure, sure." George darted into the bathroom and came out holding a box of off-brand condoms. I didn't really trust those kinds of condoms, but after making him strap on two of them, I let him in. When George felt how warm my shot was, tears rolled down his face like the river Nile. He cried, cursed, pledged his love of sweet black pussy, and some other shit I won't get into, on his way to sweet glory, while Melanie continued to lick my ass and clit. I could tell he was about to come, because his face turned beet-red, and Melanie must've known it too, because she took him out of me and snatched the condom off. Speaking in tongues, George came in Melanie's mouth and on her face. She swallowed what she was able to catch and rubbed the rest into her face like moisturizer.

"That was fucking incredible," George panted, still on his hands and knees.

"God, my legs won't stop shaking." Melanie fingered herself. "We've got to do this again!"

I slipped my sweats and T-shirt back on, stuffing my panties and bra into my pockets. "Thanks for the compliment, but I think I'll pass. I will take the rest of my bread, though," I held my hand out to George.

"Of course, of course." he scrambled to his feet. George went back to the safe and handed me $2,500. "The extra five is for being such a great fuck," he explained. "Here"—he handed me a laminated business card—"if you change your mind, give us a call."

I tucked the card into my pocket, still not sure if I would ever use it or not. "Thanks, I just might do that." I left George and Melanie in the suite to their own freakish devices while I went back to my room to take another shower and get ready for Tashee to come and get me. I had made $5,500 to put with what I had left of Slim's for under an hour's work. If all went as I'd planned, within a week or two, I'd be able to leave this bullshit alone and try to piece my life back together.

SIX

Gina

It was only eleven o'clock, and I was already pissed off. Two of the girls were no-shows, the toilet in the men's room had overflowed, and I hadn't seen Jackie since he left the house.

"Why the long face, Ms. G?" Randy walked over to where I was standing. He was dressed in a transparent yellow tank top with a pair of purple leather pants. His skin was darker than mine, but he'd highlighted it with some kind of glittery cold cream. Randy was just as gay as the day was long, but he was my brother, and I loved him regardless.

"I'm cool." I kissed him on the cheek. "What's good with you? You're working that outfit, Ms. Thing."

"Yeah, somebody has gotta show these low-class hoes how a real bitch does it." He executed a model strut.

"Boy, what're you doing over here bullshitting with me? You know them drinks ain't gonna serve themselves." I nodded at the bar, which was damn near empty except for a few drunks trying to holla at the young girl who was doing Randy's job.

"Please." He clicked his tongue. "Ain't no real money roll up in here yet, and the few muthafuckas that are here are in the back doing the nasty with these skank-ass bitches Jackie got shaking tail in this joint. Speaking of Jackie, where is the mister?"

I shrugged. "Don't start me to lying."

"Being that this is the grand opening, I thought y'all would've rolled together in the limo."

"Limo?" I asked, not knowing what the hell Randy was talking about.

"Yeah, the way I hear it, Jackie rented a white stretch limo for the event. You didn't know?"

"Does it look like I knew?" I glared at him. I wasn't mad at Randy, but Jackie wasn't there for me to take my aggression out on.

"Damn, don't shoot the messenger, Gina. I'm only telling you what I heard." He snaked his neck.

"I'm sorry, Randy. I'm just under a lot of stress right now," I told him while smoothing the sides of my wig down. It made me feel like I was wearing a furry-ass hat, but it was the best I could do at the last minute.

"So I see." He cupped my face and turned my head from one side to the other. "I love the new shade of foundation you're using." He ran his finger over the bruise on my cheek, which apparently the makeup hadn't done a good enough job of hiding.

I slapped his hand away. "Don't get cute, Randy."

"Honey, ain't nothing cute about getting your ass whipped by somebody who ain't ya mama or ya daddy."

"It's nothing—Jackie and I just had a little misunderstanding, that's all.

"Umm-hmm." He clicked his tongue. I hated when he did that. "Gina, how long has he been beating you, *this time*?"

"He's not beating me; I told you we just had a misunderstanding."

"Well, then, that makes two of us, because I'm trying to understand how a girl as smart as you can be so fucking stupid. Gina, ain't no good gonna come of this. Either Jackie is gonna kill you, you're gonna kill Jackie, or I'm gonna kill his ass for you, but all the outcomes are bad ones."

"I'm good, Randy—it's only a bruise," I told him.

"This time, but what about the next?" he questioned. "Gina"—he took my hands—"do you remember Terry and Steve?"

"Yeah, the nice couple you used to hang around with. What ever happened to them?"

"Terry was killed a few weeks ago, and Steve is on trial for the murder." This shocked me. "I had this same conversation with Terry, and he, too, was reluctant to see the writing on the wall, until his brains became the ink. You can play it off all you want, but it's never a small thing when the person you love is kicking your ass. I begged Terry to leave Steve—" His voice dropped an octave. "—but much like you, he had to stand by his man. Terry had convinced himself that his love would change Steve, but he found out different when Steve beat him to death in a jealous rage." A tear rolled down Randy's cheek and hung on his lip. "I swear, when I saw Terry in that casket with his face all made up, I thought of you."

"I'm sorry for your loss, Randy, but it's not the same thing," I said sincerely.

"Other than you being a female and Terry having been a male, what's so different about it, Gina?" He put his hands on his hips. "Big sis, since Mommy died last winter, we're all we have left. My heart couldn't take it if you left me. If Jackie was to one day kill you, as sure as my asshole points to the ground, I'd be spending my last days in somebody's penitentiary because he'd be going to sleep shortly after you did. Don't do that to us, baby, or to him."

I knew without looking into his tearful eyes that Randy was dead serious. He was a homosexual, but still a man, a man who loved his big sister and was willing to give his own life to protect her.

"Randy, it's gonna be okay, I promise." I kissed him on the cheek.

"If you say so, then I'll take your word for it, but if anything happens, you know I'm just a phone call away." He tapped the hot pink Razr clipped to his side. "All you gotta do is give me the nod, and I'll cut his dick off and stick it on a barbecue spit."

He waved his hands like he was cutting something. This got me to laugh, something that I hadn't done all day.

"I know, baby brother, and thanks." The front door opened as more girls came in. I was in the process of pointing them to the dressing room when a voice that I hadn't heard in years called out to me.

SEVEN

Princess

"Bitch, I don't know why you always gotta take forever and a day when it comes to something I wanna do," Tashee was saying for at least the fourth or fifth time that night.

"Tashee, you didn't get to my hotel until ten to eleven!" I reminded her.

"Yeah, but what if I had been there on time, and we needed to bust a move for some high stakes? Time is money, baby." This coming from a girl who had been a week and a half late for her own birth. She couldn't have been serious.

"Tashee, your ass is fried. This shit tonight ain't gonna be much more than another day at the office."

Tashee cut her eyes at me. "Umm-hmm." She leaned over and sniffed me.

"Bitch, what the fuck is you doing?" I swatted her away.

"Princess, I know you, and it couldn't have been anything but money or dick to keep you this long, so which one was it?"

I cut my eyes back at her. "Both," I blurted out, suppressing my giggle. I went on to give Tashee the short version of George and Melanie while she drove up to Harlem. Of course, her hating ass added her two cents about how I could've capitalized on the situation by robbing the couple, but that was where the difference between her and me became apparent. Tashee was a greedy bitch, and I wasn't.

For the rest of the ride we drank Cook's, smoked haze, and shot the shit. When we got off the West Side Highway and touched Harlem, I immediately tensed. I knew Slim was out there somewhere, looking for a chunk of my ass, but I couldn't let my worry make me slip. I was about to go into a den of drunken and horny wolves, strip naked, and still try to get out in one piece; being off point wasn't even an option. The parking gods had smiled on us, because we were able to find a spot a half a block away. My eyes swept the streets and darkened corners not only for Slim, but for any fool who felt like getting disrespectful that night. Slim had caught me off guard, but right then my hand was securely wrapped around the box cutter in my bag. Let the games begin, muthafuckas.

Tashee and me strode to the front of the joint like our names were on the marquee. She knew the Puerto Rican cat at the door, so we didn't have any static getting in. There was a bearded cat wearing a kufi checking the guys, and a butch-looking chick in fatigues had to frisk us. If you asked me, she took a little too much pleasure in her job, but I just smiled and let her do her thing. That hard-mugged bitch was way too gruesome for me to even think about bedding, but it was always good to get a security connect in places like that. After she got her free feels, she stepped aside to let Tashee and me in.

From the door, I could tell that the crowd was way light. The bar was damn near empty, and the dudes that were tipping the young bitches who were onstage looked like short-money niggaz. I glared over at Tashee, and she gave me the signal that everything was cool. Cool was an understatement; that spot was ice cold. Rolling my eyes at Tashee, I walked over to the girl who was playing hostess for the evening. She was a sexy redbone with a very familiar face. As I stared at her, the pieces began to fall into place, and I was taken back to Friday-night fish fries at my parents' house with my sister and her best friend. "Gina?"

EIGHT

Gina

I couldn't believe my eyes. She had way more body than I remembered, but it was her. It was the same little girl who used to try and follow me and my best friend, Audrey, when we were up to no good. From the way she had filled out, I imagined that it was her who was getting followed these days.

"Princess!" I squealed like a schoolgirl who hadn't seen her best friend all summer. I was two or three years her senior, but next to Randy, Princess and Audrey were the closest things to family I had left. "Girl, what's your little ass doing in here?" I held her at arm's length so I could get a good look at her. Princess had not only grown up, she'd grown out. She had a body so tight that after a while I felt bad about looking at her. I wasn't into girls—those two incidents in college didn't count, because we were drunk—but I was big enough to give another female her props. Princess had grown up to be a dime.

She shrugged, but maintained the familiar smile. "Trying to get a dollar."

"You're lying, when did your young ass start shaking it!" Randy butted in. At first Princess just stared at him, trying to figure out his angle, but then the tinge of recognition came over her.

"Randy?" Seeing my brother in his getup made her eyes damn near pop out of their sockets. "Look at you!" She hugged him. "You look so . . . so . . ."

"Gay?" He filled in the blanks. "No need to be shy about it, girl. I can finally say out loud what people have been saying behind my back for years. I'm gay and loving it." Randy did a crazy twirl. People were looking at him like he was crazy, but he didn't care. "So you came to get ya paper on, huh?"

"Yeah, I hear this spot is a good place for a girl to come up," Princess said.

"Or be brought down," I mumbled. "Wow, little Princess is all grown up and doing some very grown things."

"You're one to talk. I know you ain't in here because you like the food."

I know she didn't mean anything by the statement, but it still struck a nerve. Self-consciously, I tugged at the bottom of my miniskirt. I wondered who else thought I was there as a part of the entertainment. "Oh, I'm not dancing, hon, just playing hostess for the night," I informed her.

"Sorry, I didn't mean to imply—"

"It's okay," I cut her off. "If the shoe was on the other foot, I could've easily made the same mistake."

"Damn, shorty, you should think about it because you're fine as hell," the girl who had come in with Princess said. We hadn't even been introduced, and I already didn't like her.

"Tashee, why don't you have some fucking class—every bitch you meet ain't as hot in the ass as you!" Princess barked at her.

"My fault, Princess, I didn't know you were claiming her."

I looked from Princess back to her rude-ass friend. "Nobody is claiming anybody. Not only am I strictly dickly, but I'm also happily married." I wiggled my left ring finger so they could get a good look at the rock.

"Wow, congratulations, Gina. When did you jump the broom?" Princess grabbed my hand and examined my ring.

Without being rude about it, I took my hand back. "Feels like a lifetime ago. My husband is actually the owner of this place."

"I hear that, G." Princess gave me a high five. "So you must be living ghetto fabulous off this place?"

I looked around modestly. "Not really. This place is new, but Jackie's real job is as a literary agent."

"A what?" the girl named Tashee asked.

I hated holding conversations with people whom you had to translate for. "A literary agent. He matches authors and their works with publishing houses and handles their affairs."

"Aw shit, a paper pimp." Tashee grinned.

Clearly tired of her friend embarrassing her, Princess interjected. "Well, he sounds like a wonderful guy, and I can't wait to meet him tonight, but right now we gotta get ready to do our thing." She tugged at Tashee's sleeve.

I hugged the little girl I used to know and took in her scent. She smelled like weed and alcohol, but the sweetness lingered beneath. "It was so good to see you, Princess. Maybe later on we can get some drinks and I can introduce you to Jackie. He's not here right now, but I'm sure he'll be in soon."

"Sooner than you think," I heard Randy mumble behind me. I was about to ask him what he'd said, when I heard a commotion at the front door. Big José was parting the crowd, with three or four girls behind him. Bringing up the rear was my husband Jackie, with some chick I didn't know and that bitch Kim hanging from his arms.

NINE

Princess

From the tension that hung in the air and the look on Gina's face, I knew something was out of order. Security was ushering in a dark-skinned cat dressed in a three-piece suit. Two small boulders dangled from his ears, reflecting rainbows on the sides of his face whenever he moved his head. At first I thought he was just some cat coming to trick a few dollars and get his stunt on like the rest, but from the embarrassed look on Gina's face, it had to be her husband.

Jackie ambled into the spot with an expression that said he knew he was the shit. The two dolled-up broads on his arm had the nerve to throw their noses in the air and look at Gina sideways. I gave her the eye to let her know that I was with her if she wanted to beat their asses and his, but she wouldn't meet my gaze. I knew then that she was, as I had been, a prisoner of her own heart. I watched the girl who had been so very much like family to me try and raise her head and keep some shred of her dignity, but it was a hard fight.

"Hey, baby," she greeted that piece of shit. She went to kiss him on the lips, but he gave her his cheek. It took everything I had to keep from dipping in my bag and coming across that man's face. Tashee must've been feeling it, too, because I saw her Gemstar glistening between her teeth. Reluctantly I gave her the signal, and the razor disappeared back into her mouth.

"What's up, girl?" Jackie ran his hands down her sides and slapped her on the ass in front of everybody. Her face turned beet-red, but she took it like a champ. "You look good than a muthafucka tonight."

"Thanks, baby." She mustered a smile, but I wasn't fooled. Jackie was a snake, and he smelled of it.

"What's up, Jackie?" Randy spoke up. From the look in his eyes, I could tell he didn't care for Mr. Jackie either.

"How are we supposed to sell liquor if there ain't nobody manning the bar to serve the customers?" was Jackie's reply.

"Sasha will be okay for a few minutes while I talk to my sister," Randy said.

"More like gossiping," Jackie said. "I don't pay Sasha to run the bar—that's your job."

"It's okay, Jackie. He just came over to talk to me for a few," Gina interjected. When I saw the way he looked at her, I knew he was about to clown, so I tried to bow out before the bullshit popped.

"Gina, I'm about to get outta here. Are you good?" I asked her. Without even looking in his direction, I could feel Jackie's eyes undressing me.

"Yeah, thanks, Princess." Gina hugged me. When she held me, she held me close. Not like the embrace of a lover, but that of someone who really needed a hug. If you asked me, I couldn't tell you if it was more for my benefit or hers.

"And who is this?" Jackie asked. He didn't even have the common decency to hide the lust in his eyes as he looked me up and down like his wife wasn't even standing there. Slim wasn't the most loyal nigga, but even his balls weren't that big.

"Jackie, this is an old friend of mine. Princess, this is my husband, Jackie." Gina made the introductions like the good little wife, while his mistresses eyed me with contempt. I returned their glares with equal venom, because unlike Gina, I was well skilled in disorderly conduct.

"Princess—" The way he said my name made my skin crawl, but I kept it easy for the sake of my friend. "—what's good with you, ma?"

"Not a damn thing," I said very seriously. "Gina"—I gave Jackie my back, which probably only made it worse—"after I get dressed, I'll come back over and give you my number. Randy—" I gave him another hug, more out of assurance that he had an ally than from necessity. "—I'll see you in a few because I can already tell I'm gonna need a stiff drink."

"We've got the stiffest in town." Jackie tried to get fly.

I peeped Tashee about to say something crazy, so I cut it short. "It was nice meeting you, Jackie," I said, leading Tashee by the hand into the club. As an afterthought, I looked back at the girls Jackie had come in with, who were still staring at us, and capped, "Bum-ass bitches."

By the time I'd donned my heels and thong, the place had started to fill up. The part-time hustlers had pretty much ran through their paper, making way for the cats that were a little more 'bout it, but there still wasn't a Willy in sight except for Jackie, and he was off-limits. I did a lot of foul shit in my day, but Gina was like family.

I watched my long-lost homegirl for a good part of the night while she put up the farce of the happy housewife/business partner. She greeted the guests with smiles and settled disputes between the girls before they could escalate. For all outward appearances, she seemed focused, but I knew that inside, her heart was crumbling. I could never grasp why men never cherished the good women in their lives, but Jackie was twice as stupid as the rest of them. From what I remembered of Gina, she was smart, motivated, and about getting ahead in life, not to mention that she was a cutie. Gina had always been more developed than most of the girls in our neighborhood, but adulthood had done her some serious justice. She was fly in her skirt and suit jacket, showing enough skin to make the mind wonder without looking trashy. When she walked across the room, all the guys and some of the girls admired the way the mini hugged her perfectly curved hips. I could only imagine how sweet she tasted.

When I looked down and noticed my finger absently running along the edge of my thong, I knew I was tripping. Ever since I was a little girl I had thought Gina was beautiful. I had never been with a woman back then, but every now and again, I had a stray thought about what it would be like. I shook my head, embarrassed at where my mind was trying to go with it. Gina was someone who had been like a sister to me growing up, and here I was fantasizing about getting it on with her. The DJ gave me the signal from the booth, telling me it was time to go on. He cranked T-Pain's "I'm N Luv (Wit a Stripper)," and I took the stage. Before going into my routine, I took one last look at Gina and was surprised to find her staring back at me.

TEN

Gina

I was so embarrassed that I wanted to crawl under a rock and die. It was bad enough that Jackie didn't think enough to ask if I wanted to ride in the limo with him, but he shows up with Kim on his arm like she was the wife and I was the side bitch. I could tell from the look that Princess was giving me that she wanted to whip some ass, and by rights, we should've got it popping, but instead I acted like everything was good when me and everyone else knew that it wasn't. Just another sad example of how low I'd fallen.

I saw Princess watching me, but I pretended not to. I don't know if it was from the embarrassment of what had gone down with Jackie, or the thoughts running through my head. Back in the day, Princess had been a beanpole with a slick mouth, but that was a long time ago. Dressed in her stripper outfit, I could truly appreciate what she'd grown into. She stalked through the room, swinging her heart-shaped ass, making sure all eyes were on her. I couldn't believe the way dudes were fawning over her, even though she was shutting any and everybody down who didn't have a minimum of a hundred dollars in their hands. She exuded so much confidence that I felt it all the way on the other side of the room and wished I could borrow just a fraction of that.

Get a grip, Gina, I told myself, trying to slow my speeding heart rate. I was so ashamed that I felt all the color flush into my face. This was my best friend's little sister, and I was eyeing her like a piece of prime rib.

"Stranger things have happened." Randy startled me out of my daydream.

"What?"

"You know what." He placed his hands on his slim hips. "I see the way your ass is over here gawking at all that fish."

"Ain't nobody gawking at nothing, Randy. Cut that out." I know he saw through the lie, but I couldn't even draw a picture in my mind of what Randy was implying. It was too unnatural, wasn't it?

"You know they say that once you cross that line . . ."

"Randy, your ass is bugging out—you know how much I love dick!"

"Gina, I love dick, too, but that doesn't mean that I don't do a little pussy on the side when I'm feeling adventurous. It's called being bisexual."

"Randy, I'm not into girls," I told him, forcing the certainty into my voice that my heart couldn't find.

Randy raised his eyebrow, and before he said it, I knew where he was going with it. "What about freshman year?"

"Randy, that was a kiss, and it was only one time." I rubbed my sweaty palms against my skirt.

"And senior year with Rachel, after the frat party?"

Ouch.

"Randy . . . we were both roaring drunk. I don't even remember what happened between us."

"Oh, you remember, even if you wanna convince yourself that you don't." Randy folded his arms. "Gina, you wouldn't be the first victim."

"Victim of what?"

"Curiosity," he told me. "I know plenty of girls who've had rotten luck with men, so they got curious about the other side. Some of them decide to stay for a spell, and some go back to their straight lives and try to act like it's never happened."

"I'm not curious," I told him, but couldn't look him in the eyes when I said it.

"I think you are," he disputed. His eyes wandered to Princess, who was onstage giving one hell of a show. "I can't say that I blame you, though—Princess is a bad bitch."

"Cut it out, Randy."

"I'm serious. If you don't wanna fuck her, I just might." He was smiling, but I believed him.

"Randy, get yo ass back to the bar before Jackie comes over here tripping," I shooed him.

"Whatever, Gina—ain't no telling who or what that snake-ass nigga is doing right about now. I don't see him over here with you handling business."

"Watch it, Randy," I warned him.

"They say that a little truth is good for the soul." Randy snapped his finger twice. "You better get on your job, Gina, before you find yourself on the unemployment line." Randy switched back over to the bar. He took a minute to say something slick to a guy who was sitting at the bar before fixing two drinks and taking the stool beside him. My brother was off the hook.

He'd hit a sore spot when he brought up Jackie. I had just about worked myself so hard that I forgot about how he shitted on me when he came in. I could've slapped the shit out of that skinny bitch Kim for trying to style on me in my own club, but I had to be the bigger woman. This was Jackie's big night, and I didn't want to ruin it, but Ms. Plastic Titties and I were definitely gonna have some words, and deep down in my heart, I hoped that she broke fly so I could let out some of this stress on her ass. Jackie might not have respected me, but his bitches damn sure would.

I don't know if I was madder at him or me over this craziness. Every fiber of my being told me Jackie was bad news and that I needed to get away from him, but still I stayed. Why? Shit, I'm still trying to figure it out myself. I loved Jackie, but it wasn't that deep passionate love that I used to have for him.

When the fire for me in his heart died, I tried to make mine burn hot enough for both of us, but in the end, it was proving to be too much.

One of the girls came over and handed me a purple drink. I looked over toward the bar, and Randy raised his glass in salute before he and the man he'd been talking to slipped discreetly out the fire door that led to the alley on the side of the club. Looking at the man, you'd have never guessed he was a switch-hitter, but I guessed there was a little queen inside everybody. Pushing aside thoughts of Jackie and my crumbling marriage, I sipped my drink and watched Princess do her thing.

ELEVEN

Princess

I danced for three songs and halfway into a fourth when they finally pulled me off the stage. I had those tricks giving it up when I hit the scene, on my Brooklyn bullshit. The way these Harlem niggaz loved to trick bread, I couldn't see why all these bitches weren't pushing fly whips.

I took a second to stop by the bar to see Randy, but the girl told me he was on break. I ordered a Grey Goose and cranberry before scribbling my number on a napkin and asking the girl to give it to Randy when he came back. After sipping half my drink, I made my rounds, giving out lap dances and chatting with some of the guys who were spending. I ended up collecting another five hundred dollars from them before I went to the back to freshen up so I could hit them again. On my way, I caught Tashee giving the Puerto Rican bouncer a blow job in the hallway. From the way she was slurping and lapping at his rod, I hoped her jaws wouldn't be too tired for the contest. Ignoring them, I went into the dressing room and was rewarded by a far more alarming sight.

The skinny girl with the plastic titties was laying on her back on top of one of the vanity tables. Between her legs, drilling for oil, was Jackie. He hit her with quick, deep strokes while calling her everything but a child of God in his lust-driven frenzy. "Yeah, you like that, right bitch." He dug deeper while she hollered. He flipped her over and took a minute to lick her from her pussy to her ass crack before entering her from behind.

I couldn't help but be a little turned on by the way he was attacking her. Jackie's cock made a squishing sound every time it dipped in and out of her, and I could see juices dripping down the back of Kim's legs. The way she was coming, he had to be tearing the pussy up. Without even realizing that I was doing it, I slipped my hand into my thong and began playing with my clit. It started off with one finger, but before I knew it, two more had joined the party. My hand was getting soaked as I jacked myself off in time with Jackie stroking Kim. I was so caught up in my own rapture that I hadn't even realized they'd finished until I heard Jackie's mocking voice.

"Damn, you didn't have to do all that. We had room for one more." He smiled devilishly. His thick cock was dangling out of his zipper, bobbing up and down when he moved. It looked like an onyx carving, slick with Kim's cum.

I was embarrassed, but way too cool to show it in front of them. I took my hand out of my pants and examined it under the light. There was a ring of white foam around my knuckles, and my fingers were slick with my juices. I looked directly at Jackie and Kim before licking my fingers one at a time. "Nah, I did just fine on my own."

Ignoring the lustful look Jackie was giving me, and the worried one coming from Kim, I walked to the other side of the room and proceeded to towel-dry my body and wipe my pussy and under my arms with a sanitary napkin. I was applying a fresh coat of deodorant when Jackie sauntered over.

"So what's up?" he asked.

"I told you earlier, not a damn thing."

Jackie hesitated for a minute, and I knew he was looking for another angle. "So, how long you and Gina known each other? I thought I'd met all of her friends."

"We've known each other since I was a shorty." I gave him my back while I checked my makeup in my compact. Just over my shoulder, I saw Jackie's predatory eyes traveling the length of my body. I tried to ignore him, but I couldn't stop my skin from crawling.

"I hear that. So—"

"Look, I'm trying to get back out there and get my paper on, so why don't you stop bullshitting me and get to the point." I looked at him seriously.

"A'ight, bet. Dig this: I'm the owner of this joint, so I set the tempo. It can be a real sweet ride or a sour one, depending on how you play it," he said frankly.

I cut my eyes at him. "Jackie, first of all, this ain't the only club in town, so don't come over here talking that brolic shit like I'm supposed to be moved by it. Second of all, Gina is my homegirl, but I ain't into breaking up nobody's home, especially if ain't no bread coming my way in the situation. I'm in here trying to get my paper up, and I don't need no problems."

Jackie smiled. "So we understand each other." Jackie reached into his pocket and pulled out a wad of bills. He peeled off ten crisp hundreds and dropped them on the bench next to me. "I trust you didn't see anything?"

"All I see is green, daddy-o," I assured him, stuffing the money into my bag.

"That's what's up, ma. You know if you ever decided that you wanted to—"

"Jackie, you're really pushing it right now."

"Okay, okay." He threw his hands up in surrender. "Come see me later on, and I'll buy you a bottle."

I watched Jackie strut out of there with his whore on his heels and found that I was sick to my stomach. I'm not justifying what Jackie did, but men have been cheating since the beginning of time and would continue to do so until the lights went out. Still, I couldn't stand a tactless muthafucka. Not only was he fucking one of his employees at the workplace, with his wife in the next room, but that bastard had the nerve to be doing her raw. I hoped that Gina was smart enough to protect herself, because that nigga was an STD waiting to happen.

When I came out of the back, the dick-sucking contest was already under way. Tashee, along with five other girls, were lined up on their knees with six guys lining the wall. The dude Tashee had been paired with was hung like a tree trunk, but Tashee stuffed that cock in her mouth like it was the Last Supper, and the spectators went wild. Even I had to clap at the way my girl was handling her business. I was so caught up in the show that I didn't even feel him walk up on me until he grabbed me roughly by the arm and spun me around.

"Remember me, bitch?" Slim snarled. Seeing him standing in front of me, I wished those D-boys would've broken his legs instead of his hand.

All I could say was, "Damn," before the shit hit the fan.

TWELVE

Gina

It was the third time in the last week. The third time Jackie had let the sun catch his black ass outside this door. The night of the grand opening, we had gotten into a big blowout over what happened to Princess that ended up getting physical. Jackie slapped me, and I slapped his ass right back. When he looked like he was about to take it to the next level, I grabbed the water I'd been boiling for my tea and promised him on my mother's grave that I would douse his ass if he laid hands on me again. He stormed out of the house and had been coming and going sporadically ever since.

Aretha was playing softly in my CD player, and when "Tracks of My Tears" came on, I had to raise my fist in salute. On the outside I wore a smile, but if you looked close enough at my soul, you could tell it was out of place. Every time Jackie shitted on me in public, I plastered the phony smile on, but inside I was crying like a baby. It seemed like every little thing was an excuse to distance himself from me, and the incident with Princess might've been the final straw.

Princess and her boyfriend had gotten into a big fistfight, and the club had to be shut down early, and of course, it was my fault. I didn't invite her to the club, but because we were friends, Jackie tossed the blame on me. I guess any excuse was good enough if it could get him out of his own bed and into that of one of his whores. I didn't really give a shit that he had an attitude; Princess was like family.

I didn't see the blow that started the fight, but by the time José and me got there, the guy was beating Princess like a man. She got in several good licks of her own, but she was no match for him. Just before he could stomp her out, José had snatched him off his feet and started kicking his ass. Big José and his crew took that boy out to the alley with every intention of making him disappear, but Princess begged for his life. I felt so bad that I became hysterical over my friend, and when she crawled on her hands and knees and begged José not to finish him, the knife in my heart was twisted even deeper. Though I tried to tell myself I took it so hard because of how he had beaten Princess, it was really because I saw myself in her.

Randy and I had both been calling her for days to make sure she was okay, but we kept getting the voice mail, or her boyfriend would answer and say that she couldn't come to the phone. I thought about calling the police, but I didn't have any contact information for Princess other than her cell phone number. I felt like I was beating a dead horse when I tried her cell again, but to my surprise she picked up this time.

THIRTEEN

Princess

For the past few days, I've been a prisoner to my heart, my body, and my apartment. Slim's was the last face I'd expected to see at Paradise, but I should've known my karma would come back around. I fought the good fight, but ended up getting my ass kicked. When the big Puerto Rican kid had grabbed Slim, I thought God had sent me an angel. I was okay with Slim getting his ass beat, but when the Puerto Rican cat was going to shoot him, I broke down. I must've looked like a damn fool, crawling on my hands and knees, begging for the life of someone who had been trying to kill me a few minutes prior, but when you're in love, other people's opinions go out the window, even if you *are* making a damn fool of yourself.

I pulled myself out of bed, ignoring the aches and pains that plagued my body. Thankfully, Slim wasn't home, so I'd be able to have a little time for myself. I opened the refrigerator, and of course, there wasn't anything in it but some old Chinese food and a half-empty bottle of red Alizé. Slim drank so much of that shit that it was a wonder his piss didn't come out red, because his shit sure as hell did. I left the Chinese food and curled up on the couch with the Alizé.

Truth be told, I sometimes wished Slim dead. I envisioned me taking one of those damn red Alizé bottles and caving his pointy-ass skull in, and a time or two, I'd come close to doing it, but my heart always stayed my hand. I've been running the streets since I was a shorty and have come across some real boss niggaz. They showered me with paper and promises, but when they'd outlived their usefulness, I cut them off without batting an eye. They were little more than a means to an end, but Slim fucked the game up for me. I let him into my heart, and in return he stomped and pissed on it every chance he got. I'd seen this movie a thousand times with my friends, but still managed to nominate myself for the part of Best Supporting Actress. For as long as my heart continued to trump my common sense, I would be a prisoner. I totally understood why the caged bird sang.

I heard the muffled ring of my phone, but had no idea where it was because Slim hid it from me before he left. He called his self putting me on punishment, but his dumb ass didn't think to turn it off before he hid it. I found it under the cushion just before my voice mail kicked in.

"Hello?"

"Princess?" a familiar voice asked.

"Oh, hi, Gina," I said sheepishly. After what I'd caused at her husband's club, I had been too embarrassed to speak to her.

"Girl, me and Randy have been trying to reach you all week. We were worried sick." She was genuinely concerned. It was nice to have someone give a shit about me, because my man sure didn't. "We thought that maybe . . ."

"Nah, he hasn't killed me . . . yet." I tried to laugh it off, but it was no joke.

"Baby, how long has this been going on?"

I sighed. "Too long, Gina, too long."

"Princess, I had no idea that you were involved with an abusive man. Did you tell Audrey, or your mother?"

"No, they don't know, and I'd appreciate it if you didn't say anything. I don't want to worry them," I told her, but it was more like I didn't want them to call my uncle Bo. He was an old-school gangsta that was still putting in work at the age of fifty-five. There was no doubt that if word of this got back to him, there'd be no amount of begging that could save Slim.

"Okay, I'm not gonna tell them what's going on, but something has got to be done," she said.

"I know, Gina, but my head is so screwed up right now. I just need a minute to think."

"Listen, why don't you come meet me for drinks and we can talk about it," she offered.

I would've loved to go out, but Slim didn't leave me any money. "I ain't really got—"

"I didn't ask you what you had, Princess. This is on me. Give me your address and get yourself dressed, and I'll come and get you."

"No," I blurted out. "I mean, I wanna come, but we can't meet here. I don't know when Slim is coming back, and I don't want him to catch me creeping out of here."

"Okay, then this is what we'll do. Throw on some sweats and hop in a cab to Macy's on Thirty-fourth Street. I'll be there in fifteen minutes to pay for it. After that, we can do some shopping and stuff our faces while we talk about the sorry-ass men in our lives."

"Gina, you don't have to—"

"Princess, I know that all I have to do in life is stay black and die; I *want* to do this for you. Just come on, girl."

I took a few minutes to think about it. I wasn't doing anything but sitting in the house and licking my wounds, so why not go out. Slim would probably flip and give me another beating, but who the hell cared? "Okay, Gina, I'll see you in a few." Five minutes after I ended the call, I had on a pair of faded jeans and a tank top and was out the door to make it to my rendezvous.

FOURTEEN

Gina

When Princess stepped out of the taxi, my heart sank. Her lip was swollen, and I could see the bruising around her eye, even behind the dime-store sunglasses. She opened her mouth to speak, but I silenced her with a hug. I knew she needed it because she immediately began sobbing into my chest. While we enjoyed each other's embrace, I whispered to her that it was going to be all right.

After our moment on the corner, I took her inside Macy's and proceeded to spend up Jackie's money. I brought Princess a pretty violet sundress and some sandals to change into and a few outfits just to take with her. For myself, I bought the most high-end pieces I could find and bought three bed-in-a-bags for one hundred dollars apiece. When I got outside, I gave two of them away to homeless people who were sleeping on the streets and kept one for myself for the bed in the guest room, where I planned to spend the next few nights. After leaving Macy's, we decided to get a room at the Hotel New York and burn up one of Jackie's credit cards on room service.

The room was small, but it didn't matter. We came there to drink and think, not sleep. I ordered a bottle of Alizé Red Passion and Rémy Martin from the bar downstairs and two dinner platters. Princess declined the Alizé, saying it reminded her too much of Slim. I could totally understand that, because Jackie was the reason I couldn't stand cherry smoothies. Princess cracked the bottle of Rémy and attacked it with vigor. She had already taken three shots when I was still on my first. My girl had a lot on her mind.

We sat and did shots of Rémy while I listened to Princess bring me up to speed on her situation. She told me about how she'd robbed Slim, which is what led to her getting beat up in the club. She tried to blame herself for the whole thing, but I wasn't having that.

"Princess, this ain't none of your fault." I patted her on the back of her hand. "I don't care what goes on between y'all—Slim has no right to put his hands on you." I felt like a hypocrite as the words left my mouth.

"Gina, I don't know how I've gotten to this point," Princess told me with her head in her hands. "It used to be so good between us, but lately it's been like World War fucking Three. I know that there's a good man somewhere inside him, but I just can't seem to bring it out."

I tossed back my shot and looked at her. "Baby, the devil is a liar and can't no good ever come out of his mouth. The Slim who wooed you is the mask, but the nigga you bumped into at the club the other night is his *real* face."

"I'm starting to see that, but my heart tells me that there's still hope for him . . . hope for us."

"I know, Princess, but sometimes you gotta look at the writing on the wall. It started with a slap and escalated to a punch, the next thing you know you'll be collecting frequent-flyer miles at the local emergency rooms and learning how to do tricks with makeup to hide your shame and his madness."

Princess looked up at me quizzically. "Gina, I hear what you're saying, but it isn't as cut-and-dry as you make it sound. I know it might sound foolish, but I love him. You just don't understand."

Tears were in my eyes when I looked into hers. "Baby, I understand better than you think." I dug in my pocket for a wipe and rubbed the makeup off the side of my face so that she could see the slightly healed bruise. "If you're a fool, then I must be the village idiot, because I was dumb enough to marry my tormentor."

"I had no idea," Princess whispered, with her eyes still glued to my cheek. She reached out and brushed my cheek tenderly. It stung a bit, but I didn't pull away. Her probing fingers were soft, kind of like someone running a feather along the side of my face. I momentarily closed my eyes to compose myself, and when I opened them, Princess was staring at me sadly. At that moment, something passed between us. I'm still not sure what it was, but it was powerful.

"Most people don't." I reluctantly pulled away. "On the outside, it's all good, but there are fires raging in my home, too. Sister girl, let me give you a little bit of my truth." I don't know if it was the alcohol or the sense of familiarity I had with Princess, but I opened up to her in a way that I hadn't even done with Randy. I told her Jackie's and my story from start to finish, not leaving out one detail. By then we'd gotten halfway through the bottles; we were both drunk and crying on each other's shoulders.

"Gina, what happened to us?" Princess slurred. "I mean, my mother raised me and Audrey better than that, and I know your mom didn't play when it came to y'all, so how did we get to this point?"

"Because we're stupid," I said, barely understanding my own drunken drawl. "We spend our whole lives building ourselves up, just to let these sorry-ass Negroes tear us down. Ain't none of them worth the sperm it took to make them. Sometimes I wish Jackie's ass would drop dead, so I can collect the insurance and keep going with my life."

"I'll drink to that." Princess threw back her shot. "These Ike Turner–ass niggaz are like sick-ass diseases that need to be vaccinated."

"Preach, girl!" I tossed back my shot, spilling some of the liquor down my chin and onto my shirt. "I say to hell with all of them." I reached for my glass of water and ended up knocking it over. We were both feeling nice, but Princess's next statement would sober me right up.

"You know what I think," she leaned in to whisper, "I think that they all deserve to die for what they're doing to the black woman. Let's do it, Gina."

"Do what?" I asked, knowing damn well I didn't want to know the answer.

"We should kill them." She rocked on the bed. "Me and you should knock off Jackie and Slim."

I sat bolt upright in my chair and gave Princess my most serious stare. "Princess, you're tripping. I mean, I might talk a lot of shit, but I can't kill Jackie. For as much of an ass as he is, he's still my husband and a sick part of me still loves him."

"I'd do it," she blurted out.

"What?"

"I'd kill Jackie for you, ma."

"Princess, I think you've had enough."

"Yeah, I've had enough, all right, enough of these no-good dogs walking all over us. Fuck Slim and fuck Jackie with his nasty-dick ass. You might wanna go get checked out when you get a chance, too."

"What do you mean by that?" I asked. Princess told me what had happened the other night with Jackie and Kim. In my heart, I'd always known that he was fucking her, but to hear it actually being confirmed was like a slap in the face. The thought of him doing someone else was enough to make me gag, but knowing that he'd put my life at risk sent me to the bathroom to throw up. By the time I came out, Princess was sipping a glass of water and looking slightly more sober than she had been.

"I'm sorry I waited so long to tell you, Gina." Princess told me.

"It's okay, better late than never," I was a little uptight with Princess for not bringing it to me immediately, but she wasn't the one at fault; I was. It was my choice to stay with Jackie, and because of his infidelities, that choice might've cost me my life. I tried to hold it together, but ended up breaking down. "I can't fucking believe him!" I threw my glass into the wall and bawled.

"It's okay, Gina. We're strong and we'll make it through this." Princess stroked my back. Her touch was soothing to me. As she hugged me, a strand of her hair fell in my face and I breathed in the sweet scent of coconut. She began running her fingers along the back of my neck, causing me to shiver.

"I'm sorry," she said, scooting back a little but still stroking my back.

"It's okay," I said, trying to hide the shakiness in my voice. I looked up at Princess and the drunken glare in her eyes was gone, replaced by one of naked hunger. I knew what she wanted, and as embarrassed as I was about it, a part of me wanted it, too. I turned to Princess and positioned myself so that our knees were touching on the bed. Timidly, I ran my hands through her thick hair, massaging her scalp. She rolled her head back, exposing her smooth brown throat. I don't know what prompted it, but I reached over and kissed her softly on the neck. Everything after that was a blur.

FIFTEEN

Princess

When her lips touched my throat, a jolt shot through my body. I wanted it, but didn't expect it. I looked into her eyes and saw that she was afraid, so I ran my hands along the sides of her face softly. "Gina, we don't have to do this if you don't want to."

Gina's brow furrowed, and for a minute I thought that I'd probably chased away the only real friend I had in the world. To my surprise, Gina leaned and planted her rose-colored lips over mine. "I want to."

"So do I, probably more than I can even explain," I said, meaning every word of it. Moving to a kneeling position, I kissed Gina back. I could taste the alcohol on her breath as we shared a deep, passionate kiss. The reluctance in her body began to fall away with each article of clothing I removed from her. When I had stripped her down to just her panties, I laid her on the bed and admired her body. Gina was just short of a goddess. The skin on her almost perfectly proportioned body was smooth and blemish free, save for the bruise on her side. I leaned in and kissed the bruise tenderly.

"It feels good," Gina whispered.

"It'll feel better in a minute," I said devilishly. From her side I moved to her healthy breasts, planting soft kisses on each caramel nipple. Gina moaned softly as my lips left a trail down her stomach, stopping just above the line of her neatly trimmed pubic hairs. When my tongue entered Gina, she was already wet, but as I explored her sex, the moisture increased. When she came in my mouth, it tasted like honey. I slid back up the length of her body, letting my tongue and my wet pussy brush against her in various spots. When our lips met, she sucked my tongue so that she could taste herself.

"Let me do you," she breathed into my ear.

I gladly squatted over her face while she spread my ass cheeks so that she could taste every inch of me. She was a little rough with it at first, but with practice she got better. Gina licked me from my clit to my ass and back again, digging her nails into my ass cheeks. I shivered when I felt myself starting to come, and this only made her dig deeper. I looked down to see my juices saturating her face, but this didn't slow her down. Gina kept lapping out my pussy until I jumped off her and we got into a sixty-nine. I don't know how many times we came, but it had to be a lot because when it was over, all we could do was lay on the bed, smoking a joint, and looking up at the ceiling.

SIXTEEN

Gina

I couldn't believe I'd done it. I knew that the feelings I was having when I'd seen Princess naked at the club weren't natural, but I never thought I'd act on them. We lay next to each other, smoking a joint I'd stolen from Jackie's stash, both lost in our own thoughts. I could've lay there in that blissful silence forever, but Princess had something she needed to get off her chest.

"You know I was serious, right?" she asked.

"About wanting me? Yeah, I know."

"That and the other thing," she said. I propped myself on my elbows and looked at her. She was as serious as a heart attack.

"I could knock Jackie off for you, and you could kill Slim—this way, there'll be no feelings getting in the way for either of us."

I mulled it over. How would I feel if Jackie were dead? It's no secret that I'd have been happier with him out of my life, but murder? "Princess, I don't know if I'm ready to kill someone."

"Gina, you know just as well as I do that Jackie would no sooner let you leave than Slim would me. They act like they don't want us, but they don't want anybody else to have us," she reasoned. "What are we gonna do, wait around for them to accidentally kill us? Gina, I'm too young and too pretty to die early, especially at the hands of some nigga."

Princess was starting to make a lot of sense, but I still wasn't ready to entertain it. "Murder is a serious thing, Princess. It ain't like robbing somebody. You can give money back, but there's no restitution for a life."

Princess flipped over on her stomach and looked me in the eyes. "Gina, Jackie didn't give a fuck about your life or his own when he ran up Kim and God only know whoever else without a condom, so why should you give a fuck about his?" She was starting to make more and more sense. "I ain't no killer either, but it doesn't seem like we have a choice. Even if nothing comes of what happened between us today, we deserve a chance at being happy."

I sat up on the edge of the bed and looked out the window. "Princess, let's just say for the sake of argument I agreed to go along with it. How would we do it?"

Princess was silent for a few minutes. "I hadn't figured that out just yet. We could shoot the muthafuckas, but guns raise the risk of getting caught." She slid out of the bed and began pacing. "Shit, if I could slip some rat poison into that damn red Alizé he's so in love with—"

"What did you just say?" My head whipped toward her.

"I said I wished I could slip some rat poison in his drink, but he would taste it if I put enough in it to kill him."

"What if it was something else?" I asked, with a wicked plan forming in my head.

"Gina, what the hell are you up to?" she asked suspiciously.

"Nothing much, but I think I have a way to solve our problems and get away with it."

"Well, don't keep an asshole in suspense." She flopped on the bed beside me.

"Princess, how much do you know about plants?"

SEVENTEEN

Princess

"I can't say that I was surprised when you called," Jackie said smugly as he strutted around his gigantic living room. My girl Gina was living like the Fresh Princess of Bel-Air. If she wasn't my homegirl, I might've dug off into Jackie's pockets.

"Is that right?" I asked, crossing my legs. The skirt I was wearing was so short that if you really paid attention, you could see I wasn't wearing any panties.

"Yeah, when a bitch sees all this meat swinging—" He grabbed his crotch. "—she can't help but be curious. So—" He stroked his dick through his silk pajama pants. "—are you ready to satisfy that curiosity?"

"Yeah, big daddy, but first things first." I held my hand out.

"See, that's what I like about you—you're straight about your business." He dug into his pocket and pulled out an envelope, which he tossed on my lap. "You wanna count it?"

"Nah, I know a balling-ass nigga like you wouldn't short a bitch." I stuffed the envelope in my purse. "Second thing, are you sure Gina ain't gonna come home? I'd feel real fucked up if she came in here and caught us."

"Please, she went to Staten Island to see her brother, Randy. By the time they get finished shopping and having girl talk, it'll be the wee hours of the night. We've got plenty of time," he said, sliding out of his robe.

I wanted to gag at how pompous he had the nerve to be with his shit, but I had to keep up the act. In a little while, that smug-ass grin was going to get wiped right off his face. "Now that we got that out of the way—" I wiggled out of my skirt and displayed my freshly shaved kitten to him. "—let's get down to business."

Jackie wasted no time in jumping headfirst between my legs. He was nipping, slurping, and humming into my clit while stroking himself. I had to clamp my teeth down to keep from being sick. It wasn't that it didn't feel good—old Jackie ate pussy like a champ—but I couldn't get past the idea that I was about to fuck my friend's husband, even if she did cosign it.

Jackie came up for air long enough to try and shove himself inside me. I pushed him off and reached for one of the condoms I had in my purse. "No glove, no love, daddy."

"Come on, ma, I ain't got nothing," he tried to convince me, while still trying to enter me.

"Jackie, we either do it the right way or we ain't doing it," I told him. He wasn't happy about it, but Jackie put on the condom before sliding inside me. It felt like his cock was tapping my spleen as he pumped away with no finesse at all. I could only imagine how Gina felt going through this on the regular if he was as rough with her. Jackie flipped me over and did me doggystyle. Every time his dick went in, I tightened my pussy muscles around it, driving him crazy. Just as I had planned, Jackie came in under ten minutes.

"Damn, that was the best shot of pussy I ever had." He rolled onto the floor, breathing like he had just run a marathon.

"So I've been told," I smirked, taking the condom off him and stroking the rest of the nut out of him. "You ain't got no more for me, Daddy?" I pleaded while trying to stroke him back to an erection.

"Man, y'all young girls don't play. Give a nigga minute to catch his breath," he huffed.

"Tell you what, why don't I go in the kitchen and get us both something cold to drink, and then I'll see if I can get your big man to agree to another round." I kissed the shaft of his dick, making it jump.

"Yeah, that's what I'm talking about." He ran his hand over the back of my head. "Go in the freezer, and there's some cherry smoothie in a pitcher."

"How did you know that cherry smoothies were my favorite?" I gave him my phoniest smile.

"Word—mine, too. Why don't you go pour us a few glasses so we can get back to it?"

"Okay, I'll be right back." I stood up and walked to the kitchen, making sure I swung my ass the whole way. When I got in the kitchen, I rinsed my mouth in the sink. I found the pitcher of smoothie and sat it on the counter, along with two tall glasses. I peeked in the living room to make sure Jackie was still where I left him before pulling the balloon out of my bra. Gina never said how much to use, so I emptied the entire contents of the balloon into Jackie's glass. I watched the reddish-brown liquid settle into the bottom of the glass and wondered for the thousandth time if I was doing the right thing.

"Damn girl, what the fuck is taking you so long!" Jackie screamed from the living room, removing all doubt. I poured the smoothie into his glass and watched the liquid on the bottom blend in perfectly.

"I'll be right there, big daddy," I called back, stirring the fatal drink with my finger.

EIGHTEEN

Gina

I felt like such a fucking whore. I had had a one-night stand or three in the past, but this one made me feel especially dirty.

"Yo, on the real, that was some good pussy," Slim declared. He was lying on the bed beside me. On the nightstand were two glasses of Alizé Red Passion.

Princess had told me where to find him, and true to form, he showed up like clockwork at the liquor store. I was wearing some tight-ass shorts and a tank top with no bra, and of course he couldn't resist trying to lay his mack down. He was surprised that I had actually gone for the weak-ass lines he was kicking, but even more surprised that Red Alizé was my drink of choice, too. We stood in front of the liquor store talking for a few minutes before jumping in my car and heading to the hourly motel off of Fourteenth and Tenth.

Slim talked big shit the whole time, but when we got down to business, it was a different story. Granted, he was a pretty decent size, but he couldn't fuck. He tried to force his self inside me before I was even wet, and when he finally did get the pussy, he didn't know what to do with it. Slim pounded away like he was doing me, but all he was really doing was bruising my insides. I got no pleasure from sleeping with my friend's man, and was thrilled beyond words when he finally came, a half hour later.

"Good pussy for good dick." I snuggled against him and kissed his chest. His skin tasted like old bologna, but I acted like it was as sweet as candy. "Listen, why don't you go in the bathroom and wash your dick so I can show you how nasty I really get." I held my breath and let my tongue tickle the skin under his balls. "If you're nice, I might even swallow it."

Slim jumped up so fast that he almost killed his self when his legs got caught in the cheap sheets. Grinning like the ass he was, Slim ducked into the bathroom, giving me time to work my magic. I scrambled to the floor and retrieved my hoochie shorts. In the pocket, I had a prescription bottle filled with the sap from my wild cherries. As the liquid dissolved into his drink, I started to have second thoughts. True enough, I needed to be free, but it wasn't worth my immortal soul to gain it. I was about to pour the Alizé out when Slim came out of the bathroom.

He strutted around the bed, dick swinging, like he was the man of the hour. I looked on in horror as Slim snatched up the glass of Alizé and downed it. Wiping his mouth with the back of his hand, he looked down at me and said, "Now let's see about that freak shit you was talking."

"Lord forgive me," I whispered, before I knelt in front of Slim and started teasing the head of his dick with my tongue. It tasted like sweat and cheap soap, but I managed to get it in my mouth without throwing up. As I looked up at Slim's eyes rolling into the back of his head, I prayed that the poison would kick in before I had to make good on my promise to swallow.

NINETEEN

Princess

Jackie had finished off the entire pitcher of smoothie while I was still working on my first glass. Sitting there waiting for something to happen made me so nervous that I felt like I was going to shit myself. I wasn't sure how effective the wild cherry sap was, but I hoped it did what it was supposed to, because I'd hate to have fucked Jackie's repulsive ass for nothing. When he'd finished off the last of the smoothie, he started getting touchy again. He fondled my breasts while stroking himself back hard. God, not again.

"You 'bout ready to get this good dick, girl?" He slapped his penis against his leg.

"I was born ready," I lied. I slipped another condom on and straddled Jackie. I began grinding on him slowly, speeding up as I got wetter. Jackie was beneath me, pumping away, when his face suddenly went slack and I could feel his dick going limp inside me. It was finally kicking in. I leaned in and kissed him on both cheeks before whispering to him, "Gina's is the last ass you're ever gonna beat."

Jackie tried to push me off him, but I dropped my weight down on him, pinning him to the floor. He tried to take a swing at me, but the poison had him so weak that I was able to swat the blows away. The poison was killing him, but it wasn't working fast enough, so I started strangling him. I rode Jackie's cock like I was at the Kentucky Derby, while digging my fingers into his throat. When I looked down at his face, I didn't see Gina's husband, but the man who had been the cause of my misery, Slim. I didn't release Jackie's throat until vomit started spilling from his mouth and nose. It was a disgusting sight, but I was too caught up in my own rage. When I finally heard the death rattle escape him, I climbed off his dick and went to the bathroom to throw up.

After scrubbing every inch of my body, I came back and examined my handiwork. Jackie was lying in a pool of his own vomit, with his limp dick still inside the condom. Shit was pooling beneath his ass, leaving a foul odor in the air. I carefully removed the condom with a paper towel and ran a Dustbuster over his genitals to remove any hair traces I'd left. It was probably unnecessary, but I had seen it on an episode of *Forensic Files*, so I figured it couldn't hurt. After I got dressed, I sat in the far corner of the living room, trying not to look at Jackie's corpse while I waited for Gina to call and tell me she'd done her part.

TWENTY

Gina

I had been sucking on Slim's foul-smelling cock for about ten minutes when I felt his body stiffen. I ducked my head out of the way, thinking he was about to come and felt something drip onto my shoulder. I looked up and saw that there was vomit spilling over Slim's lower lip. I had read about the effects of wild cherries when they were ingested, but seeing it was something else.

Slim staggered backwards and bounced off the wall. "What . . . what?" He was trying to speak, but his throat was closing up on him.

I rolled to the other side of the bed and collected my clothes off the floor. "Princess sends her love, you bastard."

At the mention of her name, Slim's eyes went wide. "You bitches . . . you bitches set me up!" Slim tried to lunge for me, but it was uncoordinated, and he ended up falling over the bed. I ran around to the other side of the room to try and get to the door, but he managed to grab my arm and knock me off balance. I landed on the floor, on top of his pants, with something cold jabbing me in my back. I reached behind me and came up holding the small .22 that had been in his pocket.

"I'm gonna fucking kill you," he shambled toward me.

"Stay back," I warned him, trying to scoot against the wall. Even when I aimed the gun at him, he kept coming. At that moment, I saw my life flashing before my eyes and prayed for God to give me strength. From the look in Slim's eyes, I knew that he would kill me before the wild cherry sap killed him. Closing my eyes, I pulled the trigger.

I don't know how long I sat there on the floor, but my legs were starting to cramp. Slim sat on the floor, propped against the bed with vomit staining his chin and chest, while a faint stream of urine was coming from his dick. I had never seen a dead body other than in a funeral home, but even without the makeup and casket, I knew Slim was gone.

I fumbled with my phone and called Princess. When she picked up, I just started rambling. "Princess, it's me. Oh, God, oh God. I did it, Princess, he's dead. The poison wasn't working fast enough, so I took his gun and—"

"Gina, don't say another word over the phone." She had cut me off. "Listen to me very carefully: Get your shit and leave the motel room. Get to your house as fast as you can, but drive carefully so you don't get pulled over."

"But what about Slim's body?" I asked.

"Leave it there. It's an hourly motel, so they don't have any of your information. Turn the air conditioner on high and leave. By the time they find him, you'll be long gone."

"Princess, I—"

"I told you, not on the phone. Slim is good where he is, but we've gotta get rid of this mess you've got over here."

"Oh my God, is Jackie—"

"Gina, please stop asking me stupid-ass questions and get over here." She ended the call.

I jumped into my clothes, but was still afraid to leave the room. I kept having visions of the police swooping down on me as soon as I got in the hall. "Get it together, Gina." I slapped myself. There was a dead body at my feet and one in my house. What the hell had I gotten myself into?

I composed myself enough to get Randy on the line. I figured we'd need some help with getting rid of Jackie's body. I could trust my brother above all else. When he answered his phone, I could barely get the words out without having them sound like the ravings of a madwoman. The only thing he was able to understand was that there was an emergency at my house and I needed him to come over there. He tried to ask me what happened, but I ended the call. Gathering my courage, I slipped into the hall and tried my best not to break into a run as I left the motel.

When I got to my house, Princess was pacing in my living room, smoking a cigarette. Even over the smoke, I could smell death in the air. I didn't have to see what was under the sheet in the middle of my living room to know it was my husband, the man whom I had promised to love and honor, but ended up betraying.

"Are you okay?" Princess rushed over and hugged me.

"Hell no," I said, trembling. "We're murderers, Princess, *murderers*."

Princess held my face in her hands and kissed me. "No we're not, Gina, we're free. Now come help me wrap this body up so we can get him out of here."

Princess and I wrapped Jackie from his neck to his feet in an old carpet that I had in the attic, but he was too tall for his head to fit. Princess wanted to cut it off, but I wouldn't let her. We had already done enough. Instead, we wrapped it in a plastic bag and tied a pillow case over that. I was just cutting the string that we'd tied around the carpet when my front door flew open. My brother, Randy, stood in the doorway with a pistol in his hand.

"Gina, are you okay?" he asked, seeing me standing in the middle of the living room looking a hot mess. "When you called, I thought Jackie was kicking your ass again."

"Jackie won't be kicking anybody else's ass." Princess nodded to the parcel lying on the floor.

Randy's jaw dropped. "Tell me that isn't Jackie? Gina." He turned watery eyes to me. "Please tell me that y'all didn't kill Jackie."

"Randy, let me explain," I pleaded.

"Explain what, how you let this dumb bitch gas you up to go to prison?" Randy snapped. "Stupid, just fucking stupid."

"Well, I didn't see nobody else rushing to Gina's rescue." Princess glared at Randy. The tension in the air was so thick that I suddenly found it hard to breathe.

Randy paced the floor. "This is fucked up, real fucked up. I can't believe y'all killed him." His voice was trembling.

"*We* didn't do shit, *I* killed Jackie," Princess confessed. She sat on the couch and lit another cigarette. "You can call it what you want, Randy, but it was the only way Gina could've ever gotten away from Jackie. Look, I know y'all are scared, but it's gonna be okay. All we have to do is—" Before Princess could finish her sentence, her head exploded. I was so shocked that all I could do was stare at my brother as he placed the gun on the coffee table and knelt over Jackie's body.

"No, no, no," Randy sobbed, cradling Jackie's body. "You couldn't just leave him, could you? No, you had to kill him!"

"But Randy, I thought you of all people would've been happy that I was rid of Jackie."

Randy turned his red eyes toward me. "I wanted him out of your life, not dead, Gina!"

"But I don't understand."

"He was my lover," Randy spat, shocking me even further. "For the last three years, Jackie and I were having an affair."

"But Jackie hated you because you were gay."

"He didn't hate me because I was gay, Gina. He hated me because he knew that as long as he was married to my sister, we would never be more than a late-night booty call. You killed my lover, Gina!"

I felt like all the strength had been sapped from my body as I watched my brother mourn the loss of his lover, my husband. All these years, I would've never expected Jackie to be in the closet, not my Jackie. As I knelt there with my brother and the bodies of my two lovers, I realized that you never really knew someone until you knew them.

Twice in a Lifetime

ANGEL MITCHELL

For my grandmother Mellow Frankie Mitchell

Ten minutes, Marley thought as she lay staring at the ceiling with her arms folded tightly across her chest. She looked over at her latest conquest, who was snoring softly, and rolled her eyes toward the ceiling. "Come on," she whispered.

Marley stared at the small digital clock on the nightstand until the red numbers changed and displayed three thirty. Exactly thirty minutes after the sexual liaison ended. That was the exact amount of time that she needed to recuperate and not seem as if she were rushing to leave. That was one of her "regulations." She never stayed any longer than that, no matter what manipulative tactics her conquest tried to use on her. Marley had other rules as well. She never kissed on the mouth before, during, or after "the act," and she never let her date hold her afterwards. Strict rules she developed to keep her from getting caught up and to protect her heart from ever being broken again.

Lifting the covers from her body, Marley stepped out of bed and grabbed her dress from the chair. If it weren't for the light from the street that seeped through a small opening in the curtains, Marley would surely have tripped over the mess of body-building magazines, sneakers, and dirty clothes scattered around Marquez Jones's apartment.

Moving slowly and quietly, Marley grabbed her boots and her keys and made her way to the door. She softly unlocked the dead bolt and twisted the doorknob. She smiled to herself as she slowly opened the door. She was almost home free.

If Marley made it out of the house, she would cut Marquez off completely, with no questions asked. Rule number ten: Never return his calls, texts, or e-mails, and eventually block his numbers from her phones.

Marley didn't have to worry about Marquez showing up at her house or job, because her game was too tight for that. Rule number thirteen: Conquests were never invited to her home, and she never offered information about her job.

Marley's rules were carved in stone, and she never strayed away from them. Falling in love and getting her heart broken was an experience Marley vowed to never endure again. She'd been through the ultimate loss of love. To Marley, love was a far-fetched dream. Something she would never experience again. The death of DeJuan proved love *was* suicide.

"You leaving so soon?" Marquez asked with sleepiness still in his voice. He reached above Marley's head and softly pushed the door closed.

She jumped when she realized he was standing behind her. "I remembered I have something to do this morning," she said.

"What is so important that you have to leave so early?" Marquez asked, pulling her into his body. "I mean, we just fell asleep. Come back to bed."

Marley pushed away from the unwanted hug and briefly admired Marquez's naked body. Marquez was one of those men who took care of every *inch* of his body. His stomach was defined with a stunning six-pack; his back and arms showed off the rips and cuts he worked hard at the gym six days a week to define. His black hair was an endless sea of waves from front to back. The same dark hair outlined the sides of his face and ended in a small patch at the bottom of his chin. Marquez possessed smooth chocolate skin, wide dark eyes, and perfect teeth. His big feet and hands confirmed the myth. Marquez was fine. But fine didn't faze Marley Lucas in the least. She was immune to *fine*.

"Yeah, Quez, I have to meet someone. I'm sorry," Marley said. "I would have stayed longer, but I just thought about it."

Marquez hesitated and then reached for the doorknob. He leaned in to kiss Marley, but she turned her cheek to him.

"Call me," she said.

"Oh, I will."

Marley rushed barefoot down the steps and stopped at the bottom of the staircase to slide her feet into her knee-high black boots. She leaned against the unstable railing and bent over to pull up the zipper on the sides.

"You better watch who you are bending over in front of, ma."

Marley turned toward the direction of the sexy deep voice and pulled her dress down over her thick ass and thighs. When her eyes met the eyes of the good-looking stranger, her innate character took over. *Smile.*

"I'm so embarrassed," she said. *Run fingers through hair.* "I know this dress is a little too short, but I didn't expect anyone to come in." *Drop keys.*

"I got 'em, ma." The stranger bent down to pick up the keys and stared at Marley's long tanned legs as he slowly stood.

He set the keys in Marley's hand and smiled. "You live in this building, ma?"

"No, my girlfriend does. Not girlfriend, *like that* . . . but you know what I mean." *Laugh sexily. Run fingers through hair, smile. Touch him. Certified Boricua*, Marley thought as she stared at the handsome Puerto Rican gentleman in front of her. Marley eyed his huge arms, which were covered with tribal tattoo sleeves. Marley admired his light brown eyes and wavy hair while he spoke. When he smiled, his eyelids covered the corners of his eyes, which Marley found alluring. She noticed when he bent down to pick up her keys that his back was also covered with black ink. Marley loved tattooed men. Tatted with a little ink herself, Marley found the artistic form of expression addicting.

The stranger spoke with a slight accent and rolled his *r* sound often, which Marley found irresistible.

After rushed small talk with the stranger—Jay, which was short for Javier—Marley took his number and promised to give him a call. She knew that she would call at least once, but what happened after that was to be determined. Lately with Marley nothing had been certain.

Marley Lucas never had any problems turning heads. Born to a white mother who had a twisted obsession with the Jamaican-born reggae artist Bob Marley and a black father whom she'd never met, Marley had looks as exotic and unique as her name. Her long dark hair waved if she didn't use a ceramic flat iron to straighten it daily. Her eyes, light brown and wide, sparkled whenever she smiled, and she smiled a lot. Her slender nose and high cheekbones she gained from her mother's side of the family, but her dark skin, long legs, and shapely curves were definitely from her father's people. Soft-spoken, with a trace of a southern accent hidden in her words, Marley was recognized by the opposite sex as far back as she could remember. It was apparent to everyone around Marley that she exuded sexuality. Men loved the shapeliness of her legs, the roundness of her ass, and the way that she swayed her hips back and forth when she walked. She mimicked the magic that she performed in the bedroom.

When Marley walked into her condo, she threw the keys into the porcelain bowl beside the door and pressed the button on the answering machine to retrieve her messages. She placed one hand on the delete button and prepared to dismiss any voice she didn't want to hear.

"Marley, this is—" *Delete.*

"Marley, it's—" *Delete.*

"Marley, call Mom."

"Hey beautiful . . . call me." *Delete.*

Marley threw herself onto the sofa and rested her head against the back. She thought about the voice of the last caller and sighed. She leaned forward, unzipped her boots, and slid her feet out. Marley walked barefoot toward the kitchen to start a pot of Godiva French Vanilla coffee. Glancing at her watch, she decided not to even try to go back to bed. It was time to get her day started.

After she washed Marquez's scent off her body in a long hot shower, she poured a cup of coffee, mixed in two spoonfuls of sugar and French vanilla creamer, and headed toward her home office.

Marley stood in the doorway and sipped the soothing drink while she stared at the mess of folders on top of papers. Color swatches and fabric samples stuck out from underneath the home-decorating magazines spread chaotically across the desk. Adjusting the belt on her white terry-cloth bathrobe, she dragged her plush white slippers across the hardwood floor to the sliding glass door, which led to the patio. She opened the blinds. She stared at the beautiful sunrise with squinted eyes. Normally, she would gather her laptop, the paperwork, and color swatches and have coffee sitting on the balcony overlooking beautiful

Miami beach. She'd check her work e-mail first, then her personal mail. She would attempt to work, looking for unique colors, designs, and patterns that she could implement into her next project. Eventually Marley would get sidetracked and end up on one of the popular dating Web sites she was a member of. But today, clouds hovered above, there was an early morning breeze which blew through the palm trees, and the waves pounded against the shore as if rain was hastily approaching.

Marley held the coffee mug with both hands and stared at the ocean in silence until she lazily shuffled over to her desk. She crossed her legs when she sat down to start the computer. Marley took another sip of coffee and sighed heavily. She dreaded starting the work that was piled around her, but deadlines were quickly approaching, contracts had been signed, and advances already paid. She was legally bound to her duties. The same duties she used to complete long before the deadlines, making sure she put in that extra effort to ensure her clients were always fully satisfied. Now, she procrastinated until the very last minute; she did what was expected and nothing more. It had been almost ten years, but every moment of the day, Marley thought about DeJuan and what they shared and lost so senselessly.

The school zoning district unexpectedly changed right before the beginning of Marley's sophomore year in high school. The change meant that everyone who attended the small Marshall Academy was now forced to attend Northeast High School.

Marley's friends were devastated. None of them had ever ventured to that side of the city unless it was absolutely necessary, and they surely never went alone.

The Northeast school district was an entirely different world as far as Marley and her friends were concerned. Populated by mostly Latinos, African Americans, and lower-income Asians, that area of the city was infamous for its mounting drug action, violence, and criminal activity. Northeast also had the highest number of teenage mothers in the city. Many times Marley witnessed the young girls walking the streets, looking unkempt with swollen breasts and oversized bellies hanging over their supertight low-riding jeans. Many of them still tried to wear their trendy baby T-shirts. Some of the girls would be pushing a baby stroller with one hand and smoking a cigarette or rubbing her belly with the other. Instead of sympathizing, Marley and her friends drove by laughing and vowing to never look like that when they had children.

Before Northeast High School, Marley had always socialized with the white kids. She felt more comfortable around them. The few black students who attended Marshall Academy seemed to reject her, as if she weren't good enough for them. The day Nisha Brown told her that she thought she was white, Marley wanted to die. "You think you're a white girl," she said, pointing her finger directly in Marley's face. "You're *black*, Marley. I hope you realize that one day."

Deep inside, Marley knew that Nisha was right. She wasn't *just* white, but with her mother and grandmother constantly reminding her of her "Caucasian heritage," it was easy for her to pretend that she didn't have another side. Her "blackness" just didn't exist, until she looked *closely* in the mirror.

The summer before the horrifying transition, Marley spent many days tanning on the beach with her friends, talking about Northeast and what the change was going to mean to all of them. . . .

Heather removed her white bikini top and turned to lie on her stomach. Her blond hair was in a messy ponytail on top of her head, and black oversized sunglasses covered her deep blue eyes.

As Marley rubbed the SPF 50 sunblock into her best friend's already tanned skin, she confessed, "I'm kind of looking forward to going to Northeast this year."

She felt Heather's body tense before she responded. "What! Do you know what could happen to us when we get there?" she asked.

Marley laughed and continued to gently massage the oil onto Heather's back. "Nothing is going to happen to us, Heather. I'm just looking forward to making new friends and seeing what other people are like. We've been going to school with the same boring people . . . *all* of our lives."

"I happen to like those same boring people," she said without turning her head toward Marley when she moved back to her towel and removed her top. "Those are our friends, Marley."

"I know, but maybe it is time for me to make some new friends.

I've been thinking about how I need to learn more about my 'other side.'" Marley sighed while she searched through the beach bag for her sunglasses. "You know that I've always felt different. Maybe now I can feel like I belong."

Heather finally turned her head toward Marley. She took off her sunglasses and glared. "Marley, please don't give me that 'I don't belong' bullshit. You have friends that love you. You are on the basketball and volleyball team. You were voted freshman homecoming princess. You are popular, you're pretty. Come on, Marley, like, stop it already," she said.

Heather could never understand how Marley felt growing up in the shadows. Her friends were all blond-haired, blue- or green-eyed girls, and they had no idea what it was like to secretly feel like an outcast. No matter how many times she tried to explain it, Marley could never convince them of the deep sense of insecurity she'd felt through the years, even though they had the exact same conversation every day for the entire summer.

Northeast High School was more of a change than they could ever have imagined. The outside resembled much of what the inside would look like when they walked through the steel doors and on through the metal detectors. The hallways were dimly lit, and the smell of mold filled their noses as they maneuvered through the crowd to the classroom.

Northeast was filled to capacity. Each small worn-out desk seated a student. At Marshall Academy, the classes were small and comfortable and each student received personalized attention from highly dedicated teachers.

As she sat nervously in her seat, Marley glanced around at the surroundings. Huge windows bordered the classroom, but no sunlight shone through to brighten the mood inside the four bare walls. The same dim lights that failed to illuminate the halls were mounted on the dilapidated ceiling. The smell of lemon-scented Pine-Sol reeked from the shabby linoleum floors, and dust covered the bookcase, which held a minimal amount of torn reading materials.

Ms. Aiken stood timidly in front of the blackboard and began to take attendance. The stringy-haired woman was one of the few white teachers employed at Northeast. She twirled her fingers around her greasy salt-and-pepper hair and attempted to pronounce each student's name. She stumbled nervously over the articulation of many of the black students' names, which caused pandemonium in the classroom.

"Bitch, you don't know how the fuck to say my name? It's Kee-on-tay. Say it with me . . . Kee . . ." The expressive young man stood with his arms tightly folded across his chest until Ms. Aiken repeated each syllable of his name. "Tha's better. You make sure you remember that from now on, bitch," he said.

Ms. Aiken said nothing in response to Keyohanteay's disrespectful attitude, which set the tone in her classroom for the remainder of the school year. Ms. Aiken never said a word to anyone about anything.

Marley sat cramped at her desk, swinging her crossed leg back and forth swiftly, waiting for Ms. Aiken to call her name.

She prayed the teacher would have no trouble with the pronunciation, so that she could discreetly raise her hand and allow Ms. Aiken to place a checkmark in her spiral notebook before anyone noticed her. But there would be no such luck. When Ms. Aiken saw Marley's name, she paused and looked around the entire classroom.

"Muhh . . . ah . . . r . . . lay . . . yah," she said. Marley shook her head in disbelief. Her name was spelled exactly how it sounds, but Ms. Aiken managed to fuck it up, she thought to herself.

"It's Marley," she said.

Ms. Aiken seemed relieved at the simple pronunciation. She exhaled and parted her lips, revealing a small smile. Marley believed she even winked at her, but she rolled her eyes into the back of her head and looked away. Soon after her name was called, loud whistles and shouts started. The boys were giving each other high fives and repeating her name.

"I'm going to hit that, watch!" one boy said.

"*I'm* gonna get that!"

"Marley? Like Bob 'I Shot the Sheriff' Marley?" the loudest of the boys finally asked.

The class erupted into laughter when he started to sing the lyrics to the popular reggae song. She was embarrassed by all the snide remarks, but she finally said, "Yes. My mom is in love with him."

The boys stopped their ranting and calmed down as if they had been waiting for her to speak. And now they were hanging on her every word. While Ms. Aiken rummaged through the mess on her desk, looking for the assignment, private conversations took place among cliqued-up peers in every corner of the room.

The tallest of the rowdy boys walked over to Marley's desk, and his friends followed. They made a small circle around her, which intimidated her at first until the tall boy said, "That's a tight name. I like it. My name is DeJuan."

Marley smiled, recalling Ms. Aiken's ridiculous mispronunciation of his name.

"So your moms loves reggae, huh?" he asked.

"Well, she likes Bob Marley, but I'm not too sure about anyone else," Marley said.

She looked toward the front of the classroom and noticed Ms. Aiken was still engaged, or at least pretending to be. She turned toward the back and eyed three girls staring directly at her and the circle of boys. The girl sitting in the middle shot her a dirty look, and she immediately turned back to the front.

"Are you one of the kids from Marshall?" a boy asked.

"Yes," she said.

"So how you like Northeast so far?" DeJuan asked.

Marley shrugged. "It's different," she said. Marley turned her head toward the mean girls again and noticed they were still watching her every move as if trying to read her lips from afar. She could tell from the look in her eyes that the middle girl didn't like her at all.

Competition was Asia Brown's strong suit, and competition is exactly how she thought of Marley. They competed in classes, and even though they were on the same team, they competed for status in volleyball, basketball, and softball. Asia also competed with Marley for popularity, but most important, she competed for DeJuan Spencer's affection.

It wasn't long after that first conversation between DeJuan and Marley that her life started to change. Slowly her old friends faded from the picture and new friends and a new identity emerged. Marley started to dress differently. Gone were the days of preppy-looking white-girl outfits. She started wearing things that accentuated the assets that all the boys in school found enticing. She changed her hair, she started wearing a lot more jewelry than usual, and she started listening to the same music DeJuan bumped in his Chevy Caprice. Marley was having fun discovering her other side. She absolutely loved the new her.

DeJuan was one of the most popular boys in school. He wasn't the smartest, but he was loved among their classmates. When he first started flirting with Marley, she completely blew him off. She wasn't sure what to make of his actions, and with his wannabe girlfriend staring around every corner, she knew the best thing was not to act, even though she was secretly feeling the same attraction.

Marley ran her finger lightly across the top of the coffee mug and smiled. She laughed nonchalantly, and instead of grabbing Mrs. Palmer's file folder, she searched through the mess until she found the Northeast High School yearbook she looked through at least once a day. Clouds spread across the sky always reminded her of DeJuan, and when the rain started to fall, the sound of the water pounding against the cement, the smell of wet concrete and grass all reminded her of the day he whispered softly in her ear and disclosed the news that broke her heart and still breaks her heart to this day.

She quickly flipped through the pages, thumbing past the class pictures, professions of friendship, lengthy heartfelt good-byes and summer wishes written in feminine bubbled cursive writing that filled each page. A light smile parted her lips when she finally found the picture she was looking for.

There she sat under the senior-class redwood tree between DeJuan's legs, with all her innocence and identity issues. She was slightly turned toward him, looking directly into his eyes. The look of love was intense. The comments written around the photo confirmed it. "Northeast's Cutest Couple sitting under the senior tree," the caption read. Smiley faces and hearts surrounded the photo and bordered the length of the page. "You guys are so cute!" "When is the wedding?" "Perfect for each other," friends wrote.

DeJuan helped Marley find her true identity over those years, the Marley who hid behind a false character for such a long time. He exposed her to a different lifestyle. A lifestyle that was fresh and exciting. She started going to parties with DeJuan and his friends, hanging out at the local skating rink and spending nights blasting music on the deserted beach. DeJuan showed Marley things she'd never experienced, from soul food, collard greens, and homemade macaroni and cheese to hip-hop, Nas, and Jay-Z, from smoking good weed to good sex. His family showed her what it meant to have a strong family bond. She went to church with his mom and grandmother every Sunday and eventually learned to let go enough to feel the spirit in a Baptist church. Falling in love with DeJuan and his family was easy and happened fast.

Marley stared at the picture and looked into DeJuan's dark brown eyes, the same way that she had that day under the tree. Before she became too emotional, she covered her mouth with her hand and laughed out loud. Her hair had been tightly braided that day. Johnita, her new best friend, had talked her into letting her fingers work some magic on her "white girl" hairstyle, and after sitting between Nita's legs for nearly two hours, Marley had two dozen tiny braids separated by perfect zigzag parts covering her scalp. When people looked at the picture, they immediately compared Marley to the talented pianist and R & B singer Alicia Keys. Today she agreed the likeness was uncanny. As she looked at the photo, memories from what seemed like a lifetime ago flooded her mind. DeJuan was her soul mate, but as quickly as she loved, she lost.

Marley ate dinner with DeJuan and his family every Sunday. Sometimes Chris, DJ's best friend, would hang around until it was time to eat. DeJuan's mother, Miss Deidra, always "put her foot" in Sunday's meal. The dinner table looked like the scene from the movie *Soul Food*, complete with fried chicken, macaroni and cheese, collard greens, corn bread, and some special kind of cake or desert. Marley's favorite was Miss D's red velvet cake. Marley's family never ate like that on Sunday—or any day, for that matter. Tara, Marley's mother, hated to cook.

"What's your mama's name, Marley?" Miss Deidra asked.

"Why, Mama? It's not like you know the lady," DeJuan said. "Her mama is some uppity white woman. It's been two years, and she doesn't even want to meet me," he added sarcastically.

Marley wiped the corner of her mouth with a napkin and sighed. "It's not that she doesn't want to meet you, DJ. She is just having a hard time with all the changes I've made. You know?" The hair, the clothes, and the friends . . . the *boyfriend*. Marley reached for DeJuan's hand underneath the table and covered it with hers. "I'm not the same Marley I was last year. They don't like it. But this—" Marley grabbed the end of one of her braids and held it in the air. "—this is me." She leaned over and kissed DeJuan softly on the cheek. "She'll come around," she whispered.

"Are your mom and dad still together? Your dad is black, right? I know you got some black in you, even though I have to look real close!" Miss Deidra never held her tongue, and that is one of the things Marley loved about her. If she wanted to know something, she asked. If she had something to say, she said it.

"From what I know, my dad is black, Miss D, but I've never met him, and I don't know anything about him except he played football for Florida State. My mom's name is Tara," Marley said.

"Tara *what*? Where is she from? What school did she go to?" Miss Deidra sat her fork on the edge of her plate and waited for Marley to answer.

"Tara Lucas. She went to Riverbend High and she graduated from Florida State."

"She went to Florida State? Her major was?" Miss Deidra asked the question and made a statement a second later: "Interior Design," she said.

"Interior Design, how did you guess?"

"Mama went to FSU, too, so did my sorry-assed daddy who has seen me twice in my life. Once when I was born and again on my first birthday," DeJuan said. "He was some big football star, right, Mama?"

While Miss Deidra stared at Marley as if she were trying to memorize her face, she smiled and bit into a warm slice of her delicious corn bread. "It was just a guess, Marley. I think you may have mentioned it before. Boy, *you* better watch your mouth," she said, pointing at DeJuan.

"I'm sorry, Mama, but I can't stand that nigga."

"I *said* watch your mouth." Miss Deidre continued to stare at Marley. "You mean to tell me that you don't even know your father's name?" she asked.

"I don't even know his name," Marley confirmed. DeJuan and Marley cleared the table and washed the dishes as they usually did, but before she left, Miss D handed her an envelope and asked her to give it to her mother. She made Marley promise not to open it, but she couldn't resist the temptation, and as soon as she pulled out of the driveway, she steered the car into the first vacant lot and tore open the envelope. Marley pulled out the picture of a young man in a Florida State football uniform and the handwritten note.

Tara,
Our children are dating and very much in love. I think it is time that Marley knows who her father is. We need to put a stop to this. Things have gone too far. We have to tell them the truth before we cause any further devastation to these kids. It's not their fault. Please call me as soon as possible so that we can speak about how we are going to handle this fragile situation. I have enclosed a picture of Charles as you may remember him. You can give it to Marley. He is nowhere near the same man we both fell in love with. From what I've heard, drugs have taken control of his life.
Please call me.
Deidra Spencer

Marley stared at the letter and then read it over again. She didn't want to believe anything that was on the paper. She thought about all the years that had passed and left her wondering where the man who was supposed to love and protect her from everything was. She'd missed having a father in her life and wasn't open to hearing about this man Charles. Maybe he was DJ's father, but he wasn't hers. Miss D obviously had her mother confused with some other Tara. It wasn't true. Marley folded the note and placed it back into the envelope. She decided that she would never let her mother see it.

Miss D waited patiently for the phone call from Marley's mother. She asked her every time she saw her if she'd given her the note. Marley lied and told her yes every time. After one month of not hearing from Tara, Miss D decided to take matters into her own hands.

Sunday started off the same as any other Sunday: Miss D and Marley attended church, and Miss D prepared her usual Sunday spread while DeJuan and Marley hung around the house playing cards and watching movies. When they placed the plates and napkins on the table, Miss D told DeJuan to set an extra place because they were having a guest.

When the doorbell rang at exactly six o'clock, DeJuan answered it. He stood holding the doorknob and staring at the man who stood in front of him.

"Come on in, Charles!" Miss D yelled from the kitchen.

DeJuan opened the door wider, and Charles walked in. From his appearance, Marley would never have assumed he was on drugs. He even looked as if he'd put extra effort into his looks tonight. He was clean shaven, his hair was freshly cut, and he wore a pair of creased black slacks and a dark blue dress shirt and striped tie. He looked healthy.

"Come on in, we were just about to sit down to dinner," Miss D said nervously.

Marley, DeJuan, and Charles followed Miss D's voice into the dining room and took their respective seats. Marley's stomach was settled at the bottom of her feet. She sensed what the whole setup was about. Charles was her alleged father and her boyfriend's father, which made DeJuan her brother. She wanted to run out of the room screaming, but she couldn't let DeJuan or Miss D know she had any idea of what was to come. Marley held back tears while Miss D spoke.

"DeJuan, Marley, this is Charles," she said. "Charles went to Florida State. He played football. He was pretty good back then." Miss D smiled and passed the bowl of potatoes to De-Juan. "I asked him to come to dinner tonight because there is something very important that I feel you both need to know," she explained.

Marley held her breath and prayed that she was dreaming and that as soon as she exhaled, she'd wake up and everything would be normal again.

They filled their dinner plates in silence and took their first bites without a word. Everyone was processing the situation in their own way. Marley was sure that DeJuan had put two and two together and assumed this dinner was solely about meeting his father. He knew his father was a big football star at FSU and was named Charles.

"I guess I'll go ahead and start, tell you why I'm here," Charles said.

He wiped his mouth with a napkin and looked Marley and DJ over. He glanced at Miss D, and she nodded, giving him the go-ahead.

"Years ago, I was a football player at FSU. I was big-time. Probably could have played in the NFL if I wanted to," he said. Charles took another bite of his food and chewed slowly. When he was finished he continued. "Being a big-time star in college, you have women coming at you from everywhere. I've had my share of them. I've made a lot of mistakes in my lifetime," he said.

DeJuan and Marley watched Charles intently. DJ had no idea where Charles was going with his story, but Marley did, and she'd suddenly lost her appetite. She placed her fork at the corner of her plate, pushed her plate away, and waited for Charles to finish.

"One of the mistakes I made was messing around with three women and getting them all pregnant at the same time," he said. "But, I was young, and at that time I didn't know any better. I knew that I wasn't ready to be a father. I wanted what I wanted when I wanted it, and I didn't think about anyone but me back then. Every day of my life, I regret the decisions I made. I turned my back on D, Tara, and the other woman—and regardless of what they may think, I loved all of them and deep inside I loved both of you before you were even born," he said, turning his head toward Miss D.

Charles lifted his fork to his mouth, and Miss D finally looked away. DJ didn't hesitate to continue with his meal while Charles searched his mind for the next words.

"I'm sorry, DeJuan. I'm sorry, Marley. I'm sorry for missing out on your lives, I'm sorry that I was young and dumb. I'm hoping that eventually, once all of this settles that we will be able to have some kind of relationship." Charles stared into DeJuan's eyes. He sensed that DJ wasn't accepting the apology that he was trying to give. "When D told me what was going on, I knew that we had to do something."

"What?" DeJuan said. "What are you talking about, man?

You trying to tell me that you are my daddy, nigga?" DeJuan slowly stood in front of his seat. As the look of years of neglect, frustration, and anger slithered across DeJuan's face, he balled his fists at his waist, and tears welled in the corners of his eyes.

"How the fuck you gonna sit in here and eat my mama's food, nigga?" DeJuan flipped the corner of Charles's plate and watched as the uneaten food landed in his lap. "You don't deserve to eat our food! Where the fuck have you been all of these years, fool? Where the fuck were you at when I needed you, nigga? I don't give a fuck what you *used* to be. You ain't shit *now*. You don't even deserve to be in my house, nigga! Get the fuck out!"

Charles slid back in his chair and started to stand. Miss D kindly placed her hand on his arm, and he stayed in his seat.

"Calm down, DJ, we are going to talk about this like grown folk. Ain't gonna be none of that in my house. Now, sit down."

Marley sat beside DJ and watched as his anger escalated. He didn't seem to hear anything else that Charles said. It didn't quite sink in that Charles had also mentioned knowing her mom. That meant that they may be brother and sister. The only thing that DJ seemed to care about now was the fact that the man who sat in front of them eating the delicious meal Miss D prepared was his absent father. The man whom he always wished he could know and have a relationship with, Charles, was the man that DJ had cried for at night when he was a little boy.

"Charles, I think that you have my mother mixed up with some other woman," Marley said. "You don't know my grandparents. I don't think that they would have allowed my mother to date you," she said. "No offense, but that is how they are."

"They didn't *let* her date me. We snuck around. Your mom wanted to tell them, but I wasn't ready to deal with that kind of situation," Charles said. "When they found out that she was pregnant by a black man, they lost their damn minds and made her transfer to another school and everything. I couldn't talk to her, see her . . . nothing. I never heard from Tara again. I couldn't believe that they took my child away from me."

"Maybe your sorry ass should have tried harder to find your kids," DeJuan said. He looked at Marley and shook his head. Underneath the table he softly covered her small hand with his.

DeJuan was told the outcome before Tara ever received her results. The clouds were spread across the sky and the rain was approaching quickly. The temperature fell a few degrees, and a gentle breeze blew through the trees. Marley was sitting on the porch of her grandmother's colonial home when DeJuan's Caprice sped up the driveway. DeJuan threw open his door and jumped out. He walked with his head down and his hands in his pockets. They didn't exchange any words; they just slowly walked toward each other. When they were face-to-face, the couple embraced. DeJuan cried silently while Marley stood still and inhaled his scent for what was sure to be the last time. As the rain fell, he placed his mouth next to her ear and whispered, "He's my daddy." The words barely escaped. He held his breath and wiped his face with his free hand. "Baby girl, he's your dad, too, ninety nine point nine percent," he said.

Marley nearly collapsed in DeJuan's arms. "Nooo! Please no!"

She'd prayed for hours and days that the outcome would be different. She asked God to make this right. DeJuan was the love of her life. They were going to get married, have kids, and live happily ever after. She didn't want to lose him.

"I gotta go, baby girl. I can't deal with this shit," he said. He turned and walked slowly toward the car. When he reached the car, DeJuan stood in the rain behind the open door and blew Marley a kiss. She pretended to catch it and then placed her open hand to her lips. That was the last time she saw DeJuan alive. The next day, Miss D found him inside his cherished Caprice with his nine-millimeter and a bullet wound to his head. Three letters were found in the glove compartment, one for Marley, one for Chris, and one for Miss D. The situation was too much for DeJuan. He didn't feel that he would ever be able to stop loving Marley . . . his sister.

After DeJuan's suicide, Marley promised herself that she would never love again. She told herself that no man was worth giving her heart to. The experience with DeJuan forever changed Marley's feelings about love. Love was suicide.

Marley closed the yearbook and wiped her eyes. She took a sip of the coffee, which had cooled, and grabbed the telephone.

Club HEAT was one of the hottest nightspots in the area. Known for its bright lights, high ceilings, rooftop dance floors, private VIP rooms, and music, the club was frequented by many of the MIA's favorite celebrities. Athletes, models, actresses, and musicians could all be found sipping drinks and moving their bodies to the beat of the latest music.

Marley arrived at HEAT wearing a sexy backless dress that covered her ass just enough and black heels to match. Her MAC makeup was flawless, as was everything on Marley—from the French manicure on her fingernails to her long dark hair, which she straightened and parted down the middle. Her perfectly toned and tanned legs seemed endless as she walked in through a side door and up to a private VIP room reserved for the evening. Marley frequented the club with her girlfriends during her free time and was a familiar face to the security team and bouncers. Neither she nor her friends ever waited in line at HEAT.

As she sat on the plush velvet chaise sipping on a glass of Riesling, Marley started to have second thoughts. She suddenly wished she'd planned this evening with Javier instead of the person who would soon walk through the club doors.

Chris walked in, looking every bit as sexy as the last time Marley saw him. A smile immediately snuck across her lips as she looked him over from head to toe.

"Marley . . ." Chris extended and opened his arms as Marley stood to hug him. "I was wondering if you were ever going to call me again," he said.

"I've been thinking about you lately, but I've just been a little busy," she said, kissing him softly on the cheek.

"A call now and then isn't that hard, you feel me?"

"I know, and I'm sorry. You know how my schedule is sometimes." Marley sat down and slid off her heels. She curled her legs underneath her body and pointed to the empty spot in front of her. "Sit down."

After DJ's death, Marley temporarily forgot about her rules and simply enjoyed kicking it with Chris even though she quickly developed a slight reputation for being that close with DeJuan's best friend. The untimely death of her soul mate had knocked the life out of Marley. Whenever she thought of DJ and the pain he suffered and how he must have been feeling the very moment he pulled the trigger, Marley couldn't breathe; she felt as if she were being suffocated by her tears. She was often inconsolable and only found innocent solace in the arms of his friend.

Chris managed to withstand the ridiculous tactics Marley used to guard her heart. He respected her and would do anything to protect her from ever being hurt again. Chris's feelings for Marley far surpassed any feelings he'd ever felt for any other chick. He genuinely cared about her and he'd even surprised himself when he managed to momentarily knock her out of her box, as she put it, but Chris fully understood her position on his lifestyle. A hustler, a so-called thug drug dealer, was something she pledged never to allow in her life. Chris knew he was no exception, no matter how smooth and sexy she said he was.

Chris sat at the foot of the chaise and softly caressed Marley's legs. He leaned down and kissed her knee softly.

"I miss you, girl," he said.

"I miss you, too."

Chris pulled Marley's leg from underneath her body and gently massaged it while he straightened it. He slowly lifted her short dress and exposed her toned, tan thigh. Chris lowered his head and kissed her uncovered skin softly.

"Tell me you weren't falling in love with me," Chris whispered. He turned to the waitress who was suddenly standing beside the couple and ordered a Hennessy and Coke. "All those rules and shit you wrote down on that piece of paper after DJ died . . . You broke every one of them for me . . . remember?" Chris kissed Marley's soft skin again and waited for an answer.

Marley caressed Chris's smooth bald head when he kissed her thigh. When he lifted his head toward hers, she silently stared into his eyes and lost herself in a time long ago.

The day of DJ's funeral, Marley thought she would breathe her last breath also. Miss D opted for an open casket to give DeJuan's many friends and family members one last vision of his earthly shell. The display of DeJuan's lifeless body inside the shining silver casket lined with blue proved to be too much for Marley. After collapsing several times, she gathered the strength to stand over DJ's body and kiss him lightly, ending everything she knew. Her life was centered on DJ and his around her. Now he was gone, and she didn't know how she'd survive.

During the service, a superbly cleaned-up Charles sat next to Miss D and tried unsuccessfully to control her thrashing body and muffle her heart-wrenching sobs into his chest. Tara, not knowing how to help her daughter through the tragedy, quietly dabbed the corners of her eyes lightly as she sat in the back pew of the church.

Chris wrapped his arm around Marley's waist and held her tightly when her legs wobbled underneath her body. He'd been there the day Marley heard the devastating news and hadn't left her side. Chris and Marley collected their emotions long enough to stay with Miss D until the last lingering guest walked out of the door. They silently picked up trash from the floor and cleared dishes from the table until Miss D's older sister took over and forced them to go home to try to get some rest.

"I can't go home, Chris," Marley whispered once they were standing on the dimly lit porch. "I'm not thinking straight. I can't be alone. I miss DJ *already*." Marley's voice cracked slightly, and she inhaled deeply. She put her hand over her heart and gasped. She shook her head back and forth swiftly and attempted to scream at the top of her lungs, but Chris suffocated the earth-shattering sound with his body.

When Marley's body quaked uncontrollably, Chris held her and softly stroked her hair until she seemed to calm down. They walked toward Chris's Chevy in silence as Marley tried to contain her unbearable sorrow. Chris opened the car door and helped Marley into the tricked-out '97 Caprice. He closed the door after she fastened her seat belt and walked around to the other side. When gravel crunched under his Stacy Adams, Chris thought about the way the gravel crunched under his and DeJuan's basketball shoes back when they played Michael Jordan and Magic Johnson on an old basketball hoop in the driveway before Miss D saved up enough money to buy another new hoop and have the driveway paved. He shook his head and then looked toward the sky. He pounded his chest twice with his fist, kissed it, and then thrust it toward the sky.

"I love you," he whispered before opening the door and sliding into the driver's seat. Chris placed the keys in the ignition and started the car. He stared at Marley's face, studying the outline of her distinct features. He placed his hand at the back of the headrest behind Marley's head, looked over his shoulder, and backed out of the backyard. Marley continued to stare at DJ's picture on the front of the funeral program that rested in her lap and said nothing. Chris steered the car toward I-95 and pressed his foot to the gas pedal. His mind was clouded with visions from the funeral while he drove at high speed down the highway, maneuvering in and out of traffic. Inside, he wanted to break down, but Chris understood that he needed to be strong for Marley and Miss D so he held it in. He was hurting, but not only for the loss of his friend, but for the loss of his *blood*.

Finally after what seemed like an eternity, Marley spoke.

"Where are you taking me?" she whispered. Chris quickly glanced to his right when he heard the soft voice. He stared at Marley briefly, and his own eyes began to water. Marley's eyes were puffy from crying silently and blackened from the running mascara and black eyeliner. Whenever she tried to wipe away the falling tears, she smeared more of the black mess onto her cheeks.

"My brother gave me the keys to his house in Kensington Estates. They just use the house as a drop spot," Chris offered.

"No one is living there, so he told me to stay there until I got my head together and shit. You don't mind, do you? I think you could use a little time away from everyone and everything," he said.

Marley shook her head. "You are so right," she whispered. "I don't have clothes or anything, though," she said, looking down at the funeral program again.

"We'll worry about that a little later. It's been a long-ass day. We really do need to try to get some rest. We'll figure out all the details in the morning. Do you need to call your moms?"

"No, she knows I'm fine."

"All right."

When they pulled into Kensington Estates, Marley looked around the subdivision. She never expected Chris's brother's drop house, whatever that was, to look like any of the houses she was admiring. Even in the spotlight of floodlights and dimly lit walkways, Marley could make out specific architectural features on the homes, and her mind ran wild when she tried to imagine the decorating that was done on the inside of each. Chris pressed the button on the remote garage opener and slowly drove inside as the door rose.

Chris used the key to open the door and walked over to the alarm and entered the code his brother made him memorize. Marley looked around at the spacious but scarcely furnished home.

She walked around until she found the fully furnished television room. She couldn't help but laugh. The house was a typical bachelor pad. No furniture except in the bedroom and, of course, television room. A sixty-inch plasma television hung on the wall in a room complete with a plush black extended sofa and pool table.

While Marley went from room to room, Chris searched through his brother's walk-in closet for a robe or something that Marley could change into after she showered. She surprised him at the closet door after he'd found a blue Sean John terry-cloth robe. He handed her the robe and smiled.

"Towels are in the closet. I'm sure one of my brother's friends probably left some kind of smell-good shit that you women use in there."

Marley took the robe from Chris's hand and smiled. She wrapped her arms around his neck and then stepped back.

"Thanks for being here for me," Marley said before she turned and walked down the long hallway toward the bathroom. Chris watched Marley's hips sway from left to right. The way her hair hung down the middle of her bare back was the sexiest thing he'd seen in a long time. He shook his head quickly before sneaking one more glance.

Chris walked back into the closet and began removing his brother's boxed Nikes and other sneakers from the top shelf. He pulled the handle to the homemade secret compartment. He keyed the numbers into the safe, opened it, and placed money inside.

For months after the funeral, Chris and Marley retreated to Kensington Estates to get away from everything. They went to dinner and movies together. They went for picnics at the beach. Chris attended Marley's graduation and the party her family threw for her afterwards.

When the crowd dispersed, they loaded into Chris's Chevy and drove to Kensington Estates. Marley and Chris had been growing closer with each passing moment. Feelings that they could not contain were beginning to take over. It wasn't long before things got out of hand.

As Marley lay across the bed in short shorts and a tank top reading *Essence* magazine, Chris flipped through the sports channels. He tried to keep his eyes off of her ass, but each time she moved, a part of her cheek was exposed. He continued to change the channels until Marley snatched the remote and turned her back.

"Come get it," she said out of the blue. She held the remote control close to her chest but when Chris reached for it, she refused to let it go. His huge hand covered hers as they playfully struggled for the control. Finally he climbed on top of Marley and held both her wrists. He placed her arms over her head while she laughed hysterically. When she finally calmed down, they locked eyes.

"What?" Marley asked.

"Nothing," Chris whispered. He shook his head and repeated his statement.

"Kiss me, then."

"What?" Chris said.

"Kiss me."

"What? I . . . wh—Marley. D—"

"I want you to."

Chris slowly lowered his head toward Marley's waiting lips. He closed his eyes and forgot about *everything*. While he kissed

DJ's girl with uninhibited passion, he released her wrists and Marley slowly wrapped her arms around his neck and her legs around his waist. She wanted Chris. She figured it was time for her to move on with her life.

Chris grinded against Marley's lower body with his, through his basketball shorts he playfully teased her small button with his erection. When she moaned softly, he tenderly placed his mouth over hers. Together they moved their bodies in perfect rhythm until Chris suddenly jumped up.

"Yo . . . we can't do this," he said.

Chris stood at the edge of the bed and admired Marley. She was lying with her legs wide open, bent at the knee, her long dark hair was spread across the white pillowcase, and her small shirt slightly exposed her bare stomach. She looked confused, and Chris knew that he owed her an explanation, but he knew that he couldn't tell her the *truth*.

"What's wrong, Chris?" Marley asked. She sat up in the bed and stared blankly past Chris.

"This—this shit is wrong," he said.

"You're right, this is wrong. I'm sorry."

Chris couldn't believe that he'd almost taken it there with Marley. At first he was disgusted with himself when he thought about what could have happened, but after a couple of blunts and Hennessy and Coke one lonely night, Chris decided he didn't care. If his love for Marley hadn't changed after all this time, he didn't think it ever would. He called her that same night and asked her to come over.

Marley and Chris rekindled their budding romance. Chris

was falling in love with Marley without even being able to sample the goods. It wasn't about that. Chris figured it would happen sooner or later. He decided to just be patient and wait it out, but while he was being patient and falling deep in love with Marley, he was also becoming deep in the game. Chris's brother's business was growing, major clientele was established, and Chris was his right-hand man. He tried to keep his lifestyle secret from Marley, but the more he laced her with jewelry, gifts, and eventually a new car, the more inquisitive she became. It wasn't long before everything was out in the open.

"You never told me what you were into either. If I had known *that*, we would have never gotten as close as we did," Marley said. "And you know it, Chris."

After almost one year of dating Chris, Marley graduated from interior design school, and Chris's brother immediately hired her to redecorate the house in Kensington Estates. It was there that Chris's secret was exposed. When she disassembled and removed the old shelving in the closet, she found the secret hole in the wall that held the drop house's profit.

She thumbed through the crisp bills and immediately began to piece together the stories of the past. Now the answers Chris gave to simple questions didn't seem sufficient. When she asked him where his money came from, he told Marley he inherited some money when his mother passed away the prior year. Chris seemed to have a never-ending cash flow, which never seemed to bother Marley much until the very minute she sat on the floor in the closet of a drug house holding thousands of dollars. That was the demise of the relationship in her eyes.

When Marley gave Chris the ultimatum—his business or her—Chris decided he wanted to secure his future. He didn't ever want to have to work for another man. He wanted to be able to take care of his sisters and brothers. He hoped Marley would eventually come around, but she never did. In fact, when she distanced herself from Chris, he became all about his business. Nothing came before money ever again. Nothing and no one.

Chris looked at Marley with sympathetic eyes. "What can I say?" He shrugged and then reached for the clip on the side of his jeans and pulled out his vibrating cell phone. Chris held up his index finger and turned away from Marley.

"Okay, when? That's not going to work, I'm busy . . . I can't do that." Chris stood up, walked away from the chaise, and stood near the glass surrounding the VIP room overlooking the club. Marley stared at his lips while they moved, trying to read them as he spoke. She couldn't make out anything, but she assumed some kind of *deal* was being made. She watched Chris as he paced back and forth with one hand in the pocket of his jeans.

"Who was supposed to take care of that? So what now? Yeah . . . yeah I'll be there," he said. Chris ended his call and walked to where Marley sat waiting. He slowly knelt beside the chaise and ran his finger softly up and down Marley's legs. Chris kissed the back of her thigh and whispered, "I have to go, love. . . . Business."

Marley shrugged.

"I'm sorry," he said. "Let's hook up tomorrow, spend the day together or something. I should be back around twelve," he said, softly kissing her leg again.

"I don't think so. This was a mistake. Go take care of business, Chris. As usual, it comes first."

Chris shook his head and stood. He tried to kiss Marley, but she placed her hand directly in front of his face. "Just go," she said.

She watched Chris exit the room and rolled her eyes. She couldn't believe it. She'd almost let him back in. But in an instant, she was reminded of the hold his business had on him. She shook her head and pulled out her Sidekick. *I don't even know why I called him back.*

Marley flipped her screen to cover the keyboard just as Jay returned to the table. She grabbed his hand and admired him before he sat down.

"You look so good, *papi*." Marley pulled Jay close and inhaled deeply. "You smell good, too," she said.

"I have missed you, baby girl. What's been keeping you so busy these days? I was getting sick of talking to your voice mail. I'm glad that you finally decided to call me back. I was wondering if I was ever going to see you again." Jay rested his arm against the back of the chair and leaned back. He admired Marley while she sipped her wine and then slowly ran her fingers through her wavy hair. He lowered his eyelids and angled his head to surreptitiously admire the cleavage jumping out of her dress.

Marley's text message alert sounded and she shifted uncomfortably in her seat. She meant to silence it after the message. She slowly pulled the phone out of her purse and pressed the OFF button without reading the text.

"I've been working like crazy. New clients and new projects. I'm working on a doctor's office, so I've been pretty occupied," she lied. She only had to put the finishing touches on the office and she'd be done. "I'm sorry, *papi*. I'm here now." Marley leaned across the table and kissed Jay softly on the cheek. "Now, let's eat."

After dinner, Jay reached for Marley's hand as they walked across the pier that stretched out over the unusually calm ocean. When they reached the end, Jay pulled Marley close and stood behind her while they watched as the sunset over the horizon.

"I'm in love with you, baby girl."

Jay called her "baby girl" just like DJ did back in the day, and she loved it.

When Marley found out Chris's little drug secret, she slowly saw less and less of him until she wasn't seeing him at all. She'd taken a small break from the dating scene, but the more she "coincidentally" ran into Javier, the more she grew to like him and enjoy their dates. He was one of the sweetest, sexiest men she'd met in her life. Javier was easy to fall for, and for the first time in a long time she just went with the flow, no rules.

"No, you are not, Jay. You *think* that you are, but believe me . . . you don't love me. We haven't even been seeing each other that long." Marley laughed, but Jay didn't smile at all.

"I know that this is love. I think about you every day, every minute of the day. I want to be with you, Marley. I want you to meet my family and everything. I'm serious. I have never felt like this about anyone," he said.

"Wow, *papi*, you *are* serious huh?" Marley laughed.

"As a heart attack," he said.

Jay pulled Marley close to his body and looked into her eyes. When the wind blew her hair into her face, he softly pushed it away from her eyes. He kissed her softly one time on her glossed lips. "I love you, baby girl."

She smiled. "Can we go slow, Jay? You know that I have issues."

"Of course we can. Just not too slow." He laughed.

On the pier in the shadow of the sunset, Marley and Jay kissed like two newlyweds on their honeymoon. Marley's body responded to Jay's masculine touch with uncontrollable shivering. He kissed her with such force, and when he wrapped his strong arms tightly around her body, she melted and she forgot about everything. Once again, she was lost in the pure feeling. Marley experienced the typical man drama that most of her friends had endured. Marley's man drama always consisted of something drastic. Her relationships always developed from the inside out, where most of her girlfriends developed their relationships from the outside in. Back in the day, Marley embraced the difference; now she wasn't so accepting, because her relationships always ended in unfathomable circumstances. Jay and Marley walked hand in hand toward his Cadillac Escalade talking and laughing. Jay was throwing Marley's game off, and she didn't even care. He was pulling her in, and she couldn't resist. When his phone started to ring, he snatched it from the clip on his waist and pressed the TALK button.

"What's up?" Jay held Marley's hand while he talked. He started off talking in English, but by the middle of the conversation, Jay was speaking Spanish. Marley smiled and tried to make out the few words that she knew in Spanish. "Okay," he said before ending the call.

He turned to Marley and kissed her lips softly before speaking. "That was my boy. I told them not to disturb me tonight. I said it in Spanish, just in case he didn't understand when I said it in English," Jay joked.

After the walk on the pier, Jay wanted to have drinks at HEAT, but Marley knew there was a chance they would run in to Chris and his friend, and she insisted they go to Jay's place for a romantic nightcap instead. Jay set the mood by lighting the candles and starting soft music as he usually did while Marley opened a bottle of wine. She walked into the living room, and Jay pulled out two cigars, broke them open, and filled them with marijuana. After he sealed the ends closed with his mouth, Marley handed him a glass of wine and stretched her legs across his thighs as he sat on the couch. The silky sounds of Jon B. played softly in the background while Marley and Jay sat on the couch sipping pinot grigio and inhaling the relaxing treatment. Jay massaged Marley's feet gently when it was her turn to puff. Jay knew that he was falling fast, faster than he'd ever fallen for any woman, and there had been plenty of women in his past. There was something about Marley that kept him intrigued. He loved her independence, her wit and charm, and most definitely her beauty. He also appreciated the caution she took with her heart. She had taken things very slowly with him, which was also a new experience. Usually women were dying to lie in his bed, but Marley was different—she had taken the time to get to know him inside and out before she would let him have her body. Jay fantasized about making love to Marley for the first time, every day from the day he met her. Javier knew that he would feel closer to her once he was inside her.

Jay sexily puffed on the el while Marley waited for her turn. When he passed it to her, she eyed him sexily and smiled. She inhaled calmly and ran her hand down the back of Jay's neck. She stopped and lightly pulled him toward her. When he opened his mouth, she exhaled the smoke she'd been holding in her lungs, and Jay inhaled. The shotgun hastily transitioned into a long, slow kiss. Their tongues wrestled playfully while Jay exhaled the smoke through his nostrils.

Marley moaned softly when he placed his hands between her legs and tenderly massaged her spot through her clothes. They alternated positions while they kissed. Marley straddled Jay on the couch while he caressed every part of her body within reach. Between kisses, sighs, and moans Marley positioned her body at an angle. Tonight she was ready to pleasure Jay in a way she hadn't before.

Marley carefully unbuckled the belt around Jay's jeans and ran her finger back and forth against his skin under the waistline. She slowly leaned her head down and lifted his shirt. When she pressed her lips delicately against his stomach, Jay moved his hands through her hair. Marley placed her open mouth on Jay's exposed skin as she removed his pants. When he was stripped, she teasingly circled her tongue around his waiting erection. Marley was unlike any other lover he had. Her prowess and rhythmic movements left him breathless and speechless.

While Marley lay wrapped in Jay's arms, she watched the clock. She thought about what Jay had told her that night. Marley had not allowed her heart to feel love since DeJuan and Chris, but Jay seemed to be everything she wanted and needed. She was scared and confused. The numbers on the clock changed as she lay still, listening to Jay breathe behind her. Marley slowly eased her body from underneath his arm. She grabbed her phone from her purse and walked into the bathroom and locked the door. Marley turned on the shower and then sat on the toilet and turned on her phone. She scrolled through her missed calls; most were from Chris. She selected Chris's number and returned the call.

"Hey, Chris," she whispered when Chris picked up on the other end. "I'm sorry, yeah, I know. I was just trying to get some work done. I had to turn the phone off to get some peace, everyone was calling me." Marley stood naked in front of the mirror as the steam from the shower slowly began to cover it. She held the phone to her ear with one hand and examined her body for any evidence that may have been left by Jay with the other. When the mirror was fully covered with steam, Marley sat on the toilet again.

"That's cool, what time do you want to meet? . . . All right, I'll see you then," she whispered. Marley silenced her phone and set it on the sink. She piled her hair into a bun on the top of her head and stepped into the shower.

Jay knocked on the door, and Marley met him at the door smiling and wet. He immediately grabbed her around the waist and pulled her toward the shower. Jay reached up and softly loosened Marley's bun. He opened the glass shower door and lightly pushed Marley under the running water. She kissed him passionately while he massaged her shoulders.

"I love you, baby girl," he whispered between kisses. "I want you to be in my life. . . . I want you to love me, too," he said.

Marley smiled. Jay pressed her body against the wet shower wall and slowly wrapped her legs around his waist.

"*Papi*," she whispered. "We are going to go slow, remember?"

"I remember," he said. "Slow," he said, stroking Marley's insides softly with his manhood and kissing her neck. "Slow," he whispered.

"Slow," Marley repeated.

Outside of Dynasty, the sun beamed down on Marley's shoulders while she sat at a patio table waiting for Chris. She scrolled through the e-mails on her phone while she sipped on a glass of pinot grigio. She briefly looked up from her phone and pulled her oversized glasses from her face when she saw Chris walking toward the table. Marley stood as he approached. She grabbed him around the waist and softly kissed him on the cheek.

"You look so handsome, Chris. I've never seen you all dressed up like that, where are you going?" she asked.

Marley pulled off her glasses and admired Chris's slightly baggy black pants and blue-and-black-striped dress shirt. Chris wore a black tie. Marley glanced at his feet and laughed.

"I'm working now. But you know I had to throw the Tims back on before I came out in public."

Marley laughed. "A job? Like a real job?" she asked.

"Yes, a job—and yes, a real one, crazy girl," Chris joked.

"Chris, that's great. I hope it works out. What kind of job?"

"It's good to see you, too, Marley Lucas," Chris interrupted.

Chris ordered a hearty sandwich, and Marley ordered a light salad. The ex-couple caught up on each other's weekly dealings between bites.

"Marley, I need a favor. I know we haven't kicked it in a while, but I want you to come with me this weekend," Chris said. "I need you, girl."

"Where are we going?" Marley asked. "I have a ton of projects that I need to get done," she added, remembering the plans she'd unofficially made with Jay.

"It's just a little family thing—my boy's parents are having a little party, and since I'm like a son to them I think that it would do his mom good to see me with a date. Please, I don't have anyone else to take, at least not anyone that moms would approve of."

Marley took a bite of her salad and then a sip of wine. She had a feeling that Chris was not going to take no for an answer. Even though she felt awkward about doing this favor for Chris, she agreed. After all, it had been months since they'd spent any time together. They'd spent long nights talking on the phone here and there, but they both understood that until Chris wasn't mixed up in that lifestyle, they couldn't be together. *Hmmm, maybe he is trying to change. He's working, for goodness' sake.*

"I'll have to see what I can do, Chris. I've been slacking on my work lately. Clients are getting impatient."

"I can't wait for you to meet everyone, especially my boy," he said. "They are going to love you. Big Papi will probably try to hit on you, so just be ready." Chris laughed.

Marley laughed, too. She thought it was cute how Chris always used nicknames for each of his boys. Big Papi, from what Marley understood, was a big Puerto Rican dude and a big-time Realtor who'd helped Chris find his house. Dee-tox was the youngest and a hustler and rapper. The first thing Marley planned to do when she met Chris's boys was get their first names.

After lunch, Marley and Chris walked the Miami strip to go

shopping. One of the many things the old friends had in common was their love for clothes and shoes. Chris had exquisite taste, as did Marley. Marley laid her credit cards on the counter and purchased two purses and a pair of black stilettos. Marley refused when Chris offered to buy her things; she didn't want anything to do with dirty money and as far as she was concerned, Chris's paying cash for the latest sneakers and fitted caps meant his money was still dirty.

Chris walked close to Marley's side with his arms wrapped tightly around her waist as she searched the home-improvement store for tile and blinds for the Palmers' new home. She explained the layout and colors to Chris, and he listened intently, staring into her eyes as she spoke. He was enamored by her beauty, and every chance he had to tell her so, he did.

"You are still amazing," he interrupted. "You make shopping for tiles and blinds sexy," Chris said. He pulled Marley into his body and playfully kissed her neck.

"Stop it. This is serious stuff. I have to find the perfect match. You don't understand how picky Mrs. Palmer is," she said, pulling away.

They walked the entire store twice before Marley found exactly what pattern and color she was looking for. Marley handed the cashier her credit card and turned toward Chris while she swiped it.

"So, where am I going again?" Marley asked.

"I thought I told you all of this already," he said. "It's a family get-together. I want people to see me with someone like you. I'm tired of my people riding me about getting married and having kids. My cousin had the nerve to ask me if I was gay. I almost knocked the fuck out of him."

Marley nearly choked on the gum she was chewing, trying to keep from laughing. "So, you're taking me to this family get-together to prove that you are not gay?"

"Yeah, something like that." Chris smiled at Marley, and when she smiled back, that old feeling came rushing over her. This feeling was not going to go away. Chris had taken the first step to getting Marley back into his life.

He'd been taking real-estate classes and finally received his license. Chris had taken his dirty money and invested it in properties and remodeling the homes in the hood. Business was good. Chris's plan was to eventually ask Marley to join the team as the interior designer.

Chris wanted to do everything in his power to show Marley that his life had changed. He wanted to be with her, and he needed to be careful, because the one thing that he couldn't do was let Marley know the secret he was carrying. If he did, Chris would lose her forever. No questions asked.

"Why are you canceling on me?" Jay asked.

"You know, I still haven't finished Dr. Mason's office," Marley lied. "I have been putting it off for too long. I still have to get paint, tiles . . . . everything. I have to get my priorities in order before no one wants to hire me. Don't get me wrong, I want to meet your friends and everything, but this weekend is just not good."

"Okay, I understand. It's just that I've been talking about you for so long, everyone wants to meet you. They have never been excited about meeting any of my girlfriends," Jay explained.

"Maybe we can all go out to dinner next weekend or something. I promise you, I will make this up to you, Jay," Marley said.

Marley and Chris decided to meet at the house in Kensington Estates and get dressed there since it was closer to where they were going. Marley paced back and forth from the closet to the bed with a different outfit in her hand each time.

"I don't know what to wear, Chris. I don't want to be too sexy around your people. But I don't want to look too old-fashioned either. What should I put on?" Marley whined.

Chris wrapped his towel around his waist and walked toward the bed, brushing his teeth. He looked down at each of the outfits Marley chose and shook his head. "I don't like any of those," he said. "Just be yourself. They are going to love you," he said. "Wear whatever you want, Marley. It's not that big of a deal." Chris walked back into the bathroom to rinse his mouth. When he finished, he stood in the doorway and watched Marley's theatrics.

Marley fell backwards onto the bed, folded her arms across her chest, and pouted. Chris adjusted his towel and walked toward the bed. He covered Marley's body with his and laughed. He kissed her lightly on the forehead and smoothed the loose strands of hair away from her face, and Marley smiled.

"You are still funny," he laughed.

"What!" Marley screamed, fighting to free her body from Chris's weight.

He playfully grabbed her arms and opened her legs with his body. He pinned her arms behind her head. "I have my own business now," he said. He looked into her eyes and relished in her confusion.

"I know that already," Marley said sarcastically.

"For real, girl, a brother is into real estate and shit now, me and Big Papi."

"For real?"

"Yes, for real. I had to leave all that craziness alone. When they busted into the apartment in Riverton and shot my dude, that was the last straw."

Marley lifted her head toward Chris and kissed him deeply. The feeling was still there. It never left. Back then, she just wanted Chris to get his life together, and he wasn't ready. Marley refused to fall victim to the game, and that the *only* thing that destroyed their bond.

As the old connection ignited again, they kissed. Marley slowly wrapped her legs around Chris's waist and allowed him to enter her. While she moaned softly, Chris slowly stroked her body inside. She closed her eyes and finally allowed the words to leak from her lips. "I love you, Chris," she whispered. As soon as the words left her mouth, her entire body shivered. Marley didn't try to explain herself, nor did she try to recant her statement. Instead she whispered the words again and allowed herself to let go with Chris.

Marley stared out of the window in silence while they drove to Chris's friend's house. He explained the escapade of finding the perfect home, how long the renovation took, and how he'd purchased a home that was now worth over $1.5 million for less than two hundred grand.

After driving for thirty minutes, Marley and Chris drove up the driveway as Marley admired the beautiful landscape. The grass was the perfect shade of green, and beautifully sculpted palm trees lined each side of the concrete driveway outlined in brick. A six-foot black gate surrounded the home. As they drove closer to the house, Marley could see the huge white tent placed in the yard. Tahitian torches with flames blowing in the breeze surrounded the event area. Old-school tunes blared from oversized speakers, and a few guests from the older generation danced on the portable dance floor.

Chris parked his truck in the designated parking area and walked to the passenger side to open Marley's door. He reached for her hand, and she stepped out. He stared at her with wide eyes. Even though he'd watched her get dressed and driven for thirty minutes with her sitting next to him, it was something about the way that she stood with the sun setting behind her that enhanced her beauty tonight. She'd chosen a simple floor-length white linen dress with Egyptian sandals, which remained hidden underneath the dress. She'd pulled her hair back into a tight ponytail and pinned the ends into a bun. Her skin was tanned, her makeup was natural, and her gold hoops complemented the effortless ensemble perfectly. He stared at her small hands with their perfectly manicured fingernails and prayed for the day that he could place a ring on her finger.

"How do I look?" she asked.

"You look like an angel . . . just like an angel," he said.

Marley opened the back door and grabbed the bottle of wine she'd picked up for Chris's friend, and then they walked hand in hand toward the party tent.

When they walked inside the tent, Marley gasped. The decorating was absolutely beautiful. Guest tables were covered with white cloth, and small candles in votive holders were placed in the center with gorgeous white lilies surrounding them. Waiters suited in black walked back and forth quickly, serving the guests.

The old-school jams had turned into jazz, and the atmosphere was calm and mellow. They moved to their table and sat next to Chris's friend and his date. The server placed a champagne flute in front of Marley, and she sipped slowly at first, but when her eyes caught Chris's stare, she set her glass down and reached for his hand.

"Thank you for bringing me," she whispered into Chris's ear.

Chris smiled and tightened his grip around Marley's tiny hand. They held hands and exchanged seductive glances while the servers placed the evening meal in front of them. Chris and Anthony talked sports while they chewed their food as their dates listened. They dined on roasted chicken with garlic potatoes, steamed vegetables, and bread until it was time to get loose on the dance floor. Before they walked toward the dance floor, Chris stood in front of his chair and held his glass high in the air.

He cleared his throat and adjusted his shirt. "I have something that I need to say," he said. Marley sat straight up with her back against the chair and waited for Chris to speak.

"Thanks for coming with me tonight, Marley," he said. Chris knelt in front of Marley and prepared to pour his heart out to her. She reached for his hand and softly ran her fingers back and forth against his skin while he continued his speech.

"You only find true love once in a lifetime, *maybe* twice," he joked. "When you find it, you can't let it slip away. I know we have been through some shit, Marl, but through it all, I don't think that I have ever stopped loving you. You have always been right here." Chris pounded his fist against his chest right over his heart. "I want you to be in my life, Marley . . . for good . . . forever, and I just wanted you to know that."

Marley struggled to catch her breath and fight back tears. She didn't know what to say. She gently cupped Chris's face into her hands and kissed him softly. Her feelings for Chris had never changed, but it shocked her, that he still felt the same way about her.

"I will be in your life, Chris—forever, if that is what you want," she whispered. "My feelings have never really changed."

Chris lifted Marley from her seat with her arms still wrapped around his neck and spun around in a small circle. Anthony and his date stood in front of their seats and applauded. Marley was so caught up in her moment, she never noticed Jay standing in the background, watching. After the entire scene, he silently excused himself from the celebration. His heart ached as he drove home. He couldn't believe that Marley played him, but he believed that it was only a matter of time before the whole situation blew up in their faces.

"Marley," Jay said when Marley picked up on the other end of the line.

"Hey, *papi*, I was going to call you, but I got sidetracked. You know how busy I am," Marley said.

"Yeah, I know. I kinda figured you were staying away on purpose, since you are kicking it with Chris and everything."

Marley stared at the phone and then placed it back to her ear. "What?"

"I know about Chris. He's my business partner, so I know everything. I was also at the party," he said.

"What?"

"Yeah . . . I was there. So, I just wanted to wish you luck with that, baby girl. I hope that dude makes you happy."

"Jay . . . let me explain."

"No explanation needed, ma. No hard feelings. I want you to do one thing for me, though. Ask Chris about his father."

"What?"

"Just ask him about his dad. See what he tells you. Talk to you later, baby girl. Be easy."

Marley stared at the phone before she hit the END button. She had no idea what Jay was talking about. She felt sick to her stomach. She hadn't known that Jay was at the party or that he knew Chris. As usual her relationship drama was extreme.

After the party, Chris and Marley rekindled their relationship and eventually moved into Chris's new home together. Marley became a part of their team as the interior designer. She redecorated the refurbished homes once the construction was finished. In the beginning, it was awkward working with Jay, but after a few months, the shock was gone, and they were focused on the business and the business only.

Marley and Chris even talked about getting married. They were happy together. It finally seemed like the pieces of Marley's love life were coming together.

"Chris, Jay keeps asking me to ask you about your father. What is all that about?" Marley asked while she and Chris had dinner at Mr. Chow's.

"What did he say? When did he say it?"

"He's been telling me that ever since he found out about us. Today he asked me if I'd met your dad yet. It's weird," she said.

"I don't know what that dude is going through," Chris said. "I'll ask him about it."

Chris didn't know what to think at that moment. Was Jay trying to expose his secret? He knew that he should have never confided in him. Chris felt the vomit rise. If Jay spoke, it would ruin his relationship with Marley. He couldn't let that happen, but he wasn't sure how to stop it either.

When Chris arrived at the office, he threw his car keys on the desk and stormed over to Jay.

"What's all this about you telling Marley that she needs to ask me about my father? What the fuck are you trying to do, nigga?" Chris poked his chest out and balled his fist at his waist. He wanted Jay to get flip so that he could knock him the fuck out.

"Come on, dude. You need to tell that girl, before things get out of hand. That's all I'm saying. Calm down, dude. You 'bout to buck with me over this shit? You are wrong, nigga. But you know that shit already."

"There isn't shit to tell. She won't ever find out, so just keep your mouth shut, dude . . . please. I don't want no shit."

Jay turned back to his computer and pecked at the keys. He was just waiting until the happy couple's whole world came crashing down. It was only a matter of time.

"Let me handle this my way, man, I don't need any help, a'ight?"

Jay didn't respond. He glanced at the clock on the computer and continued to peck at the keys. *Just a matter of time.*

By twelve o'clock, Marley walked into the office, looking beautiful as usual. Chris was out checking on a property, and Jay was sitting at his desk, listening to his iPod. Marley walked up behind him and tapped him on the shoulder.

"What's up, Jay?"

Jay turned in his seat and waved without removing the earplugs from his ear. He glanced at the clock again and smiled.

While Marley looked through magazines for the perfect inspiration for the new property, Jay excused himself. Soon after he disappeared into the bathroom, a man walked into the office.

"Hi, Marley."

"Hi," she said, wondering how this man knew her name. She looked him over and immediately recognized his face.

"Ch-Charles?"

"It's me. I didn't think that you would recognize me—I've put on a lot of weight since you saw me last."

Marley halfheartedly wrapped her arms around Charles's neck. "I almost didn't, it's been a long time. How are you? What are you doing *here*?" she asked.

"Jay called me. He told me that he had some work for me today."

"Oh . . ."

"Where's Chris?" Charles asked.

"He's out looking at a property. Come in and sit down, Charles. Jay should be out of the bathroom soon." Marley looked around the room and hoped that Jay *would* appear soon. Even though Charles was her father, she really didn't know him or care to. His actions had turned her world upside down before; that was something she would never get over.

"So, how do you like working with my boys?" Charles asked.

"It's fine," Marley said without looking up from her magazine. "They are good guys."

"Jay is like a son to me, too. As long as I can remember, he's been hanging out with Chris. I'm just glad they left all that street business alone and got into this. I was worried about my son out there in them streets like that."

"Your son who?"

"Chris."

"Chris who?"

"Chris, the one that works in this office with—" Charles paused in midsentence and watched Marley replay his words in her mind. "Wait a minute. . . . Don't tell me that you didn't know about Chris being my son."

Marley covered her mouth with her hand. The room was becoming a blur. She tried to inhale through her nose, but it wasn't working. She uncovered her mouth and regrouped.

"He didn't tell me. Are you sure he knows?" she whispered.

"He knows. He was the only one of my kids I was able to have a relationship with. He's known almost all of his life."

"What!" Marley jumped out of her seat as tears ran down her cheeks. She'd been throwing up all morning, but she obviously wasn't finished. She covered her mouth again and ran toward the bathroom. She ran right into Jay as he was rounding the corner of the hallway. She pushed past him with her body and nearly collapsed in front of the commode. She vomited over and over until her insides were empty. She rested her head against the edge of the seat and cried hysterically until Jay knocked on the door.

"You okay, baby girl?"

"Leave me alone! Leave me alone, Jay! Get away from me!" she screamed.

Jay returned to his desk, and Charles went to check on Marley. He knocked on the door, but Marley didn't say a word.

"Marley, I'm sorry. I didn't know . . . I didn't know. I just don't understand why Chris didn't tell you. I don't know how this could have happened to you twice in a lifetime," he said, and she could hear the pleading tone in his voice through the door.

After she was sure that Charles was no longer standing in front of the door, Marley regained her composure and moved to the sink to wash her face. When she inhaled the scent of the hand soap, she felt nauseated. She turned back to the commode and assumed the position.

Marley returned to her desk, grabbed her purse and keys, and walked out the door. Jay and Charles watched silently as she stepped into her car and sped away.

Marley arrived at home still feeling nauseated. She changed into a free-flowing dress and lay across the bed. When she thought about the mess that she was involved in, she screamed into the pillow. She cried hysterically for hours until Chris finally came rushing into the bedroom.

"Marley," he said while he stroked her hair.

"Don't fucking touch me, liar!" She sat up in bed and slapped Chris across the face with everything she had. "You *knew*, and you didn't tell me shit. What kind of sick shit is that, Chris? How could you do this?"

Chris lowered his head. He'd prayed that this day would never come. He and Marley were supposed to be able to live happily ever after. "I don't know," he whispered.

"You don't know? What the fuck do you mean you don't know? All of these years, you *knew*, Chris—you knew that I was your fucking sister, and you didn't say shit! You fucked me like it was cool! You are a sick son of a bitch, Chris!" Marley said, slapping him across the face.

This time, the slap stung Chris's face and he reacted by grabbing Marley by the wrists to keep it from happening again.

"I loved you. I didn't want to lose you. I didn't know how to handle it. We have something, Marley. Do you see how we click? Do you see how our love kept leading us back to each other? I couldn't let that slip away. As sick as it sounds—I didn't tell you, because I loved you and I wanted to be with you."

Marley struggled to get free from Chris's grasp, but he had a tight grip on her small wrists. The way Chris held Marley forced her to look into his eyes.

"I'm sorry," Chris said.

"Let me go."

As soon as the words escaped Marley's lips, they were followed by another round of vomit. Chris immediately released her wrists, and Marley ran to the bathroom.

Chris wanted to take her in his arms and hold her forever. He wanted to comfort her, but for some reason, he couldn't bring himself to touch her. Chris was in shock. In an instant, his entire future was destroyed. Beads of sweat glided across his forehead and down the sides of his face. He listened to Marley sobbing hysterically in the bathroom for two minutes before he decided to console her. When he walked into the bathroom, he pulled her close and stroked her hair softly.

"How could this happen?" she cried. Marley's entire body quaked when she sobbed. Chris wrapped his arms around her tightly and allowed her to empty the pain in her heart onto his shoulder.

"I don't know. I don't know," Chris whispered.

Chris walked Marley into the bedroom and stroked her hair until she stopped shaking and crying. He kissed her forehead when she'd finally cried herself to sleep. He positioned her body comfortably on the bed, covered her with the comforter, and slowly walked into the guest bedroom.

"So, what are you going to do now, Marley? Are you going to go back to your rules and all of that madness?" Marley's friend Nina asked while they enjoyed lunch on the strip.

"I think I'm going to take a long break from dating. I don't have the strength to go through something like this again, and with my luck . . . I will," she said.

Nina nodded in agreement. She looked up from her salad and momentarily locked eyes with Marley.

"Marley, you look like you are getting kind of thick in the waist. You aren't trying to get fat so that the dudes won't approach you, are you?"

"Nina! How could you say that? Am I really getting fat?"

"Yes. I'm your girl—I'm supposed to tell you things like that," Nina said.

Marley smiled and shook her head. "I guess, but damn."

After the fiasco, Marley stayed away from all men. She didn't want to risk the chance of falling into another situation like the one she'd endured twice in a lifetime. She poured herself into her career and focused on keeping her clients satisfied.

Once she was inside her car, she checked her calendar and reached for the mail that was thrown across the front seat from the night before. She searched through her purse and pulled out her Sidekick. She searched through her messages and noticed that Jay had called. She hated Jay's not telling her sooner, but she wouldn't let that stop her from finding out just what he wanted.

Marley returned the call while she sat in the parking lot of her client's apartment complex. When Jay picked up on the other end, his voice was low and he spoke slowly.

"Charles died last night," he said.

"Oh my God!"

"He told me if something were to ever happen to him, he wanted me to make sure that all of his children laid him to rest," Jay said.

"I'll be there. I'm so sorry, Jay. Please call me if you need *anything*," she said. Tears fell from Marley's eyes as she backed out of the parking lot. She couldn't believe that Charles was actually gone.

She suddenly wished that she'd taken the months that had passed to get to know Charles instead of isolating herself from him. She wondered if he'd ever thought about her when she was younger, if he had wondered what she looked like. She wondered why Tara had kept him away. Maybe it was the drugs, but what about when he cleaned up? Why didn't she let them know and love one another? Suddenly Marley's emotions turned to anger. She was angry at Tara for keeping her father away from her. She was angry at her for allowing this facade for so long and not allowing her to experience the other side of her ethnicity.

Marley pressed the gas pedal even closer to the floor and sped ninety miles per hour down I-95 toward her condo. She was angry at DeJuan for leaving her to deal with the situation alone. She was angry at Chris for taking advantage of her vulnerability at a time when she needed comfort. She was angry at Jay for pursuing her nonstop. She was angry at Charles for not wearing a condom.

Marley couldn't think, and when her eyes filled with tears, she couldn't see. The white lines on the highway became a blur as Marley applied more pressure to the gas pedal. Maybe all of this was karma, she thought. Maybe this entire drama was caused because of the many times she'd broken some poor conquest's heart or maybe it was because of the many times she'd slipped out of someone's bed never to be seen again, with no explanation. Marley had done her share of dirt in her past. When DeJuan had died, she couldn't seem to get her life together. She was barely hanging on.

Marley's small SUV reached speeds of over ninety miles per

hour. She turned up the music full blast and screamed the words to Beyoncé's "Me, Myself and I." When Marley approached her exit, she finally slowed down. She pulled into the parking lot and opened her door. Marley leaned her head outside and vomited. Her head was spinning, and she felt hot. She slowly stepped out of the car and walked uneasily to her door.

Once Marley was inside, she threw down her purse and ran into the bathroom. She knelt in front of the toilet and lifted the lid. Marley vomited until there was nothing left in her stomach; she rested her head against the cool toilet until she felt the urge again.

The doctor walked in, holding Marley's medical chart. She sat on the stool and opened it. She flipped through the pages and looked up at Marley.

"Well, Ms. Lucas, your suspicions were correct. You are pregnant," she said.

Marley quickly covered her mouth to prevent screams from escaping. Her eyes filled with tears, and she couldn't breathe.

"According to the dates that you have given us, it looks like you are about eight weeks along, if not more. Congratulations," she said.

"Thank you," Marley whispered. She looked at the tiled floor. *The designer could have picked a better color*, she thought to herself. She looked up at the doctor. "Is it too late for me to . . . consider other options? I don't think I am ready for a child," she said.

"Marley, you still have some time, but not much. If you decide that you want to terminate this pregnancy, then you need to do it soon, but there are other alternatives to consider. Adoption is always a good option. Ultimately it will be up to you, but just remember that time is of the utmost importance in this situation."

"I understand," Marley said.

She left the doctor's office feeling as if the weight of the world had just been placed upon her shoulders. There was no way that she could have a child knowing that she and Chris shared the same blood. The risk of complications was high. At that very moment, standing in the doorway of Dr. Hines's office, she decided she would have an abortion.

Nearly two weeks passed and Marley still hadn't made a final decision about her pregnancy. She'd attended Charles's funeral and reluctantly told Chris her news. He begged her not to have an abortion. He told Marley he wanted the child and he didn't care about the risks.

Marley argued that she wasn't ready for a child, and she would handle everything on her own, but she didn't handle anything. She lay in bed and prayed all day and night.

Marley was tired of being alone. She wanted to be loved with every ounce of her soul. As her body changed with her pregnancy, she thought about the baby growing inside her and slowly began to change her perspective. No matter how high the risk, this child was a part of her. She could already feel the love.

There was no way she could get rid of the one person who would love her forever, unconditionally. She was willing to take her chance.

"Okay, Marley, are you ready to hear the heartbeat?" Dr. Hines asked as she applied gel to Marley's growing belly. She applied the fetal Doppler to Marley's stomach and moved it around in a circular motion. Marley stared at the ceiling and listened carefully.

"Oh, there it is," Dr. Hines said. "Hold on." Dr. Hines moved the instrument around a few more times and smiled. "Oh my, it sounds like two of them in there," she said. "Congratulations, Marley—it looks like you are having twins."

ACKNOWLEDGMENTS

You never know what will happen. So dream big! I want to thank God for giving me the opportunity to share my love of writing with the world. I want to thank my mother and my family for all of their support as I take this journey. Thank you to all of my friends for believing in my dream and being such major players in achieving my dream. I love you all with every ounce of me. A special thank-you goes to Shannon Holmes for offering me an opportunity that I will never forget. Your advice and belief in me has meant a lot to me. Monique Patterson, words cannot express how thankful I am to you for allowing me to work on this project with some major players. I hope we will have the opportunity to work together in the future. It has meant the world to me. Last but not least, I have to acknowledge my children, Jordynn and Jalen. I love you both more than words can ever say, thank you for coming into my life and showing me what real love is. I love you both. As high as the sky, as wide as the sea, all the days of my life. If I missed anyone, please charge it to my head and not my heart. I love you all! Thank you.